Profane Beasts

Nathan Buchholz

ISBN-9798218704049

For all of us who are pulled back to the church.

Even if we don't know what it worships anymore.

"Pull me back from all the darkness,
The pain that sets and stains the heart,
I thought I could run,
I'm not as strong as I thought I was,
Take me home now,
No matter where I go the dark finds out,
Take me home now,
Please take me home,"
-Knocked Loose

"I will die in the house I grew up in"
-Noah Kahan

Table of Contents

INTRODUCTION

Virginia 1st District Court

Convention v Faulk

.... The following records in the civil libel case of Convention v Faulk are now unsealed for public viewing. These records include all emails, recordings, voice memos, and other relevant information that went into Mr. Faulk's article posted on Medium titled "Strong Winds and Bloody Roots: The Dark Secret the Storm of the Century Concealed." The case was brought to court due to "false" and "sensationalized" reports of the events surrounding Calvary Baptist Church both before and during Hurricane Ophelia. After careful consideration of the evidence, this court found that while the eyewitness testimony, email records, and voice recordings that Mr. Faulk used for his story are remarkable, we do not find that Mr. Faulk knowingly misrepresented any of his sources or showed blatant disregard for the truth.

The investigation by Mr. Faulk has revealed key information about the whereabouts of three missing people in the wake of Hurricane Ophelia. Alice Crenshaw, Kelly Harden, and Whitney Ellington's bodies have never been recovered in the wake of the storm, and this court encourages opening new police investigations into their deaths based on the evidence that Mr. Faulk has revealed. While this court agrees that some of the more colorful pieces of Mr. Faulk's reporting may flirt with the fantastical, one does not have to believe in the strangest accounts of the events surrounding Calvary Baptist Church in order to think that local police have more work to do in bringing closure to the families of Alice, Kelly and Whitney...

Author's Note

Dear reader,

A feature of these documents that may immediately become clear to you is that unlike most evidence dumps from libel cases, these documents have been structured in the form of a narrative surrounding key people of interest such as Alice Crenshaw, Ernest Mobley, and others. In addition, the evidence is divided into three 'parts'. This speaks to a design behind the presentation of evidence, and a final document set that reads more like a pulp story or tabloid than evidence dumps from an infamous court case.

Believe it or not, the submission of evidence in this manner was not my decision, but instead insisted upon by the people trying to ruin my name and my bank account. Their claim was not necessarily that I lied about the actual content of Alice Crenshaw's voice memos or Ernest Mobley's interviews, but instead that I had "put the documents together to imply patently false information about both Calvary Baptist Church and the Convention at large." In response to the charge, I assembled the evidence together in the order that it appeared in the medium article.

As for the charge of misusing the evidence from Alice Crenshaw's phone as well as the other interviews I've collected about what exactly happened at Calvary Baptist Church while Hurricane Ophelia devastated the Hampton Roads area, I will leave that verdict in your hand's dear reader. Believe Alice and Ernest or not, it's up to you, but at least now you have the opportunity to hear their remarkable story.

Best,

-Kellan Faulk

'P.S'. As you read, you will notice several important organizations, individuals, and entities are not named, but have instead been redacted from these documents distributed to the public. I hope you can understand that as someone who has just lived through one life altering lawsuit that took my job, my home, and almost cost me my marriage, that I hope to reduce the number of future lawsuits I am exposed to by as much as possible. I deeply hope to go the rest of my life without ever seeing the inside of a courthouse again.

Thank you,

-KF

'P.S.S.' Please be advised that the following documents include depiction and discussion of neglect, religious abuse, anti-queer hate crimes, severe night terrors, self-harm, suicide, murder, mutilation, and torture. Remember that at any point if you find these pieces of evidence too harrowing to look through, that the power is in your hands to put down the book, take a sip of a preferred beverage, and go on a brisk walk during a mild day. I truly believe that reading is one of the most consensual relationships a person can have to a piece of media, and if you feel yourself reaching your limits, feel free to put this upsetting document away for a time.

I do still encourage you to read it through the end, as I believe that encountering what is inside these documents in the comfort and safety of your bedroom, study, or coffee shop is important enough to face some psychic discomfort. Alice, Ernest and all the others never had the chance to just look away from what faced them at Calvary Baptist Church, you have the privilege to take a break and step away if it gets to be too much. I expect you not to waste such a generous opportunity.

-KF

PART ONE

1

4 Months Before Hurricane Ophelia

(The following is an email exchange between Dr. Alice Crenshaw and Kelly Harden. The emails were recovered from Dr. Crenshaw's hard drive at her residence.)

Kelly Harden

to Alice Crenshaw

May 12th, 2:32 AM

Hi Alice,

It's been a few years since we've talked, so I don't know if you remember me, but we were both in the youth group at Calvary Baptist as kids. I was a few years younger, but I remember you, always volunteering and helping with the music and the service. You knew what it was like at that church, I guess that's why I'm reaching out to you, or that's one of the reasons I'm trying to reconnect.

I hate to ask, but I kind of need a favor. I haven't been sleeping and have been really in my own head lately. I know that something has to be wrong with me, but I don't really know what it is, I never got checked out or evaluated for like mental health issues. I remember my family believed that mental health wasn't really real, but instead that people who had problems were just not close enough to God. Safe to say I don't think that way anymore, but I really wanted to get some professional opinions on whether or not what's happening with me is normal. I just feel on the edge of a knife all the time, and it can be pretty upsetting.

I was looking online, and I saw your name as one of the virtual therapists for Full Cup Solutions and I wanted to reach out. I remembered you were always pretty nice to me, and church got a lot weirder after you left. I know I want to see someone to talk about, well I'm not sure how much I want to talk about, but I can't keep staying up all night worrying or else I really am going to lose it. I know therapists are busy and overbooked and everything, but I wanted to know if you could accept me as a patient before I apply. I think that knowing the person who I'm going to see, knowing they were there, in Chesapeake, it will help me start to feel a little better.

Get back to me when you can, I know it's odd to get an email from an old acquaintance at three in the morning, but I just wanted to reach out. I should be able to pay you for your services, even if I don't have a real insurance plan at the moment. Hope to talk to someone else from the 757 soon!

Alice Crenshaw

to Kelly Harden

May 12th, 11:30 AM

Kelly,

Thank you for reaching out! I do remember you from Calvary Baptist, it feels almost like another life. I know we weren't close, but I do remember that Chesapeake could be pretty tough sometimes, and there were a lot of unhealthy practices at that church. As an adult, I can look back on my time there and understand more about how unhelpful the church could be. Glad to reconnect with someone else who had the same experience growing up.

As for your question about therapy services, I would absolutely be able to provide some help. Currently I work through the Full Cup Solutions that you mentioned, I've included a link to some of the intake materials you would need in order to get seen by me. I should be able to make it so you can get a small discount if you need it and that your insurance situation shouldn't bar you from service. I'll reach out to my company and see what we can do. We should be able to set up a virtual appointment in the next few days.

Reaching out for help is a big step, and you should be proud of yourself! After we meet we can look into some next steps.

I'll let you know what I can do on the insurance front, and hope to be able to talk to you soon.

Thank you,

Dr. Alice Crenshaw
Full Cup Solutions
(Redacted)

Kelly Harden

to Alice Crenshaw

May 13th 1:30 AM

Please get me in as soon as possible. I'm having a tough time. Do you remember the trucks everyone in this town drives everywhere? Some with the six-wheel setup that look like whales menacing the interstate. I feel like someone is watching me from inside those trucks every time I leave the house. In the parking lot, driving down the street, sometimes I even think they are watching the house. Stupidly big, driven by just the worst people imaginable, designer work boots crew. But I know you remember, you know what I'm talking about.

I hope that you can help me go outside without feeling like this. I want to feel, I don't know, just alone, safe, not watched, and my rational brain knows that the problem is in my head. Really, I know it's a mental problem, not that I'm being watched, but I feel like I have eyes on me all the time.

Alice Crenshaw

to Kelly Harden

May 13th 9:05 AM

Kelly,

I should be able to fit you in for an intake appointment today at 2:30.

I do remember those trucks, I hated how they seemed to take up all the space in every parking lot, or sway on the road trying to bully me onto the shoulder. They can't be safe driving on streets with children and pets playing. You aren't crazy for being scared of them, and I want you to remember even if your "rational" brain knows it's in your head, that doesn't mean it isn't real. What I mean is that I'm sure what you described to me feels real and should be taken seriously.

But I do think it would be good to meet virtually as soon as possible. I don't want you to be suffering any longer than necessary and hope to be able to do what I can to help.

You will receive and invite to the virtual appointment later today, please confirm when you are able to. I am excited for our first session.

Dr. Alice Crenshaw
Full Cup Solutions
(Redacted)

2

3 Months before Hurricane Ophelia

(The following are session notes of Dr. Alice Crenshaw on her first tele-health session with Kelly Harden. The notes have been retrieved from Full Cup Solutions cloud storage drive.)

Client Full Name: Kelly Harden
Client Date of Birth: 07/22/1998
Exact start and end time: 2:32 PM-3:28 PM: 56 mins

Session Location: Telehealth, patient provided consent to telehealth, service performed on HIPPA compliant software.

Diagnosis:
Generalized anxiety disorder. Moderate. Several episodes. Kelly presents to initial session with reports of difficulty engaging in everyday tasks such as going to her job and the grocery store because she worries "something awful" will happen if she leaves the house. She indicates that she has had trouble holding on to employment due to her anxiety. She indicates that she had lost two jobs in the past six-month period due to tardiness, absences, and poor work performance. She worries about money and mentions something about the "settlement running out." She also expresses strong desires to leave her home city and constantly

worries about "running into someone she knows" when she leaves her home.

Chief Complaints

Patient reports feeling anxiety whenever leaving the house or being "out on the town" in her city. She reports being sleepless one to two nights a week and sleeping all day at least one day a week. She reports impulsive actions such as leaving work in the middle of the day without permission, periods of binge eating, and leaving public places like the park or the grocery store because she "thought she saw someone." Often after impulsive actions she claims that she feels "stupid" and worries that she is a "crazy person." Patient reports somatic symptoms including headaches and stomach aches when she is anxious. Patient reports childhood trauma, though she "didn't want to get into all that today."

History

-Current Medication: None
-Development: Normal per patient knowledge
-Family Psychiatric: Patient reports that "I know my parents had something, but never got diagnosed"
-Psychiatric: No previous diagnosis
-Medical: Arthritis in both wrists
-Social: Patient indicates that they have a no contact policy with both of their parents. Patient indicates they are not close with any of their extended family either. Patient states they do not have a lot of friends, and the person they see most is her roommate. The patient states, "Sometimes I go days without seeing another person."
-Substance use: None

Mental Status Exam

Appearance: Well groomed, even made up. Seemed as if she prepared for this session.
Attention: Fair
Memory: Intact
Mood: Upbeat
Speech: Fair, but scattered
Thought Content: No SI/HI. Patient reports feeling as if "someone is following her" though then walked back the statement. Patient states that

she worries she is "losing it" sometimes when she feels watched or followed.

Risk Assessment
-Suicidal Ideation: Denies at the current time. Patient reported ideation "when I was younger" and "when things were tougher" but reported no worries at this time. No prior attempts.
-Homicidal Ideation: None
-Violent/destructive behaviors: Patient reported "punching the wall" when deeply anxious or frustrated. Noted as an example of impulsive behavior.
-Current overall risk: Moderate
-Protective Factors: Help seeking, concerned about the future, other person in the house
-Static Risk Factors: Lack of social support, childhood trauma, previous SI, impulsive behavior
-Modifiable Risk Factors: Lack of coping skills, lack of medications, lack of primary care physician

Assessment
Kelly presents with symptoms consistent with mood disorder, impulsivity, and some paranoid thoughts. She describes her overall mood as "nervous" and "unhappy whenever I have to leave the house or have to prepare to leave the house." She said that being in public made her feel "watched" and that sometimes she was sure "someone was following me." Kelly reports major impacts on her quality of life as a result of her anxiety and impulsivity such as losing employment and being unable to sleep.

Therapist helped Kelly process why she feels as if she is being watched or followed, and introduced grounding coping strategies. Therapist also encouraged Kelly to meet with the medication management team for Full Cup Solutions or a local organization to start on anti-anxiety medication. Therapist also recommends Kelly take an ADHD assessment. Therapist gave Kelly a short education on anxiety to explain some of Kelly's symptoms. Therapist identified paranoid thoughts as ones to monitor in case they escalate.

Plan

Therapist will use CBT - Anxiety to help Kelly learn coping skills to manage her anxiety and impulsivity, specifically feelings of being watched or followed. Therapist recommends weekly sessions; Kelly is in agreement with this.

Electronically signed by: Dr. Alice Crenshaw

Note Signed Date: 05/27/2027

(Dr. Alice Crenshaw and Kelly Harden spoke again over email later the subject of Kelly's medication.)

Kelly Harden

to Alice Crenshaw

June 7th 11:45 PM

I went to pick up some of the medication that you had that medication appointment person set up for me, but I couldn't go into the pharmacy. Three of those big trucks were parked outside the front of the store, and I swear Alice, people were watching me. I couldn't see them behind the tinted glass, but I know they were there, just waiting for something, I don't even know what.

I don't know what I'm going to do, I can't go back there not now that they know. I'm scared, I don't know what to do.

Alice Crenshaw

to Kelly Harden

June 7th 11:50 PM

Kelly,

I am sorry this happened to you, this sounds like a very frightening experience. As a girl who grew up in Chesapeake too, I can understand not liking those trucks.

Going forward we have two options, first is for you to try and implement some of the coping strategies that we've talked about during our first session, the second is for you to try and go to another pharmacy. Let me know which one you want to try.

I know it's hard to go out and get the prescription, but I do really think it will be helpful.

Dr. Alice Crenshaw
Full Cup Solutions
(Redacted)

Alice Crenshaw

to Kelly Harden

June 20th, 2:20 PM

Kelly,

This is the second of our appointments that you missed without a call or an email to let me know that you couldn't make it. I am understanding, and can write off the first missed appointment, but I really can't do it again. Unfortunately being a no show for a therapist appointment incurs a cancellation fee of (redacted). This charge will be visible on your most recent invoice.

If you are no-show for our session next week, I will have no choice but to drop you from my patient list. Please call me at (redacted) if you need anything else. I think our sessions are productive and I think that you are making good progress. Please let me know if there's anything I can do to help.

Thinking about you,
-Alice

Kelly Harden

to Alice Crenshaw

June 20th, 2:30 PM

I'm so fucking sorry, I've been all over the place. I just got the last of the settlement money and I'm trying to figure out how to make it work. My housing should still be secure, especially with my roommate, but I'm really having trouble.

I went out yesterday and was able to turn in a job application for Food Lion down the street where I live. Hoping for a call soon, and not too many questions about my prior firings haha. I didn't see anyone I know, and didn't feel watched, it might be far enough away that they can't keep tabs on me.

I understand the cancellation fee, and I'll be at the next session, I promise.

-Kelly

(The following is a news article written by Wavy News 10 on Hurricane Ophelia's impact on Hampton Roads.)

Wavy News 10: Bodies washed ashore in Portsmouth bring closure to families preparing to celebrate the holidays

55 Days After Superstorm Ophelia

Portsmouth, Va (WAVY) – The bodies of fifteen people who washed ashore at Portsmouth City Park have been identified. The Hurricane Ophelia disaster relief force notified the families of the dead early yesterday, and families shared complicated feelings upon being informed of their loved one's death.

"I'm happy that I have a body to lay to rest, maybe help me and my family get some closure before the holidays. We've known this has been coming for a long time, but you still hold out some hope. Now we can grieve and move on," said (redacted) whose spouse went missing during the record breaking floods at Norfolk Naval Base.

The disaster relief force spoke to Wavy Ten about how many more bodies they estimate will be washed ashore in the coming days. The force said that they could not be sure, but that the volume of dead appearing on the bank of the Elizabeth River and Chesapeake Bay was much less than the days after the deadly storm.

"When we came out here at first, you'd see ten, twenty bodies every day. Now it's news when that many wash ashore. Maybe it's bleak, but I think you can see major progress being made in the recovery efforts," said (redacted) one of the task force members on the ground in Portsmouth.

The disaster relief force could not provide an estimate for how many people may still be recovered, but told Wavy that they expect to be continuing to work through Christmas and maybe beyond.

The disaster relief force work continues, as many in and around Hampton Roads are still without power nearly two months after the storm. Families who have not been given closure after the storm have expressed difficulty with waiting for news on their loved ones.

"You try to protect yourself," said (redacted) parent of missing child (redacted.) "But it's impossible not to hope that one day, (redacted) is just gonna walk through that door like nothing happened."

The fifteen recovered bodies this morning brings the total death toll of Superstorm Ophelia to 7,839 with some 30,000 still missing across the Hampton Roads area.

3

77 Days before Hurricane Ophelia

(The following was recovered from full cup solutions iCloud storage. The document below is the required progress notes taken by Dr. Alice Crenshaw in her session with Kelly Harden. Dr. Alice Crenshaw's personal calendar shows she rescheduled two other sessions to make time to meet with Kelly.)

Dr. Alice Crenshaw
(Redacted)
(Redacted)

Patient Name: Kelly Harden
Patient DOB: 07/22/1998
Diagnosis: Generalized Anxiety, Recurrent, Moderate

Date: June 27th, 2027
Start Time: 2:00 PM
End Time: 2:57 PM

Patient Chief Complaint: "I'm worried about starting my new job. I need the money, and just want to feel safe somewhere that isn't the house." Patient noted concerns about her mood, endorsing an escalating anxiety over the past month. Claimed that it "hadn't been this bad in a while." Therapist notes that worries over being followed or watched have continued for the patient, and are the key source of patient anxiety.

Clinical Observations: Patient appeared well groomed and made up for our interview. Patient's attention seemed scattered for the majority of the session, often picking up on a line of thought and then dropping them. Patient moved erratically and her eyes seemed to dart to a nearby root often throughout our session. When asked about suicidal ideation, patient at first denied ideation, but later in the session said "I think dying would be better than letting them get me again." Client did not define who "they" were.

Session Description: Patient discussed worsening anxiety stemming from a loss of income coming from a court settlement they won years ago. Patient claimed they needed to hold onto their current job because they worried without its source of income they would become housing insecure. When asked what could prevent them from keeping their job, the patient once again referred to "them," mentioning anxiety around seeing "them" at work. Patient indicated sighting people they recognized at work would result in patient quitting their job.

The patient also reported an increase in worry and anxiety stemming from their past. They shared that they were a part of the Wilderness Survival Camp (redacted) and that was the source of their sizable settlement which had kept them financially solvent until now. Patient describes sensory flashbacks including hearing events that occurred at said camp as well as feeling intense pain in their wrists. Patient linked current feelings of anxiety and paranoia to previous experience, remarking that they saw the "white truck" around town. When the therapist suggested that there are many white trucks in their mutual hometown, the patient said "I know, I know I'm going crazy." Patient quickly changed the subject after therapist input.

Patient continued to complain about the location of their pharmacy. Patient reported not going in to pick up medication because of belief they were "being watched." Patient described worry that even if the pharmacy was changed they would be followed. Patient described fear that they would be followed to work and stated "then I'd really be fucked."

Interventions/methods provided: We discussed the patient's symptoms, gave supportive counseling, identification and exploration of emotions, provided patient handout on thinking errors, brief discussion of emotional regulation, therapist proposed safety plan and patient wanted to "take a look at it in a future session."

Assessment: Patient continues to present with moderate to severe anxiety which is inhibiting daily activities such as going to the pharmacy, going to work, and socializing with others. Patient also describes several symptoms consistent with post-traumatic stress disorder resulting from time in Wilderness Camp (Redacted). Coming to the end of settlement money could be a possible trigger for auditory hallucinations for patient revolving around prior experience. Patient also displays symptoms of delusion and paranoia with reports of being followed, or tracked in her day to day movements.

Patient is at some risk for suicide. While patient denies ideation, statements such as "I won't let them take me again" or "they can't have me" display risk of suicide. Patient is at risk for further anxiety and paranoia if they do not take steps to address both, and are at risk of suicide.

Plan: Patient will acquire medications (redacted) from local pharmacy. Patient will discuss a safety plan with roommate to make sure the patient is safe at home. Patient will monitor their symptoms and will reach out if their symptoms worsen or if they feel as if they are in danger. Therapist will monitor patient response to medication at the next session.

Next Appointment: June 27, 2027

Dr. Alice Crenshaw

76 days before Superstorm Ophelia

(The following is the first of several voice memo recovered from Dr. Alice Crenshaw's icloud storage. The voice memo is dated as June 28th, 2027 and is the first to mention Kelly Harden or Calvary Baptist Church. The memo was held

by the (redacted) convention's database along with multiple other audio files of Dr. Alice Crenshaw's voice memos. Each audio file included in this report concerns either Kelly Harden or Calvary Baptist Church.)

I'm breaking so many of my own rules.

Every other therapist who survived in this job for years stresses the need for strong boundaries between you and the patient. Doubly so for virtual therapy sessions. Sometimes you'll feel like you really are making a difference and helping people work through their problems or their issues, but other times you're just paddling aimlessly through someone's inner thoughts and insecurities. It's important not to ride the roller coaster with the patient, you'll burn out, or worse. That's why professional distance is key, that's why you don't get invested.

But I know Kelly. Not just like knowing her as a friend, but I know where she grew up, I know where she went to church, and I know what she was taught and told as a kid. The same happened to me, things that I've taken years and multiple medications to work through. Supports that were denied Kelly at every turn, she had to make it on her own.

And she did! That's what's so remarkable! I don't remember the name of the school she attended at the same time she was in church, but I know that while what happened at church messed my mind up, I was only marinating in that kind of stew for a few hours a week. She soaked in all of those beliefs, all of those thoughts from the moment she woke up until she finally went to sleep.

My parents got out, it took them time, but they came around. Kelly's folks never did, not even now, cutting her support system from under her. Shipping her off in the dead of night, demanding her to change without apology or acceptance of her needs. Doing that to a kid, it's devastating, and yet she still survived.

Kelly deserves my help, as much as I can afford to give her. I wish I could've helped back then, when we could have been friends instead of just in this professional relationship. Even if I'm projecting, even if paying her therapy bill even when she cancels has more to do with me than her, I might be one of the only people who can support her, who can help her.

If there was ever anyone worth breaking rules for, it's Kelly Harden.

10 Years Before Hurricane Ophelia

4th District Court of Appeals Majority Decision

(The following is an excerpt from the court decision that awarded Kelly Harden damages for neglect and injury as a result from attending (redacted) Wilderness Survival Camp. The suit was filed hours after criminal charges were dropped over the death of Skellan Klien.)

(Redacted) Wilderness Survival Camp vs Klien et al

…This court finds (Redacted) Wilderness Survival Camp liable for damages up to two million dollars for the wrongful death of Skellen Klien. This court also finds (Redacted) Wilderness Survival Camp liable for damages up to five hundred thousand dollars to Kelly Harden, (Redacted), (Redacted), and (Redacted) to pay for medical bills from chronic injuries stemming from their time at (Redacted) Wilderness Survival Camp.

This court rejects the argument presented by (Redacted) Wilderness Survival Camp that they bore no fault for the disciplinary methods used that resulted in the death of Skellen Klien and the injury of the others listed in the case. The court finds witness testimony of the various methods used to enforce discipline such as leaving students in stress positions for extended periods of time, restricting access to drinking water, food, and medical care to be extreme and unnecessary. The court rejects the defendant's characterization of these events as "necessary" or that they fall under current regulations' understanding of "reasonable" measures that parents and guardians signed over permission to under the (Redacted).

This court determined that Skellen Klien was held without food or water in an enclosed space for nearly fourteen hours while restrained in a stress position. The negligence and failure of the defendant's employees to provide Skellen Klien with his medication that could have prevented his death is a tragedy. Recompensating his family is insufficient, but hopefully will help bring some relief to the situation they find themselves in.

Other plaintiffs' discussion of their chronic injuries as a result from similar disciplinary methods that were used at the (Redacted) Wilderness Survival Camp also require recompense.

This Court wishes to conclude their opinion by emphasizing the negligence and malice apparent in the defendant's actions to the plaintiffs. The court hopes their decision will send a strong signal to other companies such as (Redacted) Wilderness Survival Camp to be certain that they do not engage in these same disciplinary actions that were brought to light in this case...

4

Five Years After Hurricane Ophelia

(I met Ernest Mobley in a small cabin on the outskirts of Bedford. I tracked down the only survivor from Calvary Baptist Church through the counseling program of one of the major Christian conventions that Calvary Baptist church associated with. Ernest had been in their care since the storm for a variety of mental and physical conditions. Around six months before our conversation, Ernest had been discharged from (redacted) hospital and placed on hospice care for his late stage cancer. I was one of the last people besides his nurse who spoke to him before he passed.

I spoke to Ernest in several hour sessions over the course of a few weeks, and have divided up his statements to fit with the rest of the information I uncovered about what happened at Calvary Baptist Church during superstorm Ophelia. A complete recording of our conversation is available, but included in this report is the most important of his statements, and the content of which the convention finds objectionable enough to be considered libel. I ask the court to judge for themselves whether I have misrepresented or lied about Ernest, regardless of how many of his claims seem implausible.

Ernest greeted me at the door and asked me to sit by the electrical fire in the center of his home. He informed me that the convention had provided him with a large stipend to spend on his hospice care, and that a "little log cabin where no one can bother me" appealed to him the most. I took a seat, got out my recorder and pencil while Ernest sat across from me. He held in his right hand a vaporizing device that I did not recognize, and asked if he could use it during our discussions, he told me it "took the edge off." When I asked what he was using, he simply said "the good stuff" to help keep his cancer under control.

The large armchair seemed to swallow Ernest, his limbs had lost most if not all of their muscle definition and deep lines stretched the skin in his face. Blond hair grew in a fuzzy stubble on his head and his hands would shake at intervals during our conversation.

Sitting across from him, I often found myself forgetting that Ernest was only 19 years old.)

Ernest Mobley - First Recording 02/23/2032

Speakers are Ernest Mobley (referred to as "E" throughout the transcript) and Kellen Faulk (referred to as "KF" throughout the transcript)

E: If we are going to have this conversation, I need to be up front about two conditions I have before I tell you what I saw at Calvary Baptist Church. I need your agreement in writing, before I tell you anything. Either you can agree to what I want, or I can just direct you right back to the convention to get the story of what happened at that church.

KF: Why do you need these two conditions?

E: I think that will become rather apparent as I tell you about the church.

KF: You mean to say you have differences with the convention report?

E: Of course I have differences with the convention report, you also have differences with the convention report. Otherwise, what the hell would be the point of us having this conversation?

KF: I'm sorry, I was just trying to understand your conditions better.

E: You won't, not until I'm done with my story, that's why I need your agreement now, your word.

KF: Alright, name your terms.

E: Number one, whatever I say here, whatever we talk about, you keep it under wraps until I am dead, and I don't mean you think I'm dead, I mean you watched them burn my body. I mean you don't say a word of what I'm going to tell you until you can open up my urn and see my ashes. Obviously you won't keep our conversation off the record, I don't expect that, but I do expect you to have the decency to wait until I'm dead and gone. If my nurse is right, you might be able to get the story published in the next few weeks.

Number two, after I'm no longer an inhabitant of the mortal coil, you publish what I say. I don't care what your editor says, I don't care if you have to put it on some third-rate conspiracy blog. I assume as a big and serious reporter you can afford to have one bomb of a story that tarnishes your reputation. My story, what I'm about to tell you, that's what you spend whatever social goodwill you've accumulated on. I've taken one of my remaining days to talk to you, so I damn well think that what happened to me, what I did, is important.

You can disbelieve me, you can call me insane, I don't care. Just make sure the story is published, and make sure I'm dead when it hits the press. I've got the documents right here for you to sign.

(Pen scratches)

KF: Alright, signed, I agree.

E: Good, so where do you want me to start?

KF: Who were you before the storm?

E: A dumb kid.

KF: Sure, but I was hoping to get a few more details on your life before Hurricane Ophelia.

E: What, do you want me to start with my birth?

KF: No, I would just like to get some idea of why you were so invested in Calvary Baptist Church to the point you sheltered there during the storm?

E: I was there because my Father was gone on business trips every other week and my Mother knew that he wasn't actually going on business trips but instead was with another family on the west coast. The beginning of the year of the storm, my Dad's discipline finally slipped and some of his "family" photos with his west coast wife were dug up by my Mom online. The bastard didn't even apologize, he just looked my Mom right in the eye and said "what are you going to do about it?" Long story short, the answer was nothing, except drink more wine and spend more time out with her friends.

I grew up with neither of my parents being particularly interested in anything about me. I think I ranked somewhere close to ninth or tenth on their priorities list. My material needs were met, and that was about it. So, in an attempt to find belonging, to find that genuine love and affection that was denied from me, I found religion.

When you are a kid who feels like no one wants you, the idea of a God that offers love unconditionally and all you need to do is feel sorry for a bit and then you are welcomed back, well it's intoxicating. And not only does this God love you unconditionally, but there is also a community ready-made, to talk about how wonderful this God is and reaffirm your belief in him. So, instead of a home life with a Dad that was absent and a Mom that resented my existence, I spent most of my time at Calvary Baptist Church.

KF: Have either or your parents reached out to you after the storm?

E: No, not once, and I didn't expect them to. My Father was out of town the night of the storm, and as for my Mother–

(Ernest takes a deep inhale of his vaporizing device)

I'm getting ahead of myself.

I'll fast forward my life until the summer before the storm. I would have been fourteen at the time, and was spending copious amounts of my time at Calvary Baptist Church. Given my inability to operate a car at that age, I relied on two men to get me to church on Wednesday, Sunday, and every church event I could help out, hang out, or be a part of. Both were generous, until it was almost an unspoken rule that they would swing by my house to get me beforehand. I would wait at the door.

The first man was my youth pastor Alex Elington, or Mr. E as me and the other teenagers called him. Mr. E viewed me less as a living breathing person next to him, and more like a captive audience for whatever he wanted to talk about. But, Mr. E would talk, all the time. I never had to do much to keep conversation flowing in the car, and being talked at was a welcome reprieve from the silence and passive aggression back home. Mr. E filled a friendship that I needed at that point in time, a sort of older brother who I was able to use to figure out which music was cool, what politics were correct, and why the show Modern Family was the key event that signaled America's descent into degeneracy. His curly blond hair, and boyish features hid the stark age difference between us. He was in his late thirties, with a wife and two children, while I was preparing to start high school the next year. It didn't matter, when I was around him, at least I was distracted from my own mind, even if I'm not certain I spoke a single word on our drives.

The second man was Chris Durose, or Mr. Chris as I knew him. Drives with Mr. Chris were, different. He never had DC Talk albums he wanted to show me, or political rants he wanted to share, no when I entered Mr. Chris's car we were silent, listening to whichever conservative talk radio station was operating at that time of day. Mr. Chris was tall, well over six feet, and elderly, though he never told me how old, and often wore sunglasses and some vest or jacket that had marine slogans on it. A large MIA-POW sticker was emblazoned on the back hatch of his 4x4 White Toyota Tundra, and his truck smelled perpetually of tobacco.

Whenever we listened to the radio, it could be boring or even frustrating to ride with him, but every once in a while, he would tell me that I had three questions I could ask him about life. I held onto these rides with both hands, because there was an adult who listened to my questions and gave me advice. Not only that, but he remembered things I told him, no matter if they were months earlier, he was maybe the only person in my life at that time who listened, really listened to me.

The smell of tobacco still brings back that truck to my mind, and a feeling of safety and agency I didn't have anywhere else in my life. Mr. Chris never chided me for asking a sensitive, or stupid question. The worst he would say is "that's kind of personal Ernest, maybe ask me something else." That kind of stability, that kind of care, it's what I needed, and in a strange way, I'm grateful that I met Mr. Chris just for those conversations.

Once, only once I asked Mr. Chris what he would do if he was in my situation. He paused, and after a little while just said, "ah, so there it is."

When I asked him what he meant he said, "You know. Kids don't spend this much time hanging around an old guy like me if there's not something wrong."

Having a feeling, or a worry validated is one of the more powerful things you can give a teenager. I had spent such a long time pretending everything was alright, that other people had real problems, that at least my physical needs were met so I should stop complaining. I lost track of how deeply shitty what was happening to me. Mom and Dad were both a mess, but just because they were hurting didn't justify them hurting me too. Mr. Chris gave me that validation that what had happened to me was wrong, and it welled up a massive lump in my throat.

"I don't know what to tell you son," Mr. Chris said. "But there was always this passage of scripture, that I took heart in when I had some family troubles of my own. Jesus said that 'If you come to me, but will not leave your family, you cannot be my follower.' It's a difficult piece of scripture, because family is so important, but I always found some good hope in this scripture."

I asked him why, and he placed a hand on my shoulder. Let me tell you, when an adult offers you a hand of comfort, when you haven't had any for years, it affects you as a kid. I was furiously swallowing the lump in my throat when he finished his advice.

"It's a hopeful passage because it shows that even if you have a family that's not been good to you, in the end it doesn't matter. Serving Christ and following Jesus is all that matters, he will be the family you didn't have, as long as you follow him. Later he says to 'pick up your cross and follow me,' and son, you can do that whatever your family situation is."

We sat the rest of that drive-in silence. I like remembering that drive, I like remembering the smell of Mr. Chris's car, and the feeling of clarity he had for me. The feeling of finally having an answer about what to do next.

I like remembering what that drive was like before the summer,

before the storm, before I knew why Mr. Chris was taking such an interest in me. I would pick up my own cross soon, but it sure as hell wasn't
Jesus I followed.

5

Five Years after Hurricane Ophelia

(Billy Vern was the first person I ever interviewed about Calvary Baptist. Before the project consumed my life, I wanted to understand how meteorologists were so caught unaware by the superstorm Ophelia. Who better to ask than one of the area's most experienced weathermen.

Today a man in his late 80's, Billy Vern has a slight frame with a small tuft of white combed over hair, and wears a pair of wire framed glasses. He smiles when he sees me, and pours out four different kinds of tea, insisting that I try each one. The flavors are delightful, and Billy speaks lovingly of how he and his wife are planning a trip to China within the next few months and cannot wait.

When I take out my tape recorder and pull out my notebook, I see the smile drop from Billy's face.)

Billy Vern - First Recording 01/15/2032

Speakers are Billy Vern (referred to as B throughout the transcript) and Kellen Faulk (referred to as "KF" throughout the transcript)

B: Rapid intensification. That's the meteorological term for what went wrong with Hurricane Ophelia. The scientific definition is when a hurricane increases in wind strength by 35 miles per hour in a 24-hour period. Ophelia strengthened by 160 Miles Per Hour in a twelve-hour period, going from a rainy day with a few power outages, to a Hollywood blockbuster level disaster over the course of a single evening.

I could give you the set of theories as to why Ophelia strengthened so quickly, but the reality is that we really don't know. The basic mechanism is the same in every case, the hotter the ocean, the less wind shear in the air, the greater the chance of a superstorm developing overnight. Now wind shear, that is generally beyond our ability to affect as mere mortals, but rapidly warming oceans we can predict. That summer was the hottest on record, and turned the entirety of the Atlantic Ocean into a hot bath providing the necessary conditions for the hurricane to spin itself into the wrath of nature over the course of a single evening.

Now, Hampton Roads is not an area that receives a pummeling from many hurricanes. It's not Florida, or Louisiana, or even Texas that have the history of being hurricane's punching bags for the majority of the summer and fall. Usually a storm tracking north fast enough to develop into a major hurricane is either going to spin itself off to the east, or make a beeline for the Carolina's. You saw this dynamic at work with Hurricane Florence where instead of impacting the Hampton Roads area, it was pushed south into the Carolinas. But even if the hurricane stayed on target for Hampton Roads, like what happened with hurricane Isabel, it would pass over cooler waters and weaken from a colossal superstorm to something less devastating. That's part of the reason Isabel went from a record-breaking superstorm, to a storm that wouldn't have been more than a footnote in the gulf coast.

But Ophelia didn't weaken, the storm ran over some particularly hot patch of the Atlantic Ocean some hundred miles of the Virginia Beach Coast, and strengthened from a nasty tropical storm to a category five apocalypse.

I remember the night before Ophelia made landfall. As soon as I finished pointing to my graphics and giving the boiler plate warnings about tropical flooding I just had this feeling. A dread settled into my chest that I hadn't felt since I saw the projected path of hurricane Sandy some fifteen years prior. My face must have shown my worry, because the late-night shift for weather, a young kid named Rob, asked me if I was alright.

I told him about the feeling, the dread that something was wrong. He shook his head and with that confidence only a young man could really project told me "ah it'll be fine, just a bit of rain." I nodded along and shuffled off the set.

Before I packed up for the night, I asked to see the radar and tracking data we had for Ophelia again. Over and over again I went over those charts trying to see if I missed something, or if there was some reason this particular storm bothered me. Sometimes I still wonder if I had been a better meteorologist, if I had been more careful I might have been able to spot the signs that Ophelia was about to strengthen. Those extra twelve hours, how many people could have been saved? How many families trapped on I-64 might have gotten out before the floodwaters rose? Would the malfunction of the USS Gerald Ford still have taken out the HRBT? How many people who decided to stay would have had time to board up their houses? For years, I struggled with my failure to warn people about what was coming, thinking it really was my fault, that I had missed something in my old age.

But I swear that there was nothing in the charts, nothing in the radar to suggest Ophelia explosively strengthening. There was always a chance it would become more powerful, but it was beyond my imagination how strong it would become. I kept the radar for a few years after the storm, but last year I finally threw out the information. I was right, I checked everything, I was thorough, but it just wasn't enough to predict the storm in this new world we live in.

That night, the night before the storm, I went home, kissed my wife, called my grandson, and went to bed. The next thing I remember is seeing Rob's phone number on my work phone at three thirty in the morning the next day.

By the time I got into work, the whole news crew was just staring at the weather radar. Rob's mouth was gaping, the scent of morning breath mixed with bad coffee lingering in the studio. They couldn't believe what they were seeing, and neither could I.

Well, we all stood there for a moment, until I did something I'd never done at that station. I started yelling for people to get to work. I remember my manager froze while I pushed him to have us air an hour early. The faster we told people about the storm, the more people we could save. I don't know if it was my age, my experience, or the fact that I never lost my temper, but people hopped to it and we got on air by four am that morning, twenty hours before the eye passed over Portsmouth.

KF: Was anyone upset by your statements about the hurricane? You've been accused of "fear mongering" by some important people back in Richmond.

B: Not in my office. I think my news crew respected me enough not to ask questions, and it was their families who were in the path of the storm. They knew what they were seeing on the radar, and they knew what it meant for all of Hampton Roads. People from out of town, they were unhappy with me. I ignored a few calls from the governor's office that day, they dragged me out to court a year or two ago to defend my statements on air. They said I "endangered the public" with my "reckless predictions" over the severity and damage of the storm.

The Governor actually called me if you would believe that? Called my office, Rob handed me the phone saying that it was Governor (redacted) on the phone, asking to speak to me. Well, at that point I had to take the call, sending Rob to keep telling people to get out. I heard the Governor before I even put the phone to my ear, he was shouting into the receiver. Gave me an earful about how my rhetoric was "incendiary" and I could cause more harm than good if I encouraged a "panic." I knew he was full of it when I asked him what his team was projecting for the storm's impact and he got real quiet. When I told him I was going to keep sharing my expertise with the area he resorted to legal threats. At that point I hung up, and didn't take another call from him until the storm was over. Well, he was true to his word taking me to court, but the impact of his arguments over my "reckless" reporting on the storm looked deeply silly in hindsight.

Ophelia proved me right, though not a day goes by that I wish I had been "fearmongering" or "catastrophizing." A lot of people have told me that those twelve hours of broadcasting, until our power went out and we hunkered down to ride out the storm, were the finest moments of my career.

I smiled at the compliments and retired within the month after the storm was done.

Tropical hurricanes are the most destructive storms that our planet has created. They routinely exceed wind speeds of powerful tornadoes, produce more flooding than enormous nor'easters, and pummel the coast for hours or even days. The storm surge that floods into an inhabited area can exceed the height of some tsunamis, and if people aren't warned, they don't stand a chance.

The only peace I can find is that I did all I could. It's a shame it wasn't enough.

6

67 Day before Hurricane Ophelia

Kelly Harden

to Alice Crenshaw

July 1st, 2:04 AM

Hi Alice,

I just wanted to thank you for all your help and support. I know after I missed that second appointment you would have been justified to just cut me off from all contact. Thank you, I really do think that our sessions have been helpful. I left our last one feeling better than I've felt since before I can remember.

Feeling good is never a reason to send an email at 2 in the morning though haha. Mom called today. I know that we've talked about the no contact policy, and you should know that I didn't take the call. I just stared at it until the number went to voicemail like I always do. If I cut her off too early, she just keeps calling, sometimes for the next hour.

The mistake I made was listening to her message. There wasn't anything wrong with what she said, mostly just asking how I was and hoping one day that she would be able to talk to me again. This time she didn't even mention God, so that was a big plus. I guess it just seems odd to me that she knew to call now, right when the settlement money was about to run out. I know what you would say, that there was no way she could know when that money ran out, that it must be a coincidence and an easily explainable one given that she calls at least once a week. She usually calls on Fridays though, but I'm trying to do what you told me, it's just a coincidence.

I'm still up right now because I've been thinking about camp, and Mom, and everything that happened. What's bothering me isn't even some of the stuff I've talked about that they did out there, but instead what happened when I got home. I was young, fifteen or so, and I remember the white truck that dropped me off at home. I got to sit in the front, and wasn't restrained like I was on the way out to camp, and I remember seeing my Mom in the driveway waiting for me. Now I knew that she was the one who sent me to camp, I knew because her and Dad both wrote a letter detailing everything I had ever done wrong to me that I read out in front of all the other fuck up kids. Her words, cutting me up in every way a person could be cut up.

But do you know what the first thing I did when I got out of the car was?

I ran right to her. She outstretched her arms and I sunk my head into her shoulder. I cried and cried all the while she held and murmured soothing words into my ear. She just whispered "it's ok honey, Mom's got you," over and over again.

And when I finally found the words lodged in the back of my throat do you know what I said? Do you know what I fucking said to the woman who had let two men drag me out of my bed in the dead of night? I said I was sorry. I couldn't stop saying it, over and over again. All I remember is just bawling that I was sorry and relishing her tenderness and how she touched my hair. I was desperate for any sign of kindness, needed it, and mom fucking knew it. She knew that I was so messed up, so turned around, that I was ready to go back to her broken down to be built back up.

I knew a boy at school, maybe a year or two older than me, and I would constantly be over at his house because a few friends of mine were also his friends. I never liked him, but it became unbearable after he got a puppy. You see, he would never directly hurt the puppy. He wouldn't hit it or scream at it, but would just keep having "accidents." He would "accidentally" step on the puppy's foot, or cut a nail too deep, because the puppy wouldn't understand. It couldn't understand that he was actually the source of the pain, all it knew is that it hurt and needed comfort. Then the boy would offer comfort and the puppy would burrow into him for warmth and love.

The crazy thing was that he always knew exactly when the puppy was ready to reach out for comfort, for love, for reassurance in the face of whatever pain it felt. He knew how to wait for the panic to subside and be right there when he was needed. I'm just thinking a lot about that puppy right now, and how Mom always has known right when to call, to hug, to provide the love and kindness she knows I need.

Alice Crenshaw

to Kelly Harden

July 1st, 7:35 AM

Hi Kelly,

I'm sorry your Mom called. It can't be easy continuing to keep her out of your life, especially now when you might need her help. You made the right decision not answering the phone, and don't beat yourself up over listening to the message. Family can be really difficult.

It's a human impulse to seek protection in a trusted adult after a traumatic experience. As a kid, you can't hold yourself responsible for your mom's actions. She did something that hurt you, shipped you off to a place where people hurt you. That's the opposite of what a parent does, and until she apologizes, or recognizes what she did, she has to bear that hurt. Even if she apologizes, it will be up to you to decide what happens next. If that happens, we can talk about next steps, but right now you are doing the right thing and I am proud of you.

Have you been able to change your pharmacy yet? I know you were anxious about where your medication was housed earlier. I really do think that some medicine will help you right now improve your quality of life. Let me know if there's anything I can do to help.

Just as a reminder, we have another session scheduled for tomorrow at 3 PM. Let me know beforehand if you need to cancel, but we can talk more in depth about what you are feeling then.

Hang in there Kelly, you are doing great.

-Alice

Kelly Harden

to Alice Crenshaw

July 1st 11:45 PM

I changed pharmacies, but it didn't really help. Do you remember Chris Durose? We would have known him as Mr. Chris, he sometimes helped out with youth events. He was a church deacon, always around Sunday morning. Didn't say a ton but just around him there was just this feeling. He was tall, well over six feet, and you could never tell how old he was. Sometimes it seemed like he had to be in his sixties but he could move quickly and was light on his feet.

He never talked to me much, but I didn't like being around him. I couldn't read him, couldn't predict what he would do next. His face always bore the same expression, like a parent that was somewhat disappointed in you. And that was before I saw him at Camp.

He wasn't around me often, but I remember one night he came to talk to our counselors, almost as if he was their boss. I never heard of him doing that work, but he seemed like someone they paid attention to, and gave out orders.

I was out after curfew, had to pee, and was trying to sneak to the woods to relieve myself given they would only let us leave twice a night. A few girls pissed themselves early in the camp, and given I had been there for a few weeks I didn't want to be shamed. I was so startled to see Mr. Chris that I tripped and fell over an outstretched root. They were on me in a second, putting me in "timeout."

I remember Mr. Chris ran ahead of the rest of the workers at the camp. At first, I thought I could get away from him because he was older, but he was so strong.

I don't know how long I was in timeout that night, but I know the sun was starting to come up when they finally took off the restraints. My back ached the rest of the camp, and my wrists, well, they ache even writing this email.

When I went to the pharmacy today, I saw him, I saw Mr. Chris outside. He was standing next to a four by four Toyota Tundra just watching the door. I can't explain it, but it was almost like I was back at camp for a moment, and at any moment his hands could wrap around my arm like I was fifteen again.

How could he know that I changed pharmacies? How was he there at the camp?

Alice Crenshaw

to Kelly Harden

July 1st, 11:53 PM

I do remember Mr. Chris, I never liked him either. He would always wear these sunglasses whenever he would join one of the youth retreats. I didn't like that I couldn't see his eyes, I always felt like he was looking at me, or some of the other girls in the group.

I believe that you think you saw him today at the pharmacy, but let's think about a few different reasons why he might be at the pharmacy. He could have a prescription to pick up for himself, or maybe he was running in to grab some other convenience he needed. He might have been as surprised to see you as you were to see him.

I would go back to the pharmacy tomorrow and see if he is still there. Even if you do see him, remember the only person you are hurting by not getting your medication is you.

If you need to call me to help stay on the phone while you get what you need just let me know. My number is (redacted)

-Alice

7

66 Days Before Hurricane Ophelia

(The following is a voice memo recorded by Dr. Alice Crenshaw dated July 2nd at 2:04 AM)

I've been trying to sleep for an hour. I know it's my own fault, waiting for a response from Kelly and tinkering around on the Internet until after midnight. I tell all of my clients to watch out for their sleep hygiene, and here I am with blue light shining on my face until the early hours of the morning. Well, now I'm paying the price, my mind is just racing with what Kelly told me. I remember Mr. Chris too.

He seemed old to me even back then, when I left the church and headed off to college. I always felt watched when I was around him, even as a kid, and even now talking about him with Kelly got me remembering one instance in particular that never sat right with me. I've taken my melatonin twice but still feel the adrenaline and worry coursing through me. There's a reason I don't check emails so late.

But I've tried all the other strategies I've given my clients so might as well pick the scab to see if that helps settle me down. I certainly doubt that Kelly is going to email me back to set my mind at ease. I really hope she is ok, obviously she didn't see him at the pharmacy. I've several times recommended assessment for paranoia or delusion, and the Mr. Chris she would have thought would be almost twenty years older now.

No way she could recognize him. But I really didn't like him when I was in church.

I'm scattered but might as well speak about what happened. After my freshman year in college at VCU, I came back home for the summer. The church decided to take a youth trip down to Nags Head. Some Christian conference was nearby, and it was a good way to entertain teenagers out for summer break. I volunteered to chaperone, my aunt Whitney was the youth minister Alex's wife, and I had worked at a summer camp during my time in high school. We all bundled into a school bus that was rented for the occasion and me, Aunt Whitney, Alex and Mr. Chris rode down to Nags Head for the weekend. I don't remember Kelly being there, I guess I know why now.

We get down to the beach and start walking out to claim a spot for twenty plus teenagers. Safe to say, we were not the most popular people on the beach that afternoon. It was a gorgeous day, the sun was perfect and there was almost no wind on the beach keeping the sharp sand at Nag's Head on the ground instead of cutting into our legs. I oversaw the girls in the group set up camp with Aunt Whitney, and all of us set off for the water.

Alex helped the boys get setup as Mr. Chris lounged in his chair. He barked a few times for water or for a boy to help with the tent, then leaned back in his chair, face impassive and sunglasses fixed over his face.

This was not my first beach outing of the year. I had recently been down to Virginia Beach with a few friends from school. My friends had helped me pick out a new bathing suit, a wonderful two piece with frilly sleeves that left me feeling both stylish and hot enough to be unapproachable. Of course I packed my nice new bathing suit for the Nags Head trip and wore it that first day on the beach.

When I took off my cover up with the rest of the girls and headed towards the water I felt a prickle on the back of my neck. Mr. Chris's face had gone from the firm line he held most of the time to bared teeth and clenched jaw. He was angry, and while I couldn't see his eyes, I felt, I knew he must have been angry at me.

He stood up and strode over to my Aunt Whitney. I don't know what he said, but whatever it was his face was bright red with anger. Alex walked over to discuss whatever it was with him, but he was still upset and I caught him making gestures towards me. He took off his sunglasses, and I saw his eyes on me and went cold. I dove headfirst into the water, and floated out in the ocean for the next hour.

When I got back to the beach and laid out on my towel to sunbathe, Aunt Whitney sat down beside me.

"Is that the only outfit you have for the trip?" she asked.

"Yeah why?" I said, sitting up.

"Do you really think that's appropriate for a church trip?" said Aunt Whitney. "I wonder if your heart is in the right place wearing something like that, are you trying to attract attention from the boys on the trip?"

The accusation stung. I felt color flush to my cheeks. Aunt Whitney had always been someone I thought was cool, someone I wanted to impress. Her disapproval was crushing.

"I just didn't think about it," I said, bringing my knees up over my chest.

"It's alright," said Aunt Whitney, holding out my cover up. "We all make mistakes sometimes, but I don't think you're setting the best example for the rest of the girls in the group. Why don't you go back and grab your bag from the bus and change into something that is more of a godly example for the students you are chaperoning and then come back."

And I did it. I pulled on the cover up on, and it smelled like seawater the whole rest of the trip. I walked back to the bus and changed. I didn't get back in the water the whole rest of the trip, I didn't even go on the beach without shorts.

Before I left, I saw Mr. Chris turn his head to watch me go. Thankfully, I didn't feel his gaze on me the rest of the trip.

I must emphasize, I was at church maybe every Sunday and every other Wednesday. I believed that Aunt Whitney was right, and I still sometimes wear shorts on the beach because of what happened. Kelly was, well she was in that environment all day, every day. It was as natural to her as the air she breathed.

I really doubt Mr. Chris was watching her go into the pharmacy, but I'll be damned if just the memory of him stops her from getting the help and support she needs.

8

Five Years After Hurricane Ophelia

Ernest Mobley - Second Recording 02/27/2032

Speakers are Ernest Mobley (referred to as "E" throughout the transcript) and Kellen Faulk (referred to as "KF" throughout the transcript)

E: I think people have this idea of extremist churches as always outside of civilization, some sort of rural congregation, deep in the country, with a graveyard right next door. The building is isolated, miles away from any major urban centers, and inside people babble nonsense and charm snakes. That wasn't Calvary Baptist, not in the slightest.

At first glance, one might say that Calvary Baptist was in a more rural part of Chesapeake. Large properties bordered in on either side of Mt. Pleasant road towards the beach, and every few miles you would see the odd grain silo, or get stuck behind a tractor. But on all sides, Calvary Baptist was bordered by homes, and not cheap ones. Large two-story houses with between five or six cars either in the parking lot or being worked on in the back. American flags flew out in these expansive porches, and the land around them held below ground pools, trampolines, or mini skate parks depending on the age and interest of the children who filled the house. What Calvary Baptist was surrounded by was a suburb engaged in an elaborate cosplay of rural life. Any needs were met by the glitzy shopping center barely ten minutes away, but private land and the illusion of space between homes differentiated the area from a normal suburb.

In the middle of summer, Mt. Pleasant was overwhelmingly damp and humid. Higher temperatures made the place a paradise for mosquitos, and every time I was outside I could hear the buzz of their wings in the sticky, tropical air.

Calvary Baptist was built maybe a mile away from an official wetland habitat protected by the state. That's a fancy way of saying it was built right next to a swamp. During that July and August, I remember planes swooping low overhead billowing mosquito repellent to keep the population of the pests under control. The church walled off the denizens and environment of the swamps with a chain link fence that marked where civilization ended and the wild began. The opposite side of the fence bore steep edges populated by all manner of tropical ferns that would not have been out of place on the set of Jurassic Park.

The church itself was a squat, brick building pasted together from two separate structures. Protruding out on the north side of the main bulk of the edifice headed west, was a gorgeous sanctuary with a high sloped roof and tall steeple. Stained glass windows ringed each side of the worship hall, and a large window stood at the front above where the baptismal was inside. Up above the window was an upraised crucifix looming over the property. The window itself was tinted a mustard yellow, with a bloodless representation of the passion in its center. The sanctuary attached at its back end to the main bulk of the brick building that ran some ninety to a hundred feet to the south. At the southern end of the building instead of ending in a rectangle, the structure made an L shape with the bottom part of the L pointing to the wetlands and chain link fence to the east. Running along the main body of the church was a sidewalk covered by a bright white awning. Every door to the church was painted dark red, with steel reinforced glass windows at face level. The doors were made of a heavy wood composite that slammed through the whole building when closed, and squeaked on unoiled hinges. From the outside, with the stained-glass windows and heavy doors it was almost impossible to see inside the church.

Behind the church, near the fence and the wetlands beyond was a trio of willow trees. Their gnarled roots clawed above the ground creating barren spots in the grassy backyard. The willows stretched above the building, their weeping leaves brushing the chain link fence in the back. Often, during cookouts or other events, I would sit down upon the roots, only to be reminded of the reason why I never could stay. The base of those trees was always swarming with ants, bright red, and with a bite that could make a grown man yelp.

The effect of being close to the wetlands, and the willow trees blocking the view to the north where more of the exurban houses were located made the church feel like its own world. Yes, another house was just a street away, and the cemetery was a mile off instead of just in the backyard, but the property felt self-contained, like its own universe.

And I loved it, when I worked, or volunteered, or attended I felt a clarity of purpose. I knew how to interact, what to say, and who to follow when I was there. Not like home.

One week in particular I spent nearly all day at the church. Vacation Bible School, or VBS, was always a massive event. Part summer school, part bible camp, and part day care, the event lasted from the late morning to well into the evening. Later, if you were like me, and had volunteered to help tear down on the last day of the camp before the upcoming Sunday. Being in that church late that evening, waiting on Mr. Chris and his wife Ms. Pam to take me home, that I guess was the first time I grew to have some concerns about what was happening at Calvary Baptist.

KF: Concerns?

E: Well concerns probably isn't the best way to describe it, more like a worry or a fear. Something that happens that just doesn't feel right, and you think about it late into the evening. An unanswered question, where if you were honest with yourself, you don't think you want to know the answer.

KF: Yeah, ok, do you have an example?

(Ernest holds up vaporizing device)

E: Do you mind? It makes it easier to talk about.

KF: Sure, whatever.

E: (Takes an inhale of the vaporizing device and exhales) The church was built with an industrial kitchen, an eight-burner stove, sink deep enough to swim in, walk in freezer, all the appliances with the stainless steel glow and chrome plating of the 1970's. The kitchen was located inside the social hall at the opposite side of the church than the sanctuary, and had a heavy red door that led outside to where the willow trees stood. The door had a bad habit of locking every time it swung closed, regardless if you left it unlocked when you exited. Mr. Chris, Mr E, and their wives were busy lifting, moving, and pulling down the VBS decorations from across the church, and I was tired of helping. So I did what most teenagers do in that situation, I hid.

I sat in the corner, near that red door, with a pair of tweezers and a bottle of antiseptic. A large plantar wart was in the pad of my foot, and I sat there for I don't know how long, picking it out.

KF: Why?

E: Because I was bored, because I didn't like the way it felt on my foot, and because it was deeply painful.

KF: You liked the pain?

E: I liked controlling the pain. I liked being in charge of when to put the tweezers to my skin, when to grasp the roots of the wart buried deep in the pad of my foot and pull, and I liked being the one to massage the antiseptic into the deep wounds I inflicted. The sensation was akin to picking a scab, but more intense, and as I dug out the pieces of fungus it gave a sort of satisfaction.

You can identify the seed of the warts as dark little spots in the wound. Once you cut through the exterior infection you can grab these and pull. Now, it drags out some of the other skin of your foot as well, but the infection is gone. You've pulled it out from the root.

I remember being shocked by how much blood flowed out of the infected skin. There's always a moment of panic when you realize you are bleeding, made worse when the blood has that slick, watery texture to it. I was surprised and started furiously blotting the wound, wincing at the pain. The copper tang filled my nose, and I felt my fingers become slippery with the stuff. My foot wouldn't stop bleeding.

The double doors to the social hall opened, and the click of heels echoed in the long hallway. Mr. Chris's wife Ms. Pam was the only woman who would be wearing heels for VBS.

I did not want to explain the bloody mess I'd created or why I was hiding out in the kitchen. Instead, I wadded up a set of paper towels under my injured foot, slipped on my shoe, and ran out the door to the back yard. I stood there for a moment or two, when I realized that the door locked behind me.

A lot of the rest of the church was locked up at that point, and I worried that I would be left alone at the church overnight. My cell phone was lying on the kitchen counter inside, discarded so I could hold the components of my auto-surgery in my hands. I went back to the door that led into the kitchen, and I heard movement inside. Specifically, the clinking of metal, and the press of a high-powered sink.

I adjusted my shoe to hide the wad of paper towels stemming the flow of blood from my foot and pounded on the door. Spending a night outside with the mosquitos if I was left behind would have been awful. Even at nearly ten o'clock at night, the temperature was still well over 85 degrees. I imagined the church parking lot with both Mr. Chris's Truck and Mr. E's Sedan gone leaving me alone outside. I called out and knocked on the door again and again calling Ms. Pam's name. The sound of the water and the clink of what sounded like silverware continued.

Outside, in the dark, with the buzzing drone of insects in my ears, a chill throbbed at the base of my neck. The largest of the willow trees loomed behind me, and I noticed the outline of the door that was obscured in darkness was becoming more defined, in the faintest yellow light. Small fingers of the mustard glow reaching out through the small cracks where the door met the wall.

I pulled at the door one final time, and it opened, depositing me back in that kitchen, staring at Ms. Pam. The fluorescent light in the room hummed and Ms. Pam frowned at me. She was a small woman, over a foot shorter than her husband even in heels, with large, billowy white hair, and heavily veined hands. She held in her hand a long cutting knife, and the water from the faucet still poured over the blade into the sink.

I mumbled an apology and asked if there was anything I could do to help.

"No, we are done here son. Mr. E is waiting for you near the front."

I grabbed the excuse and walked past Ms. Pam, limping on my injured foot. She turned the water off and waited for me to leave. On the drying rack were nearly a full set of stainless-steel blades. A long bread knife, a short and sharp paring knife, and a set of seven serrated steak knives, all immaculately clean and glistening in the light. I went to ask her what activity the VBS students had been doing that required the utensils, when I noticed the smell.

When you smell blood, your mouth fills with the taste, and Ms. Pam and that faucet reeked of the metallic scent. Two red lines ran down the sink to the drain, fast and quick like my foot had bled moments before. Ms. Pam saw my eyes and turned the faucet back on.

"He's waiting, son," she said, pointing at the door.

When I looked back at the sink, the red lines were gone. I rode home without saying a word while Mr. E ranted about the methodist pastor down the street and his preaching on "sexual immorality." Me and his wife Ms. Whitney just politely nodded when he prompted us.

When I woke up the next morning, I still felt like I had that metallic taste in my mouth.

9

54 Days Before Superstorm Ophelia

(On July 13th, at 5:30 PM Eastern, Kelly Harden placed a phone call to Dr. Alice Crenshaw. The call lasted approximately three minutes according to the cell data recorded by (redacted) cell data company. The details of the call were recorded by NSA metadata collection. I was able to access the data through a freedom of information act, and transcribed the discussion myself. This call was the third call placed to Alice Crenshaw by Kelly Harden in three days, and the most relevant to my report.)

Kelly: They found out where I work, oh God they know where I work.

Alice: Slow down, what do you mean they know where you work?

Kelly: I can't switch jobs again; I can't quit either or I'm going to lose my housing. I have to renew the lease soon and I need some sort of income, but they know where I work.

Alice: You aren't quitting your job, what do you mean that they know where you work?

Kelly: I won't go back. I'll die first; I'm not going back.

Alice: You aren't making sense, start from the beginning.

(Sound of closing curtains, crashing cutlery.)

Alice: Kelly, you are scaring me, where are you right now?

Kelly: Home, finally. I've got the curtains drawn, I know if they come for me I'll be ready.

Alice: Who is coming for you?

Kelly: (Deep breath) I saw him today, at the store. Just while I was leaving, I saw Mr. Chris standing in the parking lot next to his truck. He was wearing his sunglasses, those stupid, clunky aviators but I knew he was watching me. He knows where I work now, they all do. When I pulled out of the parking lot, he followed me in his truck. I lost him on the interstate, but he tailed me all the way out.

Alice: Why does it matter? He can't hurt you Kelly, not anymore.

Kelly: Of course he can, him and the rest can do whatever they want.

Alice: If you are worried about your safety, it might be time to call the police. Maybe they can do something about him following you around?

Kelly: Absolutely not.

Alice: I can't help keep you safe from Falls Church, maybe they can–

Kelly: Do you think I'm stable? All there mentally?

Alice: I think that you have acted responsibly in reaching out when you need help. Now if you feel as if you are in danger, it's time to involve the police.

Kelly: (Laughs) I know I'm crazy, and the police will too. Do you know how many interactions between people with mental conditions and law enforcement end in violence?

Alice: Not off the top of my head.

Kelly: Fucking too many of them, best case scenario is that the police don't believe me, worst case is I end up gift wrapped for Mr. Chris, Mom, and the rest of the church.

Alice: The church?

Kelly: Besides, you don't even fucking believe me, why would the cops?

Alice: I believe you.

Kelly: Bullshit. You keep trying to refer me to a psychiatrist for paranoia and delusions. You'd be a shit therapist if you believed your delusional patients.

Alice: Whatever is happening to you feels real, I believe that professionally and personally.

Kelly: Mr. Chris was there, in the parking lot, watching me leave just days after my Mom calls and the payouts from my settlement from that camp ended. It's not a coincidence, they were never going to let me go.

I won't let them take me again.

(Clinking metal)

Alice: I need you to answer me truthfully Kelly, is there anyone else in the house with you right now?

Kelly: Any moment now, the white truck will come down my driveway.

Alice: Please, is there anyone else nearby that you could ask to come over to the house. I don't think you should be alone right now.

Kelly: I have to go, stay away from here Alice, no matter what, do not come back. Never come back here.

Alice: Stay on the line with me, stay on the line with me please. Everything is going to be–

(Call Ends)

10

54 Days Before Hurricane Ophelia

(Dr. Alice Crenshaw recorded the following voice memo on July 13th at 1:00 AM eastern.)

I can't keep doing this.

Every line, every rule I've made for myself to keep my mind and heart whole in this tough job I've crossed for Kelly. She called me back, after I called her over and over again, hoping she was ok. I lied to her, told her I believed everything she said, that she was being followed, being watched. I never like lying to patients but honestly, I would have done anything to keep her from hurting herself.

I've never been like this. I've dealt with worse cases and my rule of never becoming anything more than clinically invested helped me survive.

But I'm in too deep with Kelly. I've never been the one who talked someone down from whatever it was she was about to do. I didn't even know her, but I guess I see a version of myself. If my parents had been slightly less understanding, if I had not found my people in college and in grad school, I could have been her.

I know now that what I was taught at that church, about how I was a broken, wretched thing and that the only good that I could ever do was through letting God work through me is wrong. But it took a long time to get there, a long time to heal that hurt inside of me that always said that he is good he is good when there was nothing good in me.

I can't cut Kelly off because that means I can't heal from what happened to me. It means the hurt will be there forever and I can't let that happen. I have to dig to the root, and helping her, keeping her safe from her fears and herself is crucial. I don't usually have that feeling, but it's inescapable. If there is a God and we are part of his divine plan, I think becoming a therapist to help Kelly is part of that plan.

But it's killing me. I can't sleep, I'm worried sick, every day I worry that I'll see her name in the news.

I can feel it, the old anxiety, old fears creeping in every night. I'm sleeping worse, and I'm hesitant to ask for an increase in my medication. Soon I might need it though. I constantly check my phone just to make sure she hasn't texted or called.

If she did, and I didn't answer, and something happened I don't know if I'd ever forgive myself.

I have to end it, I have to end my projection, have to reestablish professionalism but I do not know how.

11

(Retired from her years working with the Virginia disaster response team, Vivian Hart chose the bustling streets of Richmond's fan district to stay connected to the city in her and her wife's old age. She offers me tea on the porch of her old Richmond home, and rocks serenely in her chair. Her eyes are closed as she begins to speak, ignoring the map of Hampton Roads I have spread out across the small sitting table outside.)

Five years after Hurricane Ophelia

Vivian Hart- First Recording 01/05/2032

Speakers are Vivian Hart (referred to as (V) throughout the transcript) and Kellen Faulk (referred to as "KF" throughout the transcript)

V: Ophelia, that was the last one for me. The disaster response team had dealt with torrential flooding from the nor'easter that hit Blacksburg and Roanoke, provided support from the truck bomb attacks in Arlington and Alexandria, and even helped the eastern shore deal with tropical storm Henry from the same year that flooded out thousands, but Ophelia, she was a different beast.

When I first got down to Emporia where most of our relief efforts started, I had some hope that the damage to Hampton Roads wouldn't be catastrophic. The Governor gave me a fairly rosy view of the situation, and was hoping that the national guard wouldn't have to come give us a hand in the clean up efforts. He was terrified that calling on the feds would make him look bad, not a lot of folks in Virginia liked the president at that time, certainly not folks in the Governor's party. So I had some two hundred full time folks, and about a thousand volunteers to clean up and provide assistance to some million odd people who were still trapped in the Hampton Roads area.

"Local support" was the phrase that kept getting used by my superiors. All we were supposed to do was link up with the local governments in tidewater, and help them get back on their feet to reestablish some basic services. Only when I got to Emporia did I realize most "local support" was nonexistent after the storm. Police, firemen, hell even the Dominion workers were in complete disarray, I'm not even certain the government was functioning inside of Portsmouth and Norfolk the storm hit them so hard. The floodwaters still hadn't receded by the time I got to Emporia, and made contacting and helping people inside those cities impossible.

On top of that, do you know how many separate cities the Hampton Roads area contains? There're seven distinct cities all with their own local battery of basic services. It was a goddamn nightmare trying to coordinate anything between them. I got seven different sets of information at all times, whether it was officials from Portsmouth hollering that over ninety percent of their people were water insecure and out of power, or officials from Suffolk grousing over why I was asking them to transport food and water to Norfolk. And God help me if I ever suggested using the resources of the Chesapeake fire department to help out Hampton or Portsmouth. I do think a few local Suffolk politicians compared me to Chairman Mao at one point because I had more of dominion's repair efforts focused on Virginia Beach where over seventy percent of people didn't have power, than getting the last few lines back up near Isle of Wight.

But the devastation, I've never seen anything like it. The speed and power of that storm took everyone by surprise, and then with what happened at the Bridge tunnel with the Carrier, it was just awful. Caskets unearthed by the flood waters floating like corks, orphaned kids without shoes trying to make their way through running brown water, houses ripped apart with their inhabitants found in a tree near a mile away. Barely anything recognizable remained.

I'll never forget when we pushed our way west towards Church-land and started draining the floodwater from 664. The Monitor and Merrimac had become the only way across the bay after the HRBT collapse, and you could just see cars backed up for miles. Thousands upon thousands of them, all packed to the brim with everything families could fit into them before the storm hit. Family pictures, plastic dolls, hot plates, stuffed animals, cat carriers, and dog toys all at the bottom of the floodwaters.

I remember standing there, looking at the line of cars, and feeling the dread of those families who hoped that they would be able to get across the river in time. You're not supposed to write the story of everyone you see die in my job, you can't, but I could just vividly see the people in these cars dread turn to panic as they decide whether to wait in traffic or take their chances on foot. Most ran, the few that didn't, well not all the cars were empty when we found them.

After we drained the rest of the interstate, I called the Governor and turned in my resignation right then and there. I was done, spent, and honestly doubted whether my expertise and knowledge would even matter in the face of such destruction.

I used to live in Hampton Roads if you would believe that. Lived there for ten years in the nineties and early aughts. There was a beach park, down on Sandbridge a little way away from the hustle and bustle up at the Virginia Beach boardwalk. Little Island I think it was called, with a fishing pier out into the ocean and a long stretch of beach where folks just sat and looked out at the Atlantic. I spent more than a few summer days stretched out on that beach listening to the ocean, the vacationing teenagers, and picnicking families until all the sound melded into a pleasant drone. When relief efforts finally got out to Mt. Pleasant and down to the beach, the pier was gone, and flood water had washed away all of the sand leaving a rocky, barren spit as all that remained.

The church you asked about, Calvary Baptist, it would have been weeks before the floods receded enough for us to get help there. Our preliminary lines of aid didn't even reach into Churchland or Hickory, and Mt. Pleasant wasn't fully restored from the storm until the end of the year. The people there faced the hurricane alone, no one was coming to save them.

12

Ernest Mobley - Second Recording 02/27/2032

Five Years after Hurricane Ophelia

Speakers are Ernest Mobley (referred to as "E" throughout the transcript) and Kellen Faulk (referred to as "KF" throughout the transcript)

E: Later that same summer I attended my first "all in" night at Calvary Baptist, and that worry, that unexplained anxiety over what I saw in the kitchen sink in the church grew into something quite different.

KF: All In night? I'm not familiar?

E: Think of it as a more intense church service. Sermons and hymns are what most people want and expect from their church ceremonies, but those can feel stilted, or even stale. Even with a high production value, booming drums, and choirs a hundred strong, something can be missing from Sunday morning. So many people who just show up every Sunday, got free childcare for an hour or two, then went on with their lives until the next week. As a teenager, I was certain that this stale, stuffy religion wasn't enough for me. I needed the old power of the revival tent, a place where true believers, people utterly on fire for God, could find community.

(Ernest takes another inhale of his vaporizing device.)

Ritual is a word that evokes a history of human religion since the beginning I guess. It conjures images of blood rites, sacrifices, foreign babbling and screaming at the sky in some misguided attempt to ensure the sun rises the next morning. When I say the word ritual, often it is consigned to the past, a foolish activity of our ancestors now only practiced by the backward or sinister places that have failed to adapt to the expectations of modern life. But it means anything you do, every day, that has significance. Coming to church on Sunday morning to worship and listen to a sermon is the definition of ritual, but it's just so ordinary. Doesn't scratch the same itch that those ancient festivals of human excess to show praise to the moon soothes. For a teenager like me, looking for something closer to that old religion, that more impactful ritual, all in night filled the void.

What was incredible was that at the time, nothing I experienced in those charged Sunday nights seemed outlandish. Only when telling another about the events, or thinking about them in hindsight, is there a strangeness to what was said and what was sung out in these rituals. When I was in the moment, when I was there, it felt rapturous, divine, even euphoric to engage in "all out worship" to God.

You've been with the convention for a while, haven't you? Or been part of their reporting office?

KF: Yes.

E: And you grew up in the church? Or were you a later convert?

KF: I grew up in it.

E: So I'll spare you all the details of what exactly was said and done at the monthly rites. There was music, loud music, that made you leap and dance for joy while you howled the repetitive words that would be in your head for the next few weeks. The band exuded the same personality as a classic rock cover group, one or two members who thought they were showmen for (redacted) and the rest a collection of the church congregation who studiously stared down at the sheet music in front of them. I stood at the front of the congregation dancing and singing with other young people, always wondering in the back of my head whether my movements were directed by the holy spirit, or a symbol of my performative faith.

Like all good rituals, the ceremonies were conducted at night. The sanctuary at Calvary Baptist could hold maybe two hundred maximum, and on 'All In' night barely half of the pews would be full. Lights that were not for the stage were turned off, making us worship in the dark with the occasional yellow glow of a spotlight, or strobe near a particularly affecting flourish of the electric guitar. In the darkness, the red velvet carpet of the sanctuary disappeared, the stained-glass windows became just a reflection of the light show on stage, and one could almost forget that this was the same stuffy, lukewarm church from Sunday morning.

If I felt useful, or purposeful at church or helping Mr. Chris or Mr. E, "All In" nights gave me an outlet for the pain of my home life, the pain of growing up, and the pain of guilt that festers and lurks inside every teenager. That feeling is still what has stuck with me today, even hearing the opening chords of (redacted) or seeing the lyrics to some of those songs, opens up a raw and ragged part of me. How the contrast between euphoria and anguish, dread and hope, outpouring love for Jesus and hatred from myself burrowed into my soul during those evenings. Sometimes, I miss it, sometimes I wonder if it would be worth it to go back, just one more time, even if I know how it ends.

KF: Worship can be deeply affecting; I recall similar feelings when I was younger.

E: Take a group of people, young and old, who have no other outlet for the raging currents of feeling inside them, who have not learned any skills around emotional regulation, and put them in a church for a few hours blasting them with praise music and emotionally charged stories, and I swear every one of them "will feel God working." I felt it, "in my heart" as they said at the meeting.

People next to me, other teenagers in our youth, people whose names I will refrain from using if you don't mind, would fall on their knees declaring endless love for Jesus. Kids I knew had grown up in the church their entire life, would constantly be kneeling in redemptive prayer, the anguish of their confessions contorting their faces into tears, cries out, and pensive silence. I was not immune, soon I was on my knees too, hands clasped, tears flowing as I felt a warmth of belonging and love surging through my mind. The singers on stage told me it was the work of the spirit, and why wouldn't I believe them, why wouldn't I think the surge of endorphins and release of repressed emotion was the work of God and not my own mind. Even today I still wonder what was actually happening inside my head as we sang the fifth refrain of (redacted.)

(Ernest rubs his head in his hands and gives me a tight grin.)

Mr. E and Pastor Phil often traded off the small amount of preaching that occurred in between the altar calls and endless loops of worship music. If the band had one or two showmen in the set of them, Mr. E and Pastor Phil were in their element. I don't remember a single scripture they bellowed from the front, but instead the constant calls to action, constant calls to repentance.

And every time they called for a confession, I shouted mine with the rest of the congregation. All of us engaged in this collective purging of whatever guilt or pain that nestled in our head like a tumor. And like pulling out the wart from my foot, it felt so fucking good.

By the end of the night my throat was hoarse, my limbs were tired, and my head throbbed from dehydration. Mr. E stood up at the front and said he was about to show a clip from a film. He spent a long time talking about how "intense" and "graphic" the clip was going to be. He explained that it was a "real" depiction of what Jesus had done for all of us and said some words about how it should convict us all to repentance. I remember the sanctuary was silent as the last of the lights faded while the band played a few mournful chords to fill the void.

The length of the video was maybe eight minutes, but it showed, in excruciating detail the torture and crucifixion of Jesus. Gasps rang out from the crowd at the escalating gore and pain that emanated from the screen. About halfway through I was on my knees with many of the other members weeping and crying in misery. I know now the film was often used by churches like Calvary Baptist, but this was my first time. When the video ended, I was a blubbering mess, no longer calling out specific confessions and sins, but instead just sitting in the nadir of pain and despair at what my savior had gone through, what, as Mr. E explained moments after the video ended, what I had done to him. I was the roman soldier who beat his back bloody and nailed him to a cross, he had to endure such things because of his love for me.

I cannot tell you the number of things that I said to the loving feeling that wrapped around my mind that night. I forgave my mother, I forgave my father, I confessed to cheating on a fifth-grade math test, I confessed to impure thoughts about women in the church, and swore my whole life to God.

The thing is, I did feel a weight lift, I did feel some relief, at least until later that evening when the hurts that I had forgiven became apparent when I spoke to my Mom and remembered Dad was still on the west coast for the next few days. But in that space, in that universe unto itself in the church, those worries were gone. For a time at least.

We came to the end of the altar call, and the worship music kicked back up calling upon all of us to cry out and confess our sins to Jesus. I shouted with the rest, in this communal display of suffering, our attempting to be "like Christ" in our pain. It's a sharp, pointed thing that sticks in my throat everytime that I think of the lyrics, or hear the slow soulful guitar of much Christian music. But right before the end, I felt something else in that sanctuary.

(Ernest takes another inhale of his vaporizing device.)

When you have dealt with an overactive mind like me your whole life, you generally do know when you are talking to yourself in your head. Even when engaged in ear splitting ritual, a small grain of self awareness knows that the vast majority of the feelings and euphoria of the evening was in my head, that it was hard to track down exactly the moment God started speaking to me. I tell you this, because right before the end of the song, a voice spoke into my head, and that wonder, that worry that it was all in my head was utterly gone.

KF: How do you know?

E: Because it felt like an intrusion, something breaking through the cacophony of my tired mind at that point in the evening, and because instead of being part of the jumbled nature of my thoughts, it sounded crystal clear.

KF: Alright, what did you think it said?

E: It didn't say anything. I looked up and saw a mustard yellow glow in one of the light fixtures, like a light bulb on its last legs. The color seemed wrong, off, and made the hair on my arms turn to goosebumps.

I looked back at the light switches at the rear of the sanctuary to see whether or not one of the lights had been left on, when cutting through my spiraling mind was the sound of a deep groan. At the time, I couldn't place the sound but now, with some more experience on myself and others, I swear that the sound was one of obscene pleasure and desire.

I spun around trying to find who made that noise in the congregation but couldn't. I looked until the end of the song, the end of the prayer, until the lights went on inside the sanctuary.

When the lights went up, I felt eyes on the back of my neck. Mr. Chris was staring at me from a vacant pew in the back, a huge grin covering his face.

13

37 Days Before Hurricane Ophelia

(The following is an email exchange between Dr. Alice Crenshaw and Kelly Harden the evening and early morning of July 30th and 31st. The emails were recovered off of Dr. Crenshaw's personal email address.)

Kelly Harden

to Alice Crenshaw

July 30th, 9:34 PM

Alice,

I'm scared.

People keep following me. I see them everywhere. I stopped going to work. I could feel them watching me. They knew my schedule, they must have known the manager.

Three men and a woman. They stood near the shopping carts. I could feel their eyes on my head. Mr. Chris and my Mom were both there, looking at me. I couldn't stand it any longer. I walked out, away from my job, and ran to the parking lot. I'll find a job somewhere else.

They want something from me, I know it, something terrible. It has to do with that sick shit they did at camp. I know in my bones that dying would be better than letting them take me again. Dying would be better than going back.

I wish you were here.

Alice Crenshaw

to Kelly Harden

Thursday July 30th, 9:40 PM

Kelly,

I know you are scared. I know what's happening to you feels real and I believe you. Are you safe in the house? Is your roommate home?

Remember some of the strategies we talked about. If people are following you, I need you to be alert and feel calm. Can you calm yourself down or do you need help?

-Alice

Kelly Harden

to Alice Crenshaw

July 30th 11:56 PM

I don't want to calm myself down. I am being followed everywhere I go. They are going to come to the house. I just know it, they are going to come to the house and then nowhere will be safe. I've been hiding in the bathroom for hours, there are not any windows, here I am as safe as possible. They can't see me here.

The white truck will roll down my driveway, and Mr. Chris will find me. This time though, I have a plan and a way to keep myself safe. I'll be safe from them forever.

If they come into the house I will be able to hear them. I won't let them take me again, no matter what.

I need your help, please come help me.

Alice Crenshaw

to Kelly Harden

August 7th 12:05 AM

Kelly,

I am available to call on my cell if you need me. I will not be driving down several hours in the middle of the night to see you. We have talked about this before.

A phone call may dissuade the people who are following you from coming to your house, and means I will know if you stop communicating. It will help keep you safe

Please reach out to your roommate, or someone else you trust to come and be with you right now. I do not think that it is good for you to be alone.

Please give me a call now so I know you are safe. I need to know you are safe.

-Alice

(The following was a voice mail left on Kelly Harden's phone. The time stamp dates the call as July 31st at 1:32 AM.)

Alice: Hi Kelly, this is just Alice, I'm just checking in. You seemed pretty scared earlier, and I wanted to make sure you were ok. I know that feeling like you are being followed is really scary. Please give me a call when you get a chance, I'm worried about you. You know that if I think you might be a danger to yourself or someone else I have to tell someone and I don't want to do that.

Please give me a call back when you can. I'll be beside my phone all night.

(Alice Crenshaw placed another call at 1:43 AM to Kelly Haden.)

Alice: Kelly, please call me back. I can't wait any longer. If you don't call me in the next five minutes, I'm going to have to call the police for a wellness check. You know I have to report anytime I think that you are a danger to yourself or others.

Please call me

14

36 Days Before Hurricane Ophelia

(The following is a phone transcript of a 9-11 call placed to a Chesapeake call center on the night of July 31st. I obtained the transcript of the entire call after multiple Freedom of Information Acts, and one sympathetic 9-11 dispatcher that I will not name here. These calls continue to follow Alice Crenshaw's attempts to establish the safety of Kelly Harden.)

Dispatcher: 9-11 what is your emergency?

Alice: My name is Dr. Alice Crenshaw. I need a welfare check for Kelly Harden at (Address redacted) due to a mental health crisis. I am a therapist and have reason to believe one of my patients may be in distress.

Dispatcher: Uh-huh, honey you know we have a non-emergency number.

Alice: I believe this is an emergency.

Dispatcher: Have you tried to contact your patient directly?

Alice: I have called her several times-

Dispatcher: But have you gone by her residence?

Alice: No, I am not local, I'm up in Falls Church. That's why I'm calling for a wellness check.

Dispatcher: You're up in Falls Church but you have a patient down here in Greenbrier? How does that work?

Alice: This is an emergency. Please just let me know when someone goes over to her address. I'd like to try and call her again before they get there, she has a history with the police.

Dispatcher: Uh huh, can't you call family? I've got a lot of cops right now dealing with several different emergencies.

Alice: This is a fucking emergency.

Dispatcher: Ma'am please calm down. I can't help you if you do not remain calm on the line. The only way to help your friend or client or whatever is to let me do my job.

Alice: (deep breath) I am sorry, but I feel like you aren't taking me seriously.

Dispatcher: Uh huh, let me see who I have available.

Alice: Please, I don't know what she has access to that she could hurt herself with. Just a quick check, to make sure she's alright.

Dispatcher: Hmmmm, I'll call it over to an officer nearby. Please hold for me while I see if I can get him to pickup. In the meantime maybe let a trusted friend, or family know. See if they can check on her since you obviously can't.

Alice: Fucking Bitc-

(Hold begins at 1:48 AM and continues until 2:13 AM)

Dispatcher: Alice right?

Alice: Did you find someone?

Dispatcher: Did Kelly call you back?

Alice: Obviously not, if she did do you think I would still be talking to you?

Dispatcher: Ah well, you think this is actually an emergency?

Alice: Yes. Why else would I call you after two in the morning?

Dispatcher: Ma'am, there's no need for sarcasm.

Alice: Did you find someone?

Dispatcher: (audible sound of keys clicking) I called Harrison, he should be able to drop by right before three. He should be able to check on Kelly, and I'll call you back with what he finds.

Alice: Please make sure to tell him it's a mental health crisis, Kelly has a diagnosis, she often is paranoid. I'll try to call her before he shows up to make things easier.

Dispatcher: Is there anything else?

Alice: Just call me back soon as you hear anything.

Dispatcher: Uh huh.

(Dispatcher disconnects call)

(Alice Crenshaw placed another call to Kelly Harden at 2:15 AM. The voicemail is recorded below.)

I called the police, Kelly. They should be by in the next thirty or so minutes. I know that this isn't what you want, I know you will probably be pretty upset when they get there but I had to do it. You've really scared me tonight. If you pick up now, or call me back I can call the cops off. They won't come by the house and it will be like this never happened. As a professional, and as someone who grew up with you, I need to know you are ok. If you pick up I can help keep you safe.

Please pick up,

(phone call continues in silence until 2:30 AM)

Please be ok.

(Call ends)

(The following transcript is of a call between officer John Harrison and Dispatcher Shelly Kharis which began at 3:23 AM outside of Kelly Harden's home.)

Harrison: I'm here at (address redacted) is this where that DC woman wanted me to check on?

Shelly: Yep that's the one, gave me some whole story about how the woman in the house was a danger to herself. Paranoid or something.

Harrison: What was her name?

Shelly: Kelly Harden.

Harrison: Oh I know Kelly, I know her parents at least, broke their heart when she stopped coming to church. She's always had some issues, a real shame, her parents bent over backwards to help her and she's never shown an ounce of gratitude.

Shelly: Ain't that some shit.

Harrison: Not just emotionally too, they sunk a bunch of money into a few of those summer camps to help kids with their problems. Now she's all grown up and thinks she can just cut them out. No calls, no visits, no nothing.

Shelly: Obviously she can't if I've got a shrink from DC begging me to check on her.

(muffled chuckles from both speakers)

Harrison: All the lights are out here, I'm not sure she's home.

(Heavy footfalls are audible on the call. A porch creaks and heavy thuds on a wooden door come through the receiver)

Harrison: Kelly? Kelly Harden? You up there? It's Chesapeake police.

Shelly: Is she answering?

Harrison: No, something weird on this door though, maybe some old damage?

Shelly: Those apartments have been there forever, could be any number of things.

Harrison: Looks like some kind of scratch, or gouge, pretty deep too, seems to crisscross all across the door.

Shelly: Do they look fresh?

Harrison: No, but there's some kind of pattern to them I think. Hold on (clicking of a flashlight) yeah I'm seeing two lines, maybe a foot or two apart, deep lines about an inch wide and an inch thick. Inside are a couple circles or something, the whole thing looks a bit like a tree.

Shelly: Anything from inside the house?

Harrison: No, not really, I'll try the door again. Kelly? Are you there? Kelly it's-

(Muffled noises, heavy footballs on the wood)

Harrison: (Inaudible) Shit

Shelly: What? Do you need help?

Harrison: (Heavy breathing) No, no I'm ok. Just saw her upstairs in the window. Startled me, that's all.

Shelly: You need backup? I can call a few of the other officers?

Harrison: No no, no need. Just got spooked, I thought I saw (long pause) Never mind. Just been a long night.

Shelly: Are you going to go into the house?

Harrison: I mean, if the DC woman said it was an emergency I guess I should.

Shelly: Oh forget her, thinking she could call down here and make you do all the work. If she was really worried she would have either driven down herself or got someone Kelly knew. Whole thing stinks of CYA.

Harrison: I did see Kelly inside the house, that usually is enough to determine that she's well enough for her to stop being my problem.

Shelly: Tell you what John, I'll call the DC lady back and tell her you went in the house and talked to Kelly. Tell her everything is all ok, and that she can go back to sleep without worrying about her crazy patient or whatever. Just say you saw her in your report and we can move on with our lives.

Harrison: All right, I did see her anyway. Thank you Shelly.

Shelly: Don't mention it, I'll call her back now.

15

36 Days Before Hurricane Ophelia

(The following is a voice memo recorded by Alice Crenshaw on July 31st at 3:40 AM)

I have the email drafted.

The full list of reasons that I need to break off my patient-therapist relationship with Kelly. I have every resource I could find, every piece of information that I thought might be helpful for her to find the support she needs. People struggle with paranoia, fear, anxiety all the time, and they either make it or they don't. I have to stop thinking that I can save her all by myself. I have to stop trying to be her only support, or else.

I believe in therapy because it helps people. Even if it's not about 'fixing' the person. Giving people a safe space and listening ear to their feelings, troubles, and worries matters. I have done that for Kelly, and now the rest is up to her.

I'll send the email in the morning. Kelly never called me back, but I'm not responsible for her, I can't be.

She is in charge of what happens next. I have done everything I can to help her navigate the trouble she endured as a kid and its effects to this day. It's time for me to step aside, it's time to let her find her support on her own.

I desperately hope she finds some peace, but I can't keep doing this.

(The following is the final email exchange between Kelly Harden and Alice Crenshaw from July 31st, 2027. The email was saved and starred in Alice Crenshaw's inbox.)

Kelly Harden

to Alice Crenshaw

July 31st 7:28 AM

Why the fuck would you call the police on me? After everything I've told you about what happened to me when I was a kid, why the actual fuck would you think the police are the best way to help me? I was in a full blown panic when I saw the flashing lights coming into the complex. I was sure I was going back to camp or somewhere worse, I thought they had come for me. I thought that my parents had called, or maybe a neighbor who was getting into my business but then I saw your phone call. How could you?

You don't give a damn about me, you never did and you never will. You don't believe me about what it's like to live here. You say all the time that you grew up here too so you understand, and for a time I thought that was true but you're just like everyone else who has tried to help me. I'm not worth believing, I'm not worth anything but the police to make sure I'm not a threat to myself or others.

A threat, ha, I've been living under threats my entire life. Followed around, bundled off in the middle of the night to dumb fuck nowhere to dig posts for six months, and now the moment you get a little worried about me you call the motherfucking police to check in. I don't even think you called because you actually cared about me, I think you called just to cover your own ass, help you keep that fancy job you got up in DC.

Well, fuck you Alice, I never want to talk to you again.

Alice Crenshaw

to Kelly Harden

July 31st 9:32 AM

Kelly,

I will not be spoken to in this way, whether over email or otherwise. I am not your friend, I am your therapist, and I think it is time for you to seek services elsewhere. I would encourage you to look for local care as it might be more suited to your needs. I am canceling your next week's telehealth appointment with me, and wish you the best of luck.

The bill for your final session should come in the mail, it is also available to pay in the online portal.

I am sorry this didn't work out,

Alice

PART TWO

16

Five Years After Hurricane Ophelia

(Anita Hernan is an easy person to find, she likes it that way. Something of a minor internet celebrity, Anita broadcasts her live political show "Whole Truth" biweekly where she speaks to crystal enthusiasts, crash diet salesmen, long shot political candidates, and a few out and out conspiracy theorists. Her audience is a couple thousand strong per her metrics.

The content of these shows includes Anita's personal political opinions along with extended advertisements for her list of increasingly 'alternative' health and wellness products to her followers. Anita leveraged her time as a meteorologist at (redacted) to build connections with the health and wellness community and establish her presence on social media. Her pushing of radical ideas, such as the belief that Hurricane Ophelia was manipulated by the US government to scare the population into taking action on climate change has isolated her from most of the journalist community, and I didn't think much more of her than another crank selling insanity to make a buck until I listened to a recording of her show where she mentioned Calvary Baptist Church.

After a terse email exchange, I agreed to fly out to Sacramento to meet with Anita and hear what she has to say about "the big one." I politely declined to be a guest on her show, but she enthusiastically agreed to talk to me about the "irregularities" surrounding Hurricane

Ophelia. I mostly wanted to just see if she had a connection to Calvary Baptist Church outside of the storm given her incessant mentioning of the name. When I arrived in her studio, she had reams of weather maps laid out on her table and was standing in front of a monitor. I sighed and pulled out my tape recorder. I had figured prying into her personal connection with the church would be contingent on me listening to her various "opinions," I just hoped it wouldn't take too long.)

Anita Hernan - 03/02/2032

Speakers are Anita Hernan (referred to as "A" throughout the transcript) and Kellen Faulk (referred to as "KF" throughout the transcript)

A: Thank you for talking to me today, the mainstream media really has done a number on me recently, going after my sponsors, peppering me with false lawsuits, but they can't silence the truth.

KF: The truth?

A: The truth about how our government keeps us passive and quiet, having all of the right opinions, and all of the right beliefs, and "government approved actions." That's why they are coming after me so much, that's why I'm constantly getting served subpoena and cease and desists and every other dirty trick in the book. Because they know I'm close to uncovering the truth. That I'm so close to figuring out the messed up way they are controlling what we think about our planet and our place in the universe.

KF: Have you shared this truth with your viewers?

A: Not all of it, they aren't ready, not yet. Deprogramming your mind from all the toxic propaganda our government pumps into our heads is a long process, and you don't want to go too fast too quickly. Most people would go insane if they knew the whole truth, so you have to bring them along gently.

KF: But you are interested in sharing this mind altering truth with me?

A: You already know about Calvary Baptist Church, you are already on the path towards truth, I would say you are much farther along than my viewers.

KF: *But what if I was to publish your "truth?" What then?*

A: (Laughs) Come on now, you and I both know you aren't publishing a word I say. I'm not stupid. Besides, all of the records and physical evidence that I've collected is staying right here with me, so if you want to stake your entire career off of my word alone, well I'll put you in the rotation of frequent guest stars. We pay 30$ an appearance, which I think you'd be needing soon.

KF: *Why Calvary Baptist Church? What's important about the place?*

A: I have here in front of you, meteorological maps of the city of Chesapeake, printed at every hour of the storm. I've got radar, rainfall averages, wind speed readings, all of the tools of the trade for the city during the entire time it was destroyed by Superstorm Ophelia. While Chesapeake never got hit by the apocalyptic winds of the eye wall that passed over Norfolk and Portsmouth, almost every populated area was flooded by the storm surge and several feet of rain that the storm dumped over the area over the two days it hovered across the city.

Look here at each of the neighborhoods. Great Bridge, mostly flooded out, Hickory, inundated, Greenbriar, buried under thirty feet of storm surge, and all the way out to Virginia Beach, Dam Neck and Princess Ann were devastated by floodwaters. These rainfall totals are beyond belief, some in the forty to fifty inches. Parts of Hickory were under pelting rain for nearly twenty-four straight hours.

Everywhere in the area was slammed by the storm, except right here on Mt. Pleasant Road.

(Alice pulls out another set of radar maps zoomed into the area around Calvary Baptist Church. Amidst the deep purples and reds of severe rainfall, the radar in a half a mile diameter around the church is clear.)

Right above the church, there's no storm. You can check every moment during the all hands on deck broadcast Billy Vern did on the storm, bless that man. Not a single drop of rainwater according to either the radar, or the rainfall gauges fell on top of Calvary Baptist. It doesn't add up, hurricanes do not selectively spare areas of impact. They aren't tornadoes, they don't skip houses, and the eye of the storm was nearly thirty miles north hovering over the Chesapeake Bay. This right here shows that there is something our government doesn't want us to know about the storm, it shows that we have the technology to stop storms from striking vulnerable areas! This is huge, it means the government has been letting people die in these superstorms while protecting their key assets in the path of the storm!

KF: Calvary Baptist church was a key asset?

A: It must have been! If the use of weather manipulation technology is confirmed, like it is looking at these maps, then they must have deployed that power at Calvary Baptist!

KF: Ok, I understand. Now I do have a question that people might ask when this goes public, I know there has to be an explanation, but I think if I was the government, I would simply claim that the weather equipment malfunctioned under the strain of the storm.

A: Oh I know, that would be how I would twist the truth too. Luckily we have more evidence that Calvary Baptist was kept high and dry while the rest of the area drowned.

(Anita holds out a picture of seagull, and places two ziplock bags with what looks like hardened bird droppings of different sizes.)

KF: What am I looking at?

A: Birdshit.

(Anita grins at me like I don't understand a convoluted inside joke.)

KF: And the birdshit means?

A: One of the cleanup crews reported an enormous amount of bird feces covering and surrounding the Calvary Baptist property within the half mile area that showed no signs of rainfall. Not only were they bird feces, but feces from terns, albatrosses, cormaments, and other species that generally range out over the Atlantic Ocean. These birds don't come as far inland as Mt. Pleasant, and they certainly don't swarm around populated areas, but the diversity and amount of birdshit around Calvary Baptist indicates that there was a huge number of sea-birds just hanging out on the property.

You see, seabirds have adapted to the faster and more powerful hurricanes we have today, they drift to the center and then chill in the eye of the storm where the winds and rains can't bother them. Often this is where we find birds who are exhausted, or who don't have the strength to escape the incredible power of the eyewall winds.

This birdshit means that those same seabirds were all congregating at Calvary Baptist, far from the eyewall, waiting for the storm to pass, confirming our radar that the church was shielded from the storm. The birds, they showed the government's hand, showed the special technology they have that can blunt the effectiveness of these superstorms. So while they go on talking about "carbon emissions" and "sea level rise" and "reduced consumption" they've got the answer right here to solve the crisis.

KF: And you are bringing them the truth?

A: It's what I do.

KF: What would you say to the families of (redacted) who recently identified the remains of their loved ones on the banks of the Elizabeth River? If I'm not mistaken, you are being sued for claiming the bodies were "made of rubber."

A: I never claimed there were no deaths related to Superstorm Ophelia.

KF: What about your statements that many people who were confirmed dead during the storm have been spotted vacationing in South America?

A: If you wish to debate me on the merits of those claims I have a few spots still open throughout this week and the next. Let me see if I can fit you in between-

KF: I think we're done here.

17

29 Days Before Superstorm Ophelia

(The following voicemail was left on Alice Crenshaw's phone by Kelly Harden on August 7th at 3:30 PM. The voicemail left on Alice Crenshaw's phone at the time of recovery for this investigative report indicating that it was not deleted. The voicemail mentions a photo that was also sent to Alice Crenshaw at 3:35 PM via text. The photograph was saved in Alice Crenshaw's photos.)

(Voicemail begins)

Alice, I'm not surprised you aren't picking up. Probably fair given all the times I let you go to voicemail. I know now that you were trying to help. I said some cruel things in the email I sent you. The more I thought about it, the worse I felt, especially after all you did for me. If I'm being honest Alice, you're the first person who seemed to genuinely want to help me. Typical of me to drive you away, it's a pattern, probably something I should talk to a therapist about.

But I didn't call you to talk about those emails, or that night. I called because I think, for the first time in years, I'm getting some answers. Answers about what happened at camp, answers about what happened at Calvary Baptist, answers about this whole fucking city. I can't tell you over the phone, they could be listening, but I've gotten to the root and I feel better than I have in a long time.

Answers are what I hoped to get talking to you. Tactics and strategies to help me be less anxious, less worried just living my life, more functional whatever that means. I know you did your best, but that wasn't enough for me, wasn't what I really needed. What I needed was to understand why, how sending me to camp, all of that poison they put in my mind was connected. Putting together the bigger picture you know? Because only once you understand why something awful happened to you can you do something about it. Now I know things. Things the people here wouldn't want to get out, wouldn't want to go public.

And that's the thing about it isn't it? Now that the hateful, dangerous center is exposed I can stop it from hurting anyone ever again. That would make my suffering meaningful.

Do you remember the testimonies that people used to give during church? Some Sunday morning where a random member of the church would talk about the "dark times" that they suffered through? I remember one time that Ms. Shelly, I guess just Shelly now that we are whole ass adults, stood up there and talked about how Jesus was the reason she had been able to leave her boyfriend. She talked about him selling pot and all the other "sins" she fell into with him. But at the end of the talk, after detailing the long list of wrongs she thought she did, she said it was all worth it because it showed her how much she needed Jesus.

Maybe it's the same for me. Maybe I was paranoid and anxious for a reason. Now I've gathered the facts and best believe me, when I'm finally ready to tell everyone what has been happening here, I'll absolutely be in the news.

I'm going to send you a photo of what happened to my door. Don't worry, I think it's good that they are trying to scare me, it means I'm getting closer to the truth. Call me back when you can so we can talk about when you are coming down to help. Make what happened to both of us mean something.

Talk to you soon!

(The message sent to Alice Crenshaw held a single photo taken in midday light outside of Kelly Harden's residence. The residence was a two story town house made out of brick nestled between two other units. In the center of the photograph is a closed blue door beside a bay window. The door bears extensive burns and gouges some over two inches wide and an inch deep.

The gouges have neat edges and are too symmetrical to be considered accidental damage. Two large gouges between two and three feet long sit around four feet apart in the center of the door. These cuts seem to bloom upwards suggesting the figure of some large tree. Shallower lines of damage appear towards the top of the door giving the appearance of limbs or branches.

Burn damage is evident in the center of the door between the two deep slashes in the door. Seven circles are placed in seemingly random order between the long cuts. These circles are blackened as if they were placed with a brand or other superheated object. At the center of each of these circles is a small point. The circles are not similarly sized with larger circles appearing at the top of the door and smaller circles appearing at the bottom of the door.

Near the top of the door are a pair of painted white clouds that are unmarked by the damage. Another set of clouds have been destroyed by the brands and cuts. Before the vandalism, the door seemed to be a pastel depiction of a sunny day one could find in a child's coloring book.)

18

Ernest Mobley Interview
Five Years After Hurricane Ophelia

Ernest Mobley - Third Recording 02/28/2032

Speakers are Ernest Mobley (referred to as "E" throughout the transcript) and Kellen Faulk (referred to as "K" throughout the transcript)

K: After that first "All In" night, did you ride to church with Mr. Chris again?

E: Not at first. Throughout the rest of July I kept some distance, riding mostly with Mr. E, and trying not to be left alone with Mr. Chris. The noise, the groan in my head, it shook me I won't lie, and it shook me that Mr. Chris knew about it. For days I ruminated on it over and over in my head, trying to convince myself that whatever I thought I heard was my own head, or one of the members of the congregation.

Eventually though, I had to ride with Mr. Chris because Mr. E was busy. It was early August, maybe that first week when I got back in his white truck to ride to church. I remember the smell of the tobacco putting me at ease, and the drone of talk radio removing the need to speak. It was comfortable, and I thought I was being foolish refusing to take Mr. Chris's offers over the past few days.

We rode in silence to the service that Sunday morning, and only on the way back did Mr. Chris finally break the quiet between us. I knew he was going to talk because he pulled over the truck a few blocks before we reached my house. He turned off the talk radio, and I felt dread of a lecture or of being in trouble freeze my limbs. He looked down at the dash and tapped his fingers on the steering wheel. Only then did I realize he was nervous.

"All In night is next Sunday, will you need a ride there?" He said, still refusing to meet my gaze.

I told him I wasn't sure, mumbling some excuse I've long forgotten. In truth, I didn't really want to go, not if there was a chance I would hear that same, outside voice. I kept that to myself, not wanting him to think I was insane, or worse.

He turned to face me, Aviator sunglasses still on, and said "I know what you heard."

The words chilled me, I asked what he was talking about.

"The voice from outside, the voice that you've been avoiding son, the voice of God."

(Ernest shakes his head and glances at the ceiling blowing out the smoke from his vaporizer.)

I told him it sure didn't sound like God.

Mr. Chris put his hand on my shoulder, and for the first time in that truck, I didn't feel safe. His grip was heavy and strong and I could see the cuts in his bottom lip from his chewing tobacco. The scent made me cough.

"What I'm about to tell you is important, son, spiritually important. I need you to listen and remember, the bible says to focus our eyes on heavenly things instead of the earth, tells us to put the flesh to death and exalt the spirit. A God who makes those commands, when he speaks to you, it can be frightening. The bible doesn't tell us to fear God for no reason."

I told him I was listening, even if I was creeping my hand over the handle of the truck.

"Now there are times, when a country, or a culture, becomes so out of step with God's vision, God's plan, that he appoints strong men to bring the world back to him. Strong men like Gideon, who he appointed with divine power to free the Israelites from the Midianites who were oppressing them. And when God spoke to Gideon, do you think it was comfortable? No, it was terrifying. He was terrified, much like I'm sure you are feeling right now."

That was when I pulled at the latch to the door. The lock was still on, keeping me in the truck with Mr. Chris. I wanted to tell him to stop talking, to tell him I didn't want to hear more, but I couldn't speak.

"Gideon called upon the Israelites to form an army to defeat the Midianites, but it was too many for God. If the Israelites won the war on their own terms, they would not have to give glory to God, so he chose a much smaller group, only three hundred to fight the Midianites. And by God's power, they won the battle and freed the people of Israel."

"I think God has chosen you son. That voice you heard, it fills you with dread, with fear, that's because it's really from Him. If it didn't shake your very bones, then why would you pay attention to the words?"

I've thought about those words over and over again. How little sense they make, how absolutely patronizing they were. I knew that whatever had happened at the last All In night was something wrong, rationally, I knew the conversation Mr. Chris trapped me in was insane.

But I grabbed onto an easy solution. A single word that stuck out from his ranting about old testament judges.

Chosen. That's what he told me, I was chosen. Now as a kid who had never felt chosen by anyone in his life, how do you think this made me feel? I had two options of what I could believe, either Mr. Chris was insane and so was I, or the experience that had haunted me for days was not a horrifying omen of me losing grip on reality. No, instead it was a sign I wasn't just loved by God, but that I was chosen for a great purpose like the ancient story Mr. Chris was telling me about Gideon.

Which story would you believe?

"God has called you son, it is up to you to decide how to respond," Mr. Chris said, taking his hand off of my shoulder and starting up the car.

Before we pulled away from the curb, I blurted out the word "yes."

Mr. Chris smiled, triumph on his face. "Yes to what, son?"

I told him that I wanted to serve God, to be one of the followers of Gideon. I don't know what vision I had in my head, maybe of me at the front doing the altar call, or preaching the word of God to thousands, various ideas about the glory God would bring me.

Mr. Chris nodded and said, "Do you mind if I pray a few words."

K: What did he say?

E: Whenever I try to remember them, I just hear the buzz of those mosquitos that summer. It's like the words don't want to be recorded, like I don't want to remember. He whispered them under his breath holding my hand, and I saw yellow light escape from the collar of his vest.

The same moan echoed in my head, louder and longer this time, drowning out the last words Mr. Chris murmured. When my mind was quiet again I heard him say "Amen."

Before he dropped me off he told me to expect strange dreams, and to be open to what God was commanding me to do. I watched his truck go and laid on my bed for hours waiting, hoping that the voice would come back, would speak to me like it did Gideon.

K: Did the voice return?

E: Yes, but not while I was awake.

19

27 Days Before Hurricane Ophelia

(The following is a voice memo recorded on Alice Crenshaw's phone at 1:04 AM on August 8th.)

I know I shouldn't have listened.

Should have just deleted the voicemail and the photograph at the same time. I told myself I was done, I had to detach. I owe Kelly nothing, I really was bending over backwards for someone who does not want to get better. Am I just an idiot or did I never learn the key lesson from my grad school?

Therapists don't save anyone, we just give them the tools to save themselves.

Still, she sounds so different in this voicemail. Energized, excited even about the future. That was never something I knew Kelly to think about. The only thing she felt about the future was just dread. My head tells me that this is typical, often people as unstable as she is can swing radically between crushing malaise and manic energy. She's just on the upswing of the roller coaster, and I cannot be responsible for what happens when she rounds the top. I am not her friend, I do not know her, and I can't keep acting and thinking like I do.

I did check back home though, and called the police station to see if there was any report placed about the vandalism on Kelly's door. As I expected there was none, not a single peep on any of the new sites about strange vandalism, certainly nothing that matches this picture. Something about it makes me feel watched. Even through the phone, God, now I'm sounding just like her.

This is why I have to delete the voicemail. It's one in the morning and I'm agonizing over a client that I cutoff a week ago and has been nothing but a drag on me in every way. Financially, personally, emotionally, hell even I'm remembering shit from back home that I wish I didn't. I got help, I fixed things, I am ok now and one of the reasons why is because I have boundaries that protect me. Boundaries that Kelly trampled all over, and I have to get them back.

Five Years After Hurricane Ophelia

Ernest Mobley - Third Recording 02/28/2032

Speakers are Ernest Mobley (referred to as "E" throughout the transcript) and Kellen Faulk (referred to as "K" throughout the transcript)

E: I thought you were a serious reporter, not a dream diviner.

K: Call it professional curiosity, you have claimed a voice from beyond your own mind spoke to you in your dreams. While the details may not make the final copy, it can't hurt to ask.

E: I'm talking to you because I want your report to be taken seriously. If you start talking about dreams I don't think anyone will think I'm anything but a madman. Frankly, I'm starting to think you view me the same way.

K: I'm interested. What else did the presence tell you in the days leading up to Superstorm Ophelia?

E: How could I remember details surrounding dreams I had five years ago? Most people forget dreams the moment they wake up.

K: Just what you can remember, that's all I'm asking for, it seems relevant to the larger discussion.

E: I don't remember that first night, the night that Mr. Chris murmured those words over me, the night he filled my head with visions of being one of God's chosen fighters.

I sat up late expecting to hear the voice. I laid in bed staring at the ceiling trying to will a bit of mustard light to creed through the window, or to hear that same moan that echoed in my head when Mr. Chris had his hand on my shoulder. After two hours of being unable to sleep, I stood up and meandered downstairs to the medicine cabinet. It was past one in the morning, and I desperately wanted to stop thinking about the encounter with Mr. Chris.

My mother, she had a strategy when she couldn't sleep, a strategy I saw her use well. Two benadryl, and she passed out on the couch, sometimes late enough that I had to wake her up to get her to drive me to school. The medication was over the counter, and simple tablets, my Mom wouldn't miss it. I pulled out three pills, meaning to bring one back upstairs if the initial dosage of two didn't knock me out cold. I forgot about this plan between the trip from the counter to the sink where I took all three.

The effects were not immediate, so I laid back on the couch in the downstairs family room, watching the ceiling fan rotate over and over again. That's the last conscious memory I have before the drugs put me into a deep sleep.

K: *So you just don't remember?*

E: Not from that night, but after three more nights of having the same dream over and over, I wrote down what I saw.

I have it here, if you want to see.

Dream Diary of Ernest Mobley

26 Days Before Hurricane Ophelia

I'm back in the church, every time I'm back in the church, in the sanctuary. Red velvet carpet crunches underneath my feet as I shift nervously in the dark. The place is backlit, the light from the hallway behind the sanctuary illuminating pews near the rear of the room where I stand, and casting the stage and the pulpit in shadow.

Near the pulpit, near the front, I know there is something in the dark. It makes sense, my mind created the dream, I'm omniscient within them, so peering into the dark fills me with dread because I know that something is there. An outline or a shape that looks back at me with malevolence and longing. No matter how much I want to turn and run, I'm forced to step forward, like the zoom in a camera pulling me deeper and deeper into the dark.

The gnarled roots and trunk of a Willow tree emerge out of the dark like a kitschy horror show. Its branches writhe and cover the ceiling of the sanctuary, the light fixtures in the structure replaced by its weeping leaves.

On its trunk, near the center, a single yellow eye opens and rolls back until I can not see its pupil. I hope that it will be quiet, I'll be able to turn and run, but like all the times before I am frozen. Screaming fills my ears, quiet at first, quiet enough for me to tell myself that the disturbed babbles have no meaning, but it grows in volume until it is unmistakable. It sounds halting, grating, like an animal in agony. At the cries loudest they are intermingled with weeping, and a woman's voice repeating over and over again that she is sorry.

Another eye opens.

And another…

And another…

Until seven yellow cat eyes rolled back in pleasure dot the trunk of the tree. Even though the thing has no mouth, I feel its voice, its presence cuts through my mind's panic and bewilderment. Overshadowing the screaming voices in my ears.

The seven eyed tree groans in pleasure and release.

That's when I wake up. When I always wake up with nausea roiling my stomach and the taste of blood stinging my mouth.

20

27 Days Before Hurricane Ophelia

(The following is a sermon from Reverend Philip Gordan, the minister at Calvary Baptist Church. The sermon was recorded and posted on the Calvary Baptist Church YouTube channel on August 8th, 2027. This sermon had the title "The Courage to Fight" and the scripture reading was from Revelation 3.)

Transcript Begins
Thank you for that worship team, really good stuff this morning. Well good morning everyone! Do you feel the spirit alive in this place today?

(Crowd calls "Yes")

Good, good, remember, the Lord says that where two or more believers are gathered he resides there as well. So before I get started I'm just going to say a quick word of prayer to the Lord over this message that I'm going to give you today. Please bow your head with me.

Dear heavenly father, please bless this message today, please speak through me to bring your word to these good people here. Please grant us courageousness to continue to show you light in a dark world, and fill us with your spirit oh Lord. Help us understand the words you have written for us, and try to apply them to our own lives today. Help us live life the way you have laid out for us, in constant thanks and belief in Jesus Christ our savior. Amen.

(Crowd murmurs Amen.)

Alright church, his week, as I've been preparing my message for you, I haven't been able to stop thinking about all of those people not just in our city, or our country, but across the world who have been lost to the dark powers of this world. While I've been thinking about these poor, lost children around the world, the Lord really laid a certain scripture on my heart today which comes from Revelation 3, if we could get that chapter up on the screen for us, ah yes there it is. Now I'm not gonna read all of it, but I will let you all know when I talk about some specific parts of the chapter.

So this is what is generally known as the "boring" part of Revelation. The rest of the book is about the persecution of God's people and the ultimate victory of the Lord which we know is coming soon Amen, but the book actually starts with a few different letters that the apostle John writes to various Christian churches across the Roman Empire. You see that in the title there, the two letters we are going to talk about today are too the Church in Sardis, and the Church in Laodocia. Now I know, I know, both of those names are funny and you might be asking yourself, "pastor, what might two ancient churches have to do with us?" But give me just a second, and I'll think you'll see what I'm saying.

You see, while I was thinking about why bad things happen, why tragedies that aren't just accidents but intentional acts of the powers of darkness occur, I couldn't help but think that the church has some responsibility for this evil. You see, we are called to put on that full armor of God, called to drive out wickedness and unrighteousness in our world and strike back against the evils of the enemy. We know, because the scripture tells us, that the final victory against the enemy is God's, but we aren't supposed to just wait around for Jesus to just come back and win that final victory, are we? No! Not at all, we are called as a church, and as Christians to still fight this battle against evil, even if we know that we will not win until God has that final victory Amen!

(Calls of Amen go out from the congregation.)

You see, in the first part of this chapter, John is calling out the church in Sardis, telling them that when Jesus returns it will be like a "Thief in the Night." Everybody isn't gonna know when God comes back to win the final victory, and the reason for that is simple. Jesus wants to see who in this world, in this country, and in this city is serious about standing up for what is good, and right. Later in the passage he says "Wake Up!" Wake up to the evil that is arranged against the church in this fallen world, and make sure that both us as a church and you as an individual are aligned against the powers, the nations, and the authorities of the enemy.

And I've got bad news folks. In America today, those enemies are more powerful than ever aren't they? Powers of division that can cut children away from their family, or the authorities that are supporting the flow of Fentanyl through our southern border, or even the fact that this nation still doesn't understand the sacred and holy nature of marriage. If God came back today, he would be so disappointed in what the church has let our country become Amen.

John tells us to "Remember, therefore, what you have received and heard; hold it fast and repent." As a nation we need to repent, and the church should be on the forefront of that effort. We have to wake up, or else Jesus could come back, and we don't want to be one of the churches that miss it do we? I want Calvary Baptist Church to be on the forefront of those whose eyes are open and are awoken to celebrating what is Godly and good and abhorring that which is of the enemy amen!

(Additional calls of Amen go out from the congregation.)

But I'm not going to lie to you all, our chances of getting our nation to repent are slim. If you look at history, if you look at the bible, one story sticks out, and that is that being a Christian is hard! All of the apostles faced persecution, faced the powers of this world, and frankly they probably thought that the enemy had the upper hand. Remember, John is writing this letter from an island prison that he will die on! Before he wrote these letters, John had survived being boiled in oil which is just a horrible way to die!

I tell you this because our country is going more the way of the enemy than the way of God. In fact, if you look to history, it's almost certain that we are going to face more persecution before God will return and win the final victory. In fact, this is already happening! Look at our culture, look at what's in the news, what's on the television, and ask yourself, does it seem like things are getting better or worse? Is this country aligning more with the truth of Jesus or the lies of the enemy? Look at the human traffickers who are transporting little girls across state lines to pour money into the abortion mills in New York and California. Look at the work of the enemy that uses music to influence our youth. The persecution is here, the powers of the enemy are here folks, and the question is what are we going to do about it, Amen.

(Loudest calls of Amen yet.)

God tells us what we should do about it through John. He says "I know your deeds, that you are neither cold nor hot. I wish you were one or the other! So because you are lukewarm, neither hot nor cold, I am about to spit you out of my mouth."

People of God, doesn't the statement "neither hot nor cold" really describe the American church to a tee? Everyone is so sensitive, no one wants to get called a bad name or hurt anybody's feelings, we've stopped our struggle against evil. And I'm telling you folks, if we don't get it together, if we don't name what's wrong with this world, soon we won't be able to. I want Calvary Baptist Church to be scorching hot for God, so devoted to righteousness and God's truth that evil can't even stand to be in our presence. I want the enemy to recoil at our very touch! That's the vision I have for this church amen!

(Pastor pantomimes an enemy being unable to stand in the presence of the congregation.)

I'll leave you all today, with a story. I heard this from one of my pastor friends who went over to China. You know, over in China being a Christian is against the law, and I can't imagine it'll be long until it's illegal here too. But he told me about this church he heard off where they had to be underground, had to be, or else the government would have shut it down or worse. Well, long story short, the government found out about this church, and when those communist agents came down on the Christians there they were not merciful. The enemy we fight hates the people of God folks, the enemy hates the words of God, and more than anything hates the way Christians understand the difference between right and wrong.

And we all are going to have a choice about whether or not we are going to stand with God or stand with the evil of this world. Those church goers in China were presented with a choice, deny God, or be killed, and do you know what happened?

Every one of those believers held fast to God, even when they were sent back to our heavenly father as martyrs.

Now I ask you all a question, were those believers lukewarm in their faith?

(Congregation calls out no.)

They were scalding hot for God, scalding hot for truth, and gave the ultimate sacrifice for their faith. I tell you now folks, the church in America has gotten soft, but a time is coming, a time of reckoning, when the true believers will be revealed. Let us resolve today, that we will stand for justice, for truth, and the will of God from now on. We give God all the glory, Amen.

21

26 Days Before Hurricane Ophelia

(The following is a news article from Wavy News 10 dated August 10th, 2027.)

Woman Severely Injured in Hit in Run

(Chesapeake Virginia)- In the early hours of morning, a woman was struck by a vehicle in a hit and run. The woman was walking down Battlefield Boulevard North bound according to Virginia state police.

On Sunday, August 10th at approximately 1:12 AM, state police received a call about a collision between a white vehicle and a pedestrian on Battlefield Boulevard.

When troopers arrived on the scene, they found a severely injured woman at the scene. Emergency personnel administered first aid at the site of the collision and transported the woman to the Chesapeake Regional Medical Center.

The woman was identified as 29-year-old Kelly Harden. She is currently in critical condition at Chesapeake Regional Medical Center.

Police were notified of the accident by a local man Chris Durose who witnessed the collision.

"Some people are just horrible," said Mr. Durose. "I saw the truck hit her without even stepping on the brakes. Just plowed right through, didn't stop to check if she was alright or not."

Police have obtained a description for the vehicle involved in the crash. The vehicle in question is a white 4x4 truck with one busted headlight. If you have any information about the said vehicle do not hesitate to contact Virginia police at (redacted.)

24 Days Before Hurricane Ophelia

(The following is a phone call placed by Alice Crenshaw to Charlotte Harden on August 12th at 2:30 PM. The full conversation was captured by Charlotte Harden's phone settings. Charlotte turned on a recording software before answering her phone. These extensions are commonly available today for most current generation smartphones, and grew to prominence after the recording of the (redacted) county teacher's controversial call home in 2026.)

Charlotte: Hello?

Alice: Kelly? Is that you?

Charlotte: No, this is her mother Charlotte.

Alice: Oh, is Kelly there?

Charlotte: No, she isn't. It's been a difficult few days. How did you get this number? How do you know Kelly?

Alice: A few months ago, we started communicating over email, and had a few phone calls.

Charlotte: So, she's your friend?

Alice: Not exactly, I would describe it as more of a professional relationship than a personal one.

Charlotte: I see.

Alice: I just saw Kelly's name on the news and wanted to check in to make sure she was ok. I understand if she can't talk right now, but I feel like I should reach out.

Charlotte: It's bad news I'm afraid. Kelly passed away late last night.

Alice: I'm so sorry to hear that.

Charlotte: The injuries from the collision, they were just too much for her body to take. It was just time I guess for her to go back to Jesus. It's still been difficult for us, even though we know she's in a better place.

Alice: I'm so sorry, do they know anything else about the person who hit her?

Charlotte: No, but I expect you'll see that on the news too if you know that Kelly got in the accident. Who are you? I feel like I would have heard Kelly talk about you if you were a new friend.

Alice: Dr. Alice Crenshaw, Kelly and I used to both attend-

Charlotte: Calvary Baptist! Oh we love it there, me and my husband Ron. I remember you Alice, now you're a doctor? What kind?

Alice: I'm a therapist.

Charlotte: Kelly didn't say anything about needing therapy. I know my daughter, and therapy, that doesn't sound like her.

Alice: She reached out a few months ago, and I was just trying to help.

(Rustling and opening sounds of a cabinet in the background.)

Charlotte: Were you giving my daughter drugs?

Alice: No, we talked about a few different medications but she hadn't started taking any of them.

Charlotte: Well there's a bunch of pill bottles here in her medicine cabinet with your name on it. Dr. Alice Crenshaw right, you said that was you.

Alice: I am sorry about the loss of your daughter, but I don't think that any of the medications I prescribed were to blame.

Charlotte: Of course you don't, oh Alice, what did they do to you after you left home? Did they tell you all these things would help? You and I both know the only thing that can help someone like Kelly.

Alice: I don't understand.

Charlotte: Do you know why Kelly was wandering around Battlefield Boulevard so late? Could it have something to do with these drugs you prescribed her? I know my daughter and she was not someone to just be walking down the street late at night.

Alice: Are you accusing me of drugging your daughter?

Charlotte: I'm not accusing you of anything Alice. I'm just wondering what happened to that nice girl that I knew back at church.

Alice: Goodbye Ms. Harden, I am sorry for your loss.

(Call Ends)

24 Days Before Hurricane Ophelia

(The following was a (redacted) post taken from Charlotte Harden's (redacted) profile. The following was posted publicly on August 12th at 6:34 PM.)

Charlotte Harden with **Ron Harden** and **12 others**

My heart is broken into a thousand little pieces over the death of my baby girl Kelly. She passed late last night after a long and courageous battle with her injuries. Thank you so much to my church family at Calvary Baptist Church, I do not know I would have survived without you. Thank you for all of the meal trains and well wishes as me and my husband walk through this valley of the shadow of death. Only through your help have we been able to keep our eyes fixed on the LORD during this time of such great grief!!! As the bible says "Set your mind on things ABOVE not EARTHLY things." While I certainly wish God had chosen someone else to be tested the way I have been, I know that it will work out for his PLAN.

Kelly was a beautiful little girl. She had such a strong heart for God, and one of my greatest joys is that I remember when she accepted Jesus into her heart. I KNOW that my little girl is in a better place, and that I will join her in heaven one day. Kelly always had some trouble, but it was because she was LIED TOO and FOOLED by the world!!! No one knows their daughter like a Mom, and Kelly was not a bad girl, she was just one who was confused and fooled by people who did not care about her. I cannot wait to see her in heaven the way I knew her, the GODLY woman I always knew that she would be.

And to the people who fooled her, the people who tempted her with promises of this worldly life, I only have one thing to say. You should have left my little girl alone. Nothing in the wild is more ferocious than a MAMA BEAR and you best believe that GOD'S JUSTICE will find YOU.

24 Days Before Hurricane Ophelia

(The following is a (redacted) post taken from Charlotte Harden's (redacted) profile. The post was made on a private group for Calvary Baptist Church. Charlotte was one of the moderators of the group. The following was posted on August 12th at 11:53 PM)

Charlotte Harden with **Ron Harden** and **12 others**

When I held Kelly's hand in the ICU, her last words to me were "mommy I'm so sorry." She knew the end was coming, and was ready to go back to her HEAVENLY home. I told her she didn't have anything to be SORRY about. All of us have STUMBLED and all of us have gone ASTRAY, in this fallen world. But the more that comes out about what happened to her just doesn't ADD UP!!! I wish she was here so I could ask her why she was on that road so late at night, but that's been taken from me. I can tell all of YOU my COMMUNITY of FAITH, that when I went through Kelly's things this afternoon I found all sorts of DRUGS in her house. I don't know where she got them but my heart BREAKS for who told her that she needed these things. No one knows their daughter like a Mother, it's a special bond, an unbreakable bond, and I know my Kelly. With how much FENTANYL comes across the border every day, I'm starting to think that my poor Kelly was a victim. Until we stop the INVASION at our SOUTHERN BORDER more Mothers will be like me, broken and GRIEVING over their dead babies. WE NEED ACTION to protect and save our CHILDREN!!!!!!!

(Underneath the status are seventy-two likes and several comments, the most relevant which have been compiled here, all comments were made between August 12th and 13th)

John Harrison: AMEN!!

Philip Gordan: Preach it! Maybe I should let you talk this Sunday instead of me!

Chris Durose: Charlotte, thank you for bringing these important issues to our attention as a community. Kelly is looking down from heaven and smiling at your posts, and we all hope that some real change in this country can be made! Even in this tough time, remember that "all things work together for good to those who love God."

Shelly Bassett: Too many Mothers have been hurt by this broken world!!!! Thank you Charlotte for being so real!

Carrie Willis: ThIS is SO reaL and So truE!

Benjamin Stile: If you all want to take some action to make the world more in the image of God, check out (Redacted) They are fighting the real fight to take this country back for God!

22

Five Years After Hurricane Ophelia

(While Kelly Harden lived in Chesapeake, she lived with a roommate named Lyn Vargas. After several inquiries to various apartment complexes in Chesapeake, I located Lyn's address. Pleasant Heights Apartments had suffered significant damage during hurricane Ophelia, but still had some records of Lyn's residence with Kelly Harden. I found Lyn off the grid on a communal farm in northwestern Oregon.

Lyn is a middle aged, non-binary person with tattoo sleeves covering both arms. On their left arm was the distinctive area code from Chesapeake of 757 crossed out. Lyn was willing to talk somewhat about their last few weeks in Chesapeake before Hurricane Ophelia.)

Lyn Vargas - First Recording 08/2032

Speakers are Lyn Vargas (referred to as "LV" throughout the transcript) and Kellen Faulk (referred to as "K" throughout the transcript)

LV: Chesapeake was never the most accepting place. We never got the horror stories out in southwest Virginia, or south across the border with North Carolina, but the dislike for people like me was palpable. There certainly were more accepting places in Norfolk, or if you went looking for them, but the whole area contained this feeling that the toleration of queer people was a passing fad. Often, I worried that the dangerous people, the people who stared at me when I walked down the street, weren't going to be constrained forever. There were cultural changes after Obergerfell, and Chesapeake wasn't a place where you'd have to worry about some county clerk who wanted to get famous and refuse your marriage license. But while civil I guess, it was never comfortable.

It's hard to explain, but there was just this feeling in the air. A vibe, as many of my younger friends called it, that the people who disliked me, who disliked us weren't gone, just waiting. The message seemed simple, "we have to tolerate you for now so have your fun, we were here before you, and we will be here after you and your kind have run out of town." I remember carrying that tension with me every day.

That's how I met Kelly. I didn't have that feeling about her, that passive aggressive, southern, bless your heart tolerance that seemed so fragile. She just accepted me as a person, and that was enough. I felt safe enough around her, at least at the beginning, so we ended up living together.

It went well enough at first, but Kelly, she didn't really have her shit together. That's ok, and I was fine helping out at the beginning, but after a year of covering more of our rent than was necessary, constant tension in the house, and a few rather frustrating romantic declarations on her part, I was over it. I was over thirty, she was almost thirty and I didn't want to be in the strange parental relationship she slotted me into. I was hoping to move farther out to Norfolk and leave the stifling environment behind. Kelly was a part of that environment, even if she didn't start out that way.

She scared me. Especially that summer before the hurricane, before I got out of Chesapeake for good. She would be on the phone crying with some woman from DC, threatening to hurt herself. That was new, I had never heard her use that particular tactic to get my attention before and it was just more validation that I had to cut her loose, I couldn't be responsible for her shit anymore.

Then, she died, and everything got so much worse.

(Lyn shakes their head and looks at the ground taking a moment to collect themselves.)

I worked at a library, Cedar Road Location, the big one I guess. This was before (Redacted) took over the library system and ripped it apart, it was actually a public service back then. I liked my job, I felt like I was making a difference, and I loved reading to the kids. I would do voices for the characters, provide strong structure, and give them a place where they could be safe for at least our reading hour. Some days, I still miss the job even with everything that happened.

We heard the stories, the book burnings, the death threats, everything else that other places around the country were dealing with, but I always thought that the people we served would be different. Yeah, it was a conservative area, but it wasn't like we were around a bunch of crazy political people. Maybe there was a high number of American flags flown outside of your average suburban areas, with maybe one or two live free or die flags. All the Confederate, NRA, (Redacted), or more overt flags were saved for people's timeshares out in Nags Head.

Then Kelly died, and I had the pleasure of meeting her parents.

I tried to go see Kelly at the hospital, once, but was informed that I wasn't on the list of approved visitors. "Only family" is what I was told, which didn't seem right given Kelly had told me several times how she had gone non-contact with her parents. When I walked out of the hospital, Kelly's parents were leaving at the same time.

One look from them was all it took to recognize that same tight, barely restrained contempt at who I was. The man, Kelly's father I guess, hid it better. He just looked away, but her Mom would not stop staring. A look that didn't even have the polite facade to cover her hostility at me just being in the same hospital as her, breathing the same air.

She gave me the same look when I opened the door to the apartment for them to clean out Kelly's stuff.

The door was all messed up, I had to put in a work order due to the cuts and marks that dotted the door. I would have put in a police report, but I still have to think that Kelly made those marks herself. Part of one final manic episode that led her to wander out late the night it happened. I knew Kelly's feelings about the police, we shared some of the same politics on that issue and I wasn't about to bring them to my home willingly. If I wanted two jackasses to show up and say "damn that's weird, good luck" I'd just call my uncles.

While they packed up all of Kelly's stuff, I stayed mostly to myself. Hid in my room, busied myself with checking email, that kind of thing. A few times I thought about leaving, but everytime I would move to go,

I would hear a creak in the hallway or muffled voices in the stairs. I didn't want to interact with them anymore than absolutely necessary, so I just waited.

I fucked up when they went to leave. I thought I was safe, but Kelly's mom stayed in the hallway, just for an extra minute looking around. She had a box of Kelly's things, keepsakes she collected over the past few years. I saw in the box one of my gifts, an embroidered notebook full of quotes that I hoped could help her get some healing as well as a book of Rupi Kar poems. Kelly was always pretty ironclad about identifying as a woman, and I thought some of those poems could be helpful for her. Anyways, something like anger must have crossed my face, because even though I was exhausted with Kelly, and was ready to move away from her, I knew that the last thing she would have ever wanted was her parents poking around inside her life.

She told me about living with them, the nightmare of the camp, and honestly what she went through was all that was keeping me around her at that point. Kelly was frustrating, and manipulative, and hurt me more times than I can count, but even I couldn't argue that she had a rough go. There's a hope you hold onto, that if you just stay with a hurt person long enough, you can put them back together, especially when you're young. I wasn't so young anymore, and was realizing what I guess all of us do at some point.

You can't put people back together, they have to do it for themselves.

Kelly hadn't done that, now she was gone, and people she never wanted to see again had their hands on what was left of her life. I wanted those things out of her Mom's hands. I offered to take them to the car, thinking maybe I could swipe one of the two booklets I gave her. The thought of this woman in a "Jesus Saves" t-shirt looking through Kelly's thoughts in that inspirational quote journal made me see red.

Kelly's Mom shook her head, and stared at me the same way she had at the hospital. She was this skinny woman with blonde hair, some sort of plastic surgery on her face, and beach tanned skin. She just kept staring for I don't know how long, until a smile crossed her face. Now, after what happened, I know that was the moment she recognized me, and believe me, I wish I had just stayed inside my room. Maybe it wouldn't have mattered, maybe she would have figured out where I worked anyway, but either way I had this awful pit in my stomach that the tight-lipped tolerance of me was coming to an end.

The next day at work, I sat down, opened my email, and hated that I was right.

23

23 Days Before Hurricane Ophelia

(The following is a voice memo recorded on Alice Crenshaw's cell phone. The memo is dated August 14th at 1:23 AM.)

Why was Mr. Chris the one who reported Kelly's accident?

I've tried everything. I'm taking my meds. I'm going out, I'm trying to live life, but I can't stop thinking about that man's sunglasses. I'll be out with Sean and friends, and in the middle of dinner I'll just be locked back in the memory of Mr. Chris staring at me in my two-piece bathing suit with contempt and rage. Mr. Chris at the front of the youth group talking about the importance of "glorifying God" with our dress while his eyes lingered on me. Mr. Chris standing at the doorway of the church bus, checking in each student without saying an additional word, but just this presence, this menace that loomed over me.

I imagine Mr. Chris staring at Kelly as she tried to enter the pharmacy to pick up the medication that I know would have helped her, that might have stopped her from wandering down that street late at night. A small piece of me starting to doubt her death was a random hit and run.

Damn it, I'm sounding like her emails. Like her last emails. She was a paranoid, delusional patient, and that's that. I can't start connecting dots, I'm going to lose it. I know Sean is noticing me sneaking out late at night to keep looking at the picture she sent me, listening to the voicemail again. He can be patient, but for how long? How long can I keep acting this unhinged before well, before it's over?

That picture she sent me, on her door. I've looked every night for something similar but nothing comes up. I've looked on old occult forums, hindu temple engravings, and even had a cursory visit to the church of Satan's website, but nothing even resembles that symbol. The tree with seven eyes, seven eyes I swear are in a different place every time I open up the photo.

I showed it to Sean, he didn't feel the same and then got that tense jaw that he does whenever he's upset at me about something. He said the marks were random, that he didn't see any shapes, that I was projecting. He's stopped even responding when I try to bring the conversation back to Kelly. Sometimes I wonder if he's right, and I'm making up the arrangements of the marks, trying to find meaning where there is none. I want him to be right, so I can get rid of this God-awful feeling.

Mr. Chris being the one to report Kelly's fatal accident doesn't mean anything, I have to believe that. Yes, it's strange, but it's just a random dot connecting. I tell the people I work with all the time, connecting the dots, figuring out the grand key to how everything works, it never helps. The world is chaotic, full of coincidence, and events that feel like they should mean something often don't mean anything at all. I have to remember that. Kelly was dealing with trauma from her past and un-medicated mental illness. She already had a history of seeing people from her past in contexts that didn't make sense. Mr. Chris was not at that wilderness camp, and there's no reason to believe he was at the pharmacy, it's a pattern of Kelly's paranoid delusions. I have to, I need to, get it together.

But, they had a picture of him, of Mr. Chris. It's been over fifteen years since I've seen him, and he wasn't a young man when I was at church. He looks the same, not just like he's aging well, he looks identical. There's no hunch in his well over six-foot-tall frame, no softness in his chest or belly, not even the gaunt look in his face that people who have to be in the seventies start to get as they age. He looked like the same imposing presence that would keep "those youth boys" in line.

I should call Aunt Whitney. She might know more about what's going on, I don't think there was a single event at Calvary Baptist that she didn't have a hand in. Vacation Bible School, Youth Lock Ins, All In

Night, she would be there. I like to believe that maybe in a different place, or a different church, we would still talk often. It might just feel good to talk to her, I always felt better after I talked to her, brings me back down to earth, even if we have some pretty big disagreements. I don't know what I want her to say, but just to talk to someone normal from Chesapeake would be helpful.

24

Five Years After Hurricane Ophelia

(Pastor Blake Harkness sits in the green room of his church (redacted.)
An older man with a personable grin in a button up shirt without a tie,
he was happy to talk to me about Calvary Baptist, more specifically its
minister, Phillip Gordan.)

Blake Harkness - First Recording 05/2032

**Speakers are Blake Harkness (referred to as "BH" throughout the tran-
script) and Kellen Faulk (referred to as "KF" throughout the transcript)**

BH: Pastor Gordan? Phillip Gordan? Yeah, I knew him, was one of the
best associate pastors I ever had here at (Redacted.) Being a minister is
a difficult job, it requires strong people skills along with an excellent
biblical understanding. If that wasn't enough, you also have to be a really engaging teacher. Frankly, I only have the biblical understanding
and the people skills, finding a man of God who has all three together is
exceptionally rare.

Phillip had it all. He could make you feel like whatever was happening, whatever you were going through, it was the most important
thing in the world. He set people at ease, let them talk about what was

actually on their heart. You know, the longer I do this job, the more I think it compares to some combination of the hardest jobs in the world. A full-time therapist might not hear half the things a person will say to their pastor in moments of spiritual vulnerability. Those secrets, they can be a heavy thing to carry. I always wonder if maybe the Catholics have it right, training people how to deal with confession instead of the denomination's plan of just seeing who can handle bearing your brothers and sisters in Christ's deepest secrets and who can't.

Pairing that ability with a sharp mind for scripture, and an almost theatrical presentation, my point is Phillip was lightning in a bottle. He was close to outshining me whenever he spoke to our congregation, and the more I watched him the more I knew that he had big things ahead of him.

It didn't take long, but a job offer to be a senior pastor came from Calvary Baptist. The church had a moderate size congregation, and after his visit Phillip raved about how engaged the members of the church were. He spoke highly of the deacons, music minister, everything, his eyes big with dreams of finally being "the guy" for a church.

I remember I just asked him whether or not he felt God's call to Calvary Baptist.

Phillip didn't like that question. You see, even with his exceptional levels of talent, I always sensed in him that, to not put too fine a point on it, he liked telling people what they wanted to hear. I tried to discipline him out of this urge, and we got into some roaring disagreements over what was and was not appropriate to say from the pulpit. I'd say something like, "the different politics or desires of people will pass, but the word of God endures forever."

He always called me old fashioned for that idea.

I had suspicions about Calvary Baptist. They were still a card-carrying member of the denomination, and I had started the painful process of leaving. Not only that, but the last minister got forced out of Calvary Baptist for reasons that were never completely clear to me. Phillip always blew past that when he spoke about the job opportunity, and I never had time to look into it further.

Even with my caution though, he went ahead and took the job. Before I knew it his family, which I grew accustomed to seeing every Sunday was uprooted and moved out to Chesapeake. I added him to my prayer list, and tried to keep some tabs on my very talented young pastor. For a few years that was it, we'd exchange emails, get coffee at a conference, and talk about theology.

I kept some discreet tabs on him, so I saw the August before the storm, when Calvary Baptist got embroiled in the protests over that library. A few days into the political firestorm, I got a message from Phillip asking to meet over coffee. I had to drive a few hours to see him, but I felt obligated. To be honest, I also wanted to give him a piece of my mind over what he was doing in Chesapeake. It would be the last conversation I had with him.

(Pastor Harknesses's brow furrows and he taps on the table.)

Philip did not look well. His face was gaunt, massive bags underneath his eyes, and he kept fidgeting. He'd lost weight, and kept looking at the exits of the small cafe we met for coffee. He thanked me for coming down and after a few pleasantries about each of our families he started to tell me about how well Calvary Baptist was doing.

Even before being in the national news, he had grown the church as I had expected. They were close to double their previous attendance, expanded their parking, and were considering sending mission trips to Uganda and the Dominican Republic. Whatever my worries were about the congregation hurting his trajectory as a talented and strong minister seemed disproven.

And that was before the president shouted out Calvary Baptist in a speech, and all those elected officials threw their support behind his church. Enough money was flowing in that Philip was talking about building a whole new complex with a gymnasium, Christian school, and to turn the place into a full on community center. He said this all with a manic energy, tumbling over his words as he talked about his successes. A less kind part of me wondered if he had asked me down here just to boast and perhaps win an old argument over whether or not the church was a better witness for God if it embraced or eschewed politics.

When he finished listing his accomplishments I gave him the warmest smile I could muster and said, "well Phil, if things are going so well, why couldn't you wait to give me these updates at the next convention?"

My annoyance at Phillip for his list of achievements evaporated when he took the same pensive look he had when he was my pupil. He murmured something about how he was worried about some of the people in his congregation, how some of the things they said scared him.

KF: Was this about the Cedar Library Case?

BH: Yes, and more. He seemed to dance around specifics, but he seemed disturbed by some statements by the people in his congregation. He wasn't sure how it happened, but a lot of the more radical believers from the city had started coming over the past few years. "Crazy attracts crazy" he said barely at a whisper. He also mentioned a (redacted) group that had some "non-Christlike" images and statements that were circulated.

Philip wasn't alone in this issue. Every church was dealing with political extremism in one form or another. My own church had just been through a pretty messy divorce with local politicians who wanted to use the pulpit as a space for their stump speeches. I lost a few members over that tiff, as well as when I left the convention but we survived and moved on. Conservative churches weren't the only ones with these issues either, rainbow flag waving progressive churches also had complicated problems to navigate. I always tried to make my church a place based on the word of God, not politics.

I asked Philip point blank whether what he was teaching from the pulpit was the truths of God or the truths of man. He looked away for a second and it gave me my answer.

Turns out that Philip had followed his congregation's worst impulses. He found that every time he talked about politics his attendance went up, whereas whenever he tried to actually engage with the scripture, his attendance fell. I've watched some of his sermons, and it's undeniable that he was less biblical and more political than he should have been. The Cedar Branch episode was just that coming to a head.

I gave him what advice I could, told him that it might hurt for a little while, but the more he let these "crazier" characters lead him the worse things would get. I told him I would pray for him and clapped him on the shoulder looking for my car to leave. I didn't have much more to say, and part of my heart broke both at how much he had compromised to achieve riches in this life just to have to pick between those riches and the kingdom of God.

Before I left, I'll never forget our last exchange. He said "but wouldn't it all be worth it? Doesn't God often ask people to listen to strange people to show their faith in him? Isn't it worth a few crazies to reach the community with the school, the gym, and the new building?"

"Well Phil, are you building those things for God or for yourself?"

The words were out of my mouth before I could think about them. Sometimes when I pray, I worry I was too harsh, to direct, and that it hurt my ministry to Phil. On the other hand, it was the truth. One look from him and he knew it too, and he stormed out the door.

25

22 Days Before Hurricane Ophelia

(The following phone record is between Alice Crenshaw and Whitney Ellington. It is dated August 15th at 2:04 PM. Alice Crenshaw's phone was set to record the conversation using a similar software that Charlotte Harden used to record Alice during their conversation.)

Alice: Aunt Whitney?

Whitney: Alice, oh thank God, it is good to hear your voice.

Alice: Are you alright?

Whitney: Well, if you had called me a few weeks ago I think I would tell you that I was fine, but now, no Alice I'm not alright, not alright at all.

Alice: What happened?

Whitney: It's hard to talk about (muffled sob) Oh Lord, I can't believe you call me for the first time in years and the first thing I want to talk about is my problems. I want to hear about you, I know you didn't want to talk, but your Mom has given me some updates. Nothing specific, I just know you're doing well for yourself up in DC.

Alice: I'm doing fine, I was calling about church, it's a long story but can wait for a moment. I'll ask you again what happened?

Whitney: (Laughs) Well, I'll do my best, but I haven't been to church in a couple of weeks. I'm not sure how much I can help you.

Alice: You love that church, why haven't you been? Did something happen?

Whitney: I did didn't I, I gave them so much, every event, all of the late hours, all the volunteer work, and well that's all done now. I'm not sure what I'm going to do.

Alice: Did Alex leave too?

Whitney: No, um, he was the uh reason I had to leave. I don't know how exactly to tell you this Alice, but Alex hasn't been faithful to me if you understand my meaning.

Alice: What?

Whitney: About a month ago he confessed to me that there were a few different women he slept with. He didn't give me all the details, but when I kept pressing him, it had to do with the conference he attends every year. The youth pastor one in June, apparently there were several women he was with, and as I kept pushing him the list got longer.

Alice: I'm so sorry, how long was this going on?

Whitney: A long time, a really long time. That's what's made it so difficult, maybe just one mistake I could understand, but he kept doing it, over and over again. I just don't know what I did wrong, why he didn't think I was enough for him.

Alice: His choices are not your fault.

Whitney: I know, it's just hard not to wonder, you know, maybe if I had done something different then he would have stayed, we could still live the life that we had just a few months ago. I wish I didn't know.

Alice: Why did he tell you?

Whitney: I guess he finally felt guilty enough, or someone he was with was going to expose him so he wanted to get ahead of it. Maybe he just was angry over something I said or did so decided that revealing his indiscretions was his way to win an argument. I don't know honey, but he told me and we've been separated ever since.

Alice: I would hope so, that kind of pattern, you can't have a relationship with someone you don't trust.

Whitney: It's been difficult, he keeps asking for forgiveness or "grace" as he calls it. He tells me he's changed, that he won't act like that again. I can't get away from him entirely until the divorce case actually finishes, mostly because of the kids. They've been with me most of the time since we've separated, but I'm having to let them stay with him recently. I hope to get just supervised visitation, but that will be up to the judge.

Alice: I understand how that would be a reason to stop going to church.

Whitney: (laughs) Oh, I still haven't told you why I left the church, why I won't set foot in that building ever again.

Alice: I mean if Alex betrayed you after all you did for him, all you did for the congregation, makes sense to me.

Whitney: It was awkward the first few Sundays, but I can handle that, I'm a big girl Alice and the kids still enjoyed Sunday school. I could stand a few awkward interactions. But about two weeks ago, pastor Phil came over and asked me to see him in his office. I hoped he would offer some condolences, or maybe spiritual guidance during this time. Most people in the congregation knew we were splitting up at this point, and as much as it hurt my pride to admit, being a single Mom meant I probably was going to need some community help. I had stocked the food kitchen so often, it was almost embarrassing that I might have to ask for some of the canned vegetables myself.

Alice: That's nothing to be ashamed of, you've offered help to so many people who needed it, they should be there for you when you are the one in need.

Whitney: I appreciate it honey, but I don't think that's going to be an option. I headed back there, already feeling weepy, hoping I could confide in a man of faith. When I entered the pastor's office, who do you think was in the room with him?

Alice: You're kidding, no way did he have–

Whitney: I wish I was honey, but on the other side of the desk sat Alex, his curly haired head bowed in that same fake prayer stance he gave every time he led a youth event. The pastor shut the door behind me and offered me a chair on the other side of the desk.

Alice: You didn't stay right, please tell me you didn't stay.

Whitney: Well, I was angry enough that I, it's not very Christlike of me, but I guess I had this hope I could embarrass Alex. Maybe Pastor Phil wanted to get my side of the story and I could convince him to fire Alex, or take my side.

Alice: If he was already in the room, it meant they must have talked beforehand.

Whitney: Believe me, I know, I've gone over the whole thing in my head a dozen times. Well, turns out Alex had confessed to Pastor Phil, not all the affairs of course, just the most recent one, and as soon as Pastor Phil started talking about forgiveness my heart just sank.

Alice: My God.

Whitney: You know, I don't know if that counts as taking the Lord's name in vain Alice or if it just describes what happened, it was just horrible. But about halfway through I got an idea, here we were and Alex was confessing to the affair and I thought that might be useful in the divorce proceedings so I recorded a good amount of the conversation.

Alice: Aunt Whitney! That's incredible.

Whitney: I thought it was smart. I listened to both of those men restate their case for me to come back to Alex, told them I would think about it, picked up the kids, and haven't been back since.

Alice: I'm sorry this is happening, I'm sorry I didn't call earlier.

Whitney: I think going through this whole divorce, I'm seeing some of the reasons you didn't want to talk to me. It makes sense Alice, you had to figure out the person you were going to be, and I wasn't a part of that.

Alice: Thank you.

Whitney: I just feel so lost right now, Alex and I were together for almost twenty years. I was active in the church for the past twelve after the kids didn't need me every moment of every day. That he would lie to me for so long, and that I couldn't see it, it doesn't feel good.

Alice: Well, I'm not usually one to endorse spite, but it will probably feel good to play that recording in court.

Whitney: It will won't it? (giggles) Starting over is hard, but I think I can do it, I'll figure out the rest later. Thank you for calling, it's good to hear your voice.

Alice: Anytime, and if you see anything weird, anything that makes you feel uneasy, please call me.

Whitney: I'll be careful honey, I can look after myself.

26

Five Years After Hurricane Ophelia

Ernest Mobley - Fourth Recording 02/29/2032

Speakers are Ernest Mobley (referred to as "E" throughout the transcript) and Kellen Faulk (referred to as "KF" throughout the transcript)

KF: So after your dream, and the encounter in Mr. Chris's car, you continued to attend the church?

E: Attend, invest, obsess over, you name it. I took Mr. Chris's words about being chosen by God to heart. I had to show my devotion, my heart for God for him to keep speaking to me. The best way I thought to accomplish that was by investing more instead of less into the church

I got involved helping put-on All-In night, and I should have known something was strange when it was only Mr. E and not him and his wife, Whitney, who picked me up. I didn't say anything about it as Mr. E lectured me about the problems with modern women. I was passive and wished that Mr. Chris had been the one to pick me up instead when we pulled up to the church. Mr. E stopped speaking, and gave me a grin like a mischievous older brother.

"Do you want to see something cool?"

I agreed and Mr. E pressed a button on his dash that unlocked the hatch of the small sedan. I followed him around the back of the car to look down into the trunk and saw an unmarked black box. Beside the box was a green metal case about a foot tall and three feet wide. Two large bullets sat in the space between the case and the cloth interior of Mr. E's trunk. I started to feel sick as Mr. E clicked the two metal clasps on the sides of the black box to the open position. Mr. E looked at me in expectation, like a magician wanting a reaction from their latest magic trick and threw open the case.

Nestled in the felt interior of the hardshell was a polished handgun. The weapon looked brand new with its clear chrome exterior and un-blemished grip. The barrel was nearly a foot long, and the blocky con-struction of the body gave off the appearance of heft and weight. The sight of the weapon made me shiver in the August heat. I was never around weapons, especially not firearms, and my imagination spun around everything that could go wrong with the weapon tucked into the back of Mr. E's car.

I told him that it looked very neat, and went to walk into the church building. Before I'd taken a step he said, "Wait, do you want to hold it?"

When I turned around he had the gun in his hand, waving it around like a dumb teenager who would end up on the news later in the week. One of the few things I had devoted to memory my parents told me was to never let a friend play with firearms. Mr. E was an adult, but I still felt uncomfortable with the blase way he waved the gun around.

I told him that I didn't know how to hold the gun.

"Oh that doesn't matter, neither do I really, Chris is going to take me to the range later this week so I can start learning."

The idea of Mr. Chris with a gun horrified me. I wondered if the night he prayed over me, the night he talked about Gideon and God and told me I was chosen, did he have a weapon right there to silence me if I didn't say the right thing?

"We have to start getting ready, the time is coming soon Ernest," said Mr. E. "The time when good God-fearing men like you and me will have to be ready to fight for what we believe in."

Mr. E's finger rested over the trigger while he made this declaration. I nodded in agreement like I always did to his rants, and waited for him to lock up the gun in his case and let me into the church. I didn't say anything the rest of the evening until All In night began.

KF: And at this point, you were unaware that Alex Ellington and Whitney Ellington were in the process of separating?

E: I knew that I hadn't seen Whitney in a few weeks, and I knew that Mr. E was acting weird. But I did not know that papers had been filed, did not know that their split was inevitable.

KF: But Mr. E's purchase of the firearm still disturbed you? It was out of character?

E: I had never seen or heard him talking about owning a gun before. I wrote it off in the moment, deciding that he was just getting older, or into different hobbies, or maybe (Redacted) told him to purchase a gun for the coming days, but after the immediate discomfort around the encounter ended I tried to put it in my mind.

Now of course I can put together a few of the pieces surrounding a suddenly embittered man purchasing a gun, but I was 14 at the time. 14 and completely locked into impressing Mr. E. In fact, what I worried about the vast majority of the time before All In night began, was whether or not he was somehow insulted by my refusal to hold and examine the gun he brought to church.

KF: And what about Mr. Chris? Was he in attendance for this All In night?

E: Of course. He was there, the Hardens were there, the teenage regulars, the deacons, Pastor Phil, it was one of the best attended All In nights ever according to Mr. Chris when he drove me home.

KF: And what about the voice you claimed to hear?

E: The voice I did hear. I'm getting to that, you see, tonight was a very special night for Mr. E, important for him to keep his job as the youth minister at Calvary Baptist. It was the night of his confession.

I didn't know, wasn't prepared for the words to come spilling out of him as soon as he took the stage. The music cut out entirely, which was strange, usually during an alter call one of the band members was fingering some set of minor chords or scales to pull on our heartstrings.

It was right at the halfway point of the service, after an hour of the soul rending music, and several stories of the power of God all across the world. A few videos stressing the importance of spiritual warfare between armies of angels and armies of demons, and a pastor with spiked hair repeating the fact that the universe is very large with increasingly absurd comparisons. All of this was foreplay of course, the songs everyone in the congregation knew were held until the end of the service, and Mr. Phil and Mr. E had yet to start preaching on God's power and grace which always brought the congregants to their knees.

The voice in my head had not groaned once, and I felt a sense of impatience and restlessness in my own bones. The point of All In night was to break from the stuffy services of Sunday morning service in order to find real connection with God. The first hour or so that hot August evening felt just like any other church service, just at a different time and with louder music. The disappointment in the air was palpable, and in my mind, I felt that voice and presence from outside drifting further and further away. Part of me wanted it to leave forever, but the desperate part of me, the part of me that wanted to be a part of something greater clung to the voice and begged it to stay, begged it to remain just a little longer.

Then Mr. E took the stage. His face was ashen, and his eyes downcast. Behind him to his left, Mr. Phil stood without his typical smile, and Mr. Chris walked over to flank him to the right.

My heart quickened as Mr. E cleared his throat. Something bad was about to happen, some conflict, confrontation, my body tensed in anticipation. The downcast faces, the simmering anxiety over secrets being revealed. Those were familiar to me, like when my Mother confronted my Father over the revealing of his secret family. The faces on the stage looked the same.

"Church, I've got a few confessions to make," said Mr. E. "I've seen a lot of people share their testimony on this stage over the years and describe their brokenness and their slavery to sin in stark terms. I only hope that I can be half as eloquent as they were in speaking to you tonight."

As Mr. E spoke, the voice in my head seemed to wake and rouse. A few low moans raced through my mind as Mr. E spoke about his grief and shame.

"Yes," murmured the voice in my head. "More, please."

"Congregation, people of Calvary Baptist Church," said Mr. E. "I have sinned. I have gone against God's teachings and rejected his undying love for me. Even in the light of all that God has done for me, I have still turned my back upon him, and now am at his mercy."

A few calls went out from the crowd in support of Mr. E, but Mr. Chris and Pastor Phil stayed stone faced.

"What sin," said Pastor Phil, stepping towards the front of the sanctuary.

Mr. E looked down from the congregation and bit his bottom lip. The voice in my head moaned louder at his obvious and all-consuming discomfort.

"I have committed the sin of lust, I have coveted those who are not my wife, I have been with those who are not my wife, and I have given into my own pleasure through online women time and time again," Mr. E looked upward to the Congregation, I fixed the spotlight on his face, able to see the red flush of his cheeks. "The bible says that a man who looks upon a woman with lust has committed adultery, and I have done so hundreds of times while in my position of leadership. Only by the power of God's grace have I not been struck down by his hand, like so many others who disobey his commands."

Mr. E's voice went up an octave as he finished the invocation, and a small piece of mustard yellow light started to shine in the front of the stage. It illuminated the ceiling of the sanctuary in an odd shape of two nearly perpendicular lines with seven circles between the edges.

"Do you confess your sins to God almighty?" said Pastor Phil, stepping to Mr. E's side. "And do you ask for his undying grace to forgive you of your sins."

"I do," Mr. E said, holding his hands above his head in a sign of surrender.

"Do you confess to your sins in the company of believers, so we may know and help you walk in righteousness?" said Pastor Phil motioning Mr. Chris to come to the other side of him.

"I'm sorry," howled Mr. E. "Lord Jesus, I am sorry for what I have done, I'm so sorry for what I've done with this perfect gift you have given me."

Mr. E wore pain on his face like I'd never seen. As I reflect on what happened next, what Mr. E would do in the coming days before the storm, I wonder if the whole thing was an act. A last-ditch effort by a pathetic man to save face after a life of casting aside all the good things that came to him. A sort of ritual humiliation he had to endure to keep his job and standing in the church.

But those moments where he howled for forgiveness, I often believe they were genuine. That whatever else was about to happen in the next few weeks, Mr. E was in incredible pain when he begged for forgiveness in front of the church.

The voice from outside certainly noticed, it's grunts and moans in my head growing louder and more frantic.

"Do you repent?" cried Pastor Phil.

"I–" Mr. E started, but before he could finish the next word Mr. Chris's hand whistled through the air and struck Mr. E on the mouth. Mr. E fell to his knees, his eyes closed and his hand going to his bleeding lip.

"Do you repent Alex Ellington?" bellowed Pastor Phil.

"I repent," Mr. E screamed before the next blow struck the back of his head. Mr. Chris's fist was closed for the strike, and instead he shoved Mr. E to all fours.

The yellow glow on the stage brightened until I could make out the iris's in each of the seven circles on the ceiling. None of the congregation looked towards the ceiling, they all were looking to the stage.

Pastor Phil crouched over Mr. E like some prehistoric insect and his face twisted in anger while he bellowed, "do you repent?"

"MORE" screamed the voice in my head, the voice from outside, the voice I still thought was from God.

"I'm sorry," hollered Mr. E, covering his head against the next blow. Mr Chris stepped back, and Pastor Phil leaned down to lift up Mr. E's chin.

"Then in the name of Jesus Christ," said Pastor Phil. "I declare you free from the sin, and as he said to Mary Magdalene who was also afflicted by the sin of lust, I tell you go and sin no more!"

The congregation erupted in applause as Pastor Phil raised Mr. E up to his feet. The band came back in with a refrain from (redacted) and the swing of euphoria lifted all to their feet.

Everyone except me, in the back of the room, running the sound system. My eyes were still fixed on the yellow glow in the ceiling of the sanctuary, the yellow glow that changed from the symbol of seven eyes to just one great yellow eye looking down directly at Mr. E.

And I swear to you on everything holy, I saw that eye blink.

27

19 Days Until Hurricane Ophelia

(The following was a (redacted) post by Charlotte Harden recovered from the private Calvary Baptist Church (redacted) group. The post is dated August 17th at 1:32 PM. The post includes a picture of Lyn Vargas taken from Charlotte Harden's phone, as well as a picture of two books one titled (redacted) and other title (redacted)

Charlotte Harden with **Ron Harden** and **twenty others**

Praise God, but I think I am finally finding some ANSWERS to what happened to my DARLING Kelly. Not only did I find DRUGS in her apartment, but I was able to meet her ROOMATE. I know Kelly was around some INTERESTING characters, but I wasn't prepared for the person Kelly was living with. Safe to say, I'm adding another LOST soul to my prayer list. But it got me thinking, that I thought I RECOGNIZED the roommate from somewhere.

Turns out I did. She works at the CEDAR branch of the Chesapeake Library. Now I'm not trying to judge, or hate anyone, but I wanted to check on what the library was providing. While I was looking through the books I saw the following two titles shelved in the KIDS section. Now I don't HATE anyone, but I think all reasonable people can see that these two books are NOT appropriate for young children. As pastor said on Sunday, we have to WAKE UP and see that this is what is being allowed in our COUNTRY.

MAMA BEAR is AWAKE and ready to protect our CHILDREN. No one should have to go through what I went through with Kelly. This is how it starts, CHILDREN who get confused on what is RIGHT and what is WRONG, like my sweet little girl. This is WRONG and we need to say something!!!!

Lyn Vargas' interview continued...

(Lyn Vargas washes their hands and rubs their sore arms. I've been with them for the past few hours as they have hoed, weeded, and pruned on the communal farm along with a set of other queer folks. As the sun starts to dip below the deep red sky. A few anxious residents check a weather app to see the direction of the raging wildfires to the north. Lyn turns her attention back to me as I ask a question about Kelly's medication.)

LV: I never saw her take any and never saw any in the house. When I spoke to Kelly's mother, there weren't any pill bottles in her box. Honestly, that was one of the reasons why I resolved to leave Kelly on her own. Even when she was able to do her therapy, her medicine appointments, everything on the internet, she still wasn't getting help. Instead she would tell me some story about why she was unable to leave the house, why she couldn't go to the pharmacy. At the time, I thought it was just a vicious cycle. Kelly had mental health problems that made it difficult for her to get help for mental health problems. A tough situation, but the stuff she was prescribed was fairly intense, not things someone could just pick up for her. New state regulations and penalties also made the risk of getting caught for helping her out just too high.

We had a few fights about my refusal to risk my safety and freedom just because she didn't want to leave the house. Those really scared me, not for my safety but Kelly's too. She was hurting, bad, and scared, and maybe I was being too cautious but the last thing that I wanted was to attract the wrong kind of attention. I did not wish to be perceived in public, not until I found a home somewhere else.

If only I had known that a few weeks later I'd be at the center of the latest culture war firestorm.

(Lyn slaps their gloves down on the table.)

I just don't understand, the people at Calvary Baptist, the people across the country that rallied behind them, the fucking president, they weren't actually in any danger. They had won, overwhelmingly. The culture was theirs again, and while some states still had some protections in place, it was only a matter of time before they folded. It was the golden age for those people, and it didn't matter in the slightest.

They all came for me.

Meme pages, pickets, my face with devil horn poorly photoshopped on. A reposted call for my death by multiple elected officials, and just being unable to do my job. I worked with the summer reading program, I was excited every year to work with kids on their reading. I really prided myself on helping them fill in the gaps in their learning from the school year. I remember constantly telling people that and it just being drowned out in hateful derangement.

I think my favorite theory that was floated was that I was some sort of Fentanyl trafficker. I was giving all the kids in my reading circle Fentanyl to get them hooked on it in the future. Obviously, I had fooled everyone else at my work, that was the only reason they would let someone like me teach or help the children. The reason they couldn't fire me was of course that I had MS-13 sleeper agents inside the library, or holding the library board's family members hostage.

That mask, that veil of civility was utterly gone, and finally I was feeling the city, the real city trying to cast me out like some sort of disease.

KF: How long did this last before you got out?

LV: I wasn't planning on leaving. That's the funny thing, after this storm of accusations and hate crested into my work, I resolved to stay in my position. I couldn't stop thinking of those few kids I had met who were still discovering themselves. Trying to let kids see themselves reflected in you is a strong incentive to stay, and I just decided that the hateful stuff had to blow over eventually.

Besides, I would be lying if spite wasn't a big part of the reason I stayed in my position. My manager was behind me, and the library was able to operate normally, especially when it was just those people from Calvary Baptist Church who were picketing outside. Things almost got back to normal after a week or two.

Then, they came to my home.

(Lyn takes a shuddering breath and their eyes go distant.)

I had a flag, just a rainbow one. Got left out after pride, and I was happy to keep it out a little longer. After the stuff with the library started, that same spite kept me flying it outside. Stupid on my part even though I'm not sure it would have mattered. I'm not making any accusations, but Charlotte Harden knew where I lived. Given Charlotte was the one who lurked in the library and targeted me, let's just say I have suspicions of her involvement in what happened next.

My alarm hadn't gone off on time that morning so I was rushing around the house looking for my keys and such. I remember looking up at where I had the flag flying and thinking it must have blown off. It was an old thing, having been with me since high school, lasting past both the target themed pride mech, and when most companies stopped selling "controversial materials" in the later 2020's.

The heat that day was stifling. I itched in my work clothes, and almost turned around to go back inside for some anti-perspirant. Instead my heart stopped at what was arranged on my porch.

My flag was there, some of it scorched black but most of the colors were still shining through. The fabric was arranged, and it took me a second to recognize the oval shape that was on my porch.

There's a feeling you get when something you dread, something you've told yourself can never happen, something so awful you repress thinking about it at every turn, faces you in the real world. An unreality, a realization, someone I knew once described the feeling as "when the other shoe dropped."

My mind still wasn't processing the shape, but there were words in the center laid out on my porch in thick red paint. It was a slogan, an old one that made the rounds in the late 2000's and early aughts. Safe to say one of the words was "hates" one of the words was "God" and the last word was a particularly vile slur. Below the words was a symbol, two slashes with seven circles inside, the same mark I found before Kelly disappeared. I think that was what brought me back to myself, remembering Kelly for a split second, that symbol activating the adrenaline, and finally shocking me out of my freeze response to the rainbow noose outside my door.

I think if it had just been the hate symbols outside my door, I might have stayed. Who knows, the spite and need to help those kids at the library might have overridden my fear at the very clear sign the community was sending me. Maybe then I would have a memorial named after me or something. I don't think I'd like that, troubling me after I'm dead with more of this stupid fight over who is allowed to actually be a person. But my fear turned to terror when I saw, in the parking lot across the street from my apartment complex, a 4x4 white pickup truck, and three people standing outside.

All three were men I recognized from protests outside the library.

One towered over the other two, his hair was gray but his physique showed no sign of his age. Next to him was a man with a boyish face and blond curly hair, a poorly concealed handgun down the front of his pants. The last person was barely a teenager, his mop of sandy hair unkept and blowing in the wind. All of them were looking at me the same way, "you've had your fun, but now's time to go. You never belonged here, and you will leave, one way or the other."

I went inside, gathered a few of my possessions, got in my car, and drove away as fast as I could. People in my circle came together, family surprised me with their support, and I made the trek across the country to here, where a lot of people have gotten a new start. I was even able to get some of my stuff shipped across from my old apartment.

That time after Kelly died, it was the worst pain I've ever been through. In my clearer moments, I know that I wouldn't wish it on anyone, but sometimes when I'm not feeling so forgiving my thoughts turn darker.

Sometimes, I wish that those waters that came up from the hurricane were still there, burying that whole fucking city.

28

13 Days Before Hurricane Ophelia

(The following is an audio recording taken by Whitney Ellington while at Calvary Baptist Church. The audio recording was submitted as evidence by Whitney Ellington in her divorce with Alex Ellington. Whitney Ellington's consul claimed the evidence painted a picture of a toxic environment for their two children, and should be considered in custody decisions by the court. Ms. Ellington also used the recording as evidence that Mr. Ellington had engaged in infidelity against her.

Three speakers are identified. The first is Whitney Elington herself, the second is Reverend Philip Gordan, and the final speaker is Alex Elington, Whitney's husband.)

Speaker 1 (Whitney): Pastor, I'll be honest, I'm feeling angry right now.

Speaker 2 (Phillip): All good Christians are angry when confronted by sins. I'm glad you are angry, I'm angry too, going against God's word and God's will always has consequences.

(Whitney): I'm just surprised, I don't understand why you didn't tell me Alex would be here.

(Philip): Would you have come back to talk to me if I told you?

Speaker 3 (Alex): No way.

(Whitney): What's there to talk about Alex? You made a promise to me, twenty years ago, that I was yours and you were mine. Now I find out that you broke that promise over and over again. What's there to talk about?

(Alex): It was only once, I swear.

(Whitney): That's not what you said to me when we weren't in front of the Pastor.

(Alex): That's a lie and you know it.

(Whitney): I'm the only one here who isn't lying.

(Philip): Peace, peace you two. I understand that there has been heartbreak, I understand that there has been hurt. We are fallen people, living in a fallen world, and often we stumble. Any marriage will involve some amount of mutual hurt, mutual pain on both sides. Whitney, I know that what Alex has done hurt you deeply. His sin is not one that can be easily reconciled, but God does not call us to just do what is easy, Jesus's sacrifice on the cross was not easy, it was painful, it was difficult, but through it there was healing and forgiveness.

(Whitney): You want me to forgive him? For the lies? For the betrayal? And just continue like this never happened?

(Philip): We are called to forgive Whitney. What I see here, is two broken people who are made full only by the grace of God through his son Jesus Christ. Your husband has admitted to a great sin, and you have revulsion and hatred of his sin. That is good and right, a great testament to the woman of God you are, but ask yourself. What would be a greater testimony to God's forgiveness, for you two to give up on this beautiful marriage? Or for you to just do what everyone else does in our fallen world. Will you let resentment separate and fracture your family? The scripture says "what God has joined together, let not man separate."

I call on you to do something difficult Whitney, to go against what this world says you should do and focus your eyes on heavenly things instead of things of this world.

(Whitney): But you admit it Alex? Admit the affairs?

(Alex): I admit that I have made mistakes.

(Whitney): For me to even think about forgiveness, you have to tell me what I'm forgiving you for.

(Alex): It's always like this with you, not enough to just win, but you have to humiliate me as well, you want me to crawl on my belly for you.

(Whitney): I'm not the one who hid in the pastor's office to surprise his scorned wife.

(Philip): Let's stay focused, Alex, she's right. In order for there to be forgiveness there must be a confession of sin.

(Alex): Is this really necessary?

(Whitney): Oh, I think it is Alex.

(Alex): Fine, I slept with (redacted) while I was married to you Whitney. I broke my marriage vows to you and to God, and ask for your forgiveness and for God's forgiveness as well.

 (Philip): Amen.

(Whitney): Thank you, I need to pray about it, but thank you for that Alex.

(Philip): I will pray for this reconciliation as well.

(Rustling as speakers get up to leave)

(Philip): Oh, one last thing Whitney, this is a holy place and a holy conversation. I do not think it would be prudent for it to leave the walls of this office. Can I trust in you, sister in Christ?

(Whitney): Absolutely pastor, now excuse me I need to pick up the children.

(Alex): I'll give you a hand.

(Whitney): I've got it, I have a few more days like we agreed.

(Alex): Can I at least–

(Recording ends)

(The following is a voice memo recorded by Alice Crenshaw. The memo is dated August 23rd 4:37 PM)

I can't imagine what Aunt Whitney is going through.

A divorce is bad enough, especially a divorce with kids, but that church was her entire life. I remember during Vacation Bible School she would be there for hours both before and after the events. She would be the one to put together the list of activities for students, she would be the one working tirelessly on bulletin boards. The church needed her, and she I think, needed the church.

Now that whole community is just gone. If she can't feel safe there, can't worry about getting pulled into some ambush meeting with the pastor and her hopefully soon to be ex-husband, then she won't ever step through those doors again. Her friends, her people she relied on, they are all there, and now the only story they are going to hear is the one Alex wants to tell.

The fact that Alex is still working with the youth is nuts to me. How many times did I sit there in a youth group and hear about how sex and intimacy was a holy act? How many times did we split based on gender so Aunt Whitney or some other woman from the church could talk about modesty, or Godliness, or purity? How many videos did we watch where whenever a boy or girl ended up "sinning" the consequences of teen pregnancy, suicide, and drug addiction collapsed around their head?

What makes me angry, makes me livid, is that I bet they are still teaching those lessons that to engage in "sexual immorality" as the bible says will end teenagers' lives, but Alex gets "forgiveness" not just from the pastor and God but also from the church.

"Grace" and "forgiveness" weren't part of the equation when I was there, but for Alex, he tries to intimidate his wife into forgiving him. The good, God-fearing woman who did everything right that he betrayed.

(Deep Breath)

I'm also worried for Whitney. We didn't talk about Kelly, but her shadow hovered in my mind. I'm trying to put it out of my head, but I just keep seeing a headline with Whitneys' name and the phrase "tragic accident."

Alex always had an edge of anger about him. A lot of the congregation would often comment on how well behaved and respectful the youth were in church, and a lot of that I think had to do with Alex. He was a filter of sorts, the kids who stuck around were kids like me, ones who would stay even if they were screamed at.

I remember one time we were setting up for a youth car wash, and I came to help out a good fifteen to twenty minutes late. I had stopped for a coffee beforehand, and rolled in to find him and a few other kids setting up. As soon as he saw me, his face turned red and his jaw clenched. In a different context, if I was a different kid who could just let adults be upset at me, the situation would have been funny. This short, baby faced man in flip flops and a shark bathing suit turning beat red with anger. But that wasn't me, or any of the other kids there. Alex made the youth group so uncomfortable that anyone who talked back to him didn't stay.

I was sixteen, had just gotten my license and was one of the older kids there. I don't know what was going through his head, but Alex didn't say a word to me. I started to stammer and apologize when he reached out and slapped my drink out of my hand. I don't really remember what he said next, but I remember trying not to cry.

One of the other kids picked up the coffee and threw it away, but they all stayed silent while Alex tore into me verbally. We were there early enough that there weren't any other adults around yet, so no one could have told him to calm down.

And I just took it. I stood there, let him say his piece, then did the car wash. It didn't even occur to me to tell my parents what happened, mostly because I thought I deserved to get "chewed out a little" for being late. Alex came by next time we were at church and started to apologize for what happened, but I cut him off and apologized for being late. I still thought that slapping the cup from my hand, humiliating me in front of my peers, was all fair game because I dared to get a coffee before volunteering at the car wash.

What Whitney is doing, she's making him very angry I'm sure. She has every right to, but I just worry. I worry about leaving her alone right now. She's posting on social media which is good, especially since from all outward appearances it looks like she is having a good time. But the comments are disabled on all her posts, that doesn't happen unless someone has said something to her. I can imagine some of the bile she might have to deal with from people she used to consider her community.

I might need to go home, to help her, or maybe just to keep her safe.

29

Five Years After Hurricane Ophelia

(Sean Clark is an unassuming man in his late thirties. Wearing khaki slacks, a white button up and a speckled tie he eats his Mediterranean salad in small bites during his lunch break. He has agreed to meet with me to discuss his time where he was involved with Alice Crenshaw. He places his keys and IT badge down on the desk and rubs his eyes before he begins.)

Sean Clark - First Recording 06/15/2032

Speakers are Sean Clark (referred to as SC throughout the transcript) and Kellen Faulk (referred to as "KF" throughout the transcript)

SC: So like, you're a real journalist? Not like some tabloid or clickbait writer? I don't want to end up on some worst boyfriends list. That stuff happens all the time you know, tell the wrong person the wrong details about your private life and bam you're on billboards as "the worst man on (redacted)" or you find out the reason you weren't able to get any dates is because you were in the wrong woman's little black book of "toxic men."

KF: I'm writing a story about Calvary Baptist Church and how they weathered

Hurricane Ophelia. Alice went down to the church, didn't she? Before the storm?

SC: Promise I'm not going to end up on an online listicle or in a (redacted) short video?

KF: I'm hoping to get a better understanding of Alice in the months before the storm. People break up all the time, relationships fail, I'm not here just to gossip about your love life.

SC: Good, good. I'm glad you get that. A lot of people, I don't know, any relationship that goes sour they have to put a label on it. It's difficult to accept, I guess, that sometimes it just doesn't work out, not really anyone's fault, but two people who thought they were compatible, just aren't. It's an easier story to tell yourself for sure, that the partner who you couldn't make it work with was abusive, or narcissistic, or whatever label we want to put on failed relationships these days.

The reality was that me and Alice, we just weren't going to work under substantial stress. Honestly there was a part of me that was grateful the things ended when they did, because I could see a world where the two of us ended up married for years before the first major bump in the road caused everything to fly apart. A lot of people I know ended up like that, when times were great everything went well. The first few bumps in the road were overcome, but then a serious decision would appear, jobs in different cities, family commitments, whatever, and that was just the end. Either of the marriage, or of any genuine love between the partnership.

You want a relationship that can last through a serious compromise, or a serious problem, and me and Alice, we failed that test. I'm sort of glad we failed it too early instead of too late.

We were a bright burning couple though. There's a kind of freedom in dating someone in your late twenties, or early thirties on her part. Both of you are full people, have developed a self-concept and everything independently, so you can see a little bit more of the actual person you are interested in. Also, even though people do get married a bit later, when you're older, things just get serious so much faster. Neither me or Alice were interested in dicking around trying to figure out if we were "the one" for each other. The questions were much more utilitarian.

You make me feel good, I make you feel good, our lives seem compatible so what's the point of waiting.

I even had a ring. I was thinking of asking her that summer before the storm, before everything ended up going south. I remember going to the same jewelry store we had looked into before as a joke. "Oh, look at how much dumb kids spend on fancy rocks," kind of nonsense. Alice would have called it "ideating" or playing with the idea of getting engaged. Well I remembered the one ring where she hadn't had a joke prepared. An elegant twist, with an modest, but glittering diamond. A week later, I bought the ring, and was just waiting for the right moment. That moment never came.

Look, Alice had a very different upbringing than I did. Both of our parents were middle class, and all our needs were met but mine didn't really do church. Alice's did, and did church like a lot. She said that they had changed, but still seemed like they were always at arms distance from her. I never totally understood it, but it did cause some issues when we were intimate. We had a few conversations about whether we were compatible, and generally were able to work through it. But being close was a sore spot for both of us.

This all got a lot worse when she got that email from Kelly.

(Sean stabs his salad with his fork and grits his teeth.)

Kelly Harden, back from the deepest of Alice's repressed memories, and really the person to blame for why me and Alice didn't work out.

It started harmless enough. Alice would talk about the new patient she had and I thought she was more energized, more excited to help someone than I'd seen her in a while. We had recently moved in together, and hearing about her sessions with patients started out as a highlight of my day after I came home. Soon though, I started only hearing about Kelly, like there were no other patients who existed for Alice. Gently, I told her that she was starting to fixate, starting to get stuck on just the same patient. She got really quiet, like she knew I was right, and told me that she knew she needed to take a step back from Kelly for a bit. That's when I heard more about that church you mentioned, Calvary Baptist. I didn't understand all that much about what Alice said, but I held her hand, listened, and assured her that getting some distance was the right thing to do. She agreed, and I thought that was that.

Then the phone calls started.

Alice would drop everything, mid conversation, just to answer her phone if Kelly called her. The calls were never anything good. Always some crisis. I almost got bored with the cycle, Kelly would call Alice, after that Alice would pick up, and finally I would hear all the details about the current problem. Alice even considered going down to Chesapeake, driving the eight hours round trip just to check if Kelly was ok.

I had never seen Alice this worked up before. Absent minded in all our conversations, glued to her email and her phone. Things came to a head I think in July before the storm, the night that Kelly called Alice in an utter panic. It woke me up, and I had work early the next morning. I remember grinding my jaw so hard that it ached the whole next day.

The next morning, Alice was asleep as I was preparing for work, and started trying to apologize for the night before. I said, something I wasn't proud of, and walked out of the house.

KF: Did the tension escalate after that conversation?

SC: No, I think that instead I just started isolating myself. I started to, well, I was a young man and not the most mature at the time, but uh I started finding my intimacy in other places.

KF: Other women?

SC: Virtually. I started being in some chat rooms, paid for a few pieces of stuff that catered to my tastes. It made sense to me at the time. Alice was ignoring me, marginalizing my presence in her life, but I wasn't mature enough to actually confront her about the issue so instead I just pouted and spent more time alone.

Alice knew, maybe not about exactly what I was looking at, but definitely that I was pulling away. Early August I think, she sat down at the table and laid out the last conversation she had with Kelly. She told me that I was right, she was letting this particular patient run most of her life, and needed to cut her off. Alice asked me to forgive her.

I said the words, but I was still hurt, doubly so because I told her so many times exactly what she was telling me. Like it could have been a direct transcript. I think that was when I really knew that our fling, intense feelings, were done. Not even six months in, I resented some-thing she did, and I held it inside myself, nurturing it like a flame.

Now I look back, and I think a lot of it was because while she apol-ogized, I never did for all the money I paid for things on the internet. In order for me to justify keeping that stuff from her, she had to still have done something wrong, something that justified my habits. So, I was dishonest, I said I forgave her when I still held onto how she had made me feel.

For a few weeks, things got back to normal, until Kelly died.

(Sean spins the ice in his soft drink before taking a sip.)

If Alice was fixated before Kelly's death, she became obsessed. I tuned out most of her wild conversations around Kelly when Kelly was still just Alice's patient. After though, it got unhinged.

Maybe Kelly wasn't hit by the car, maybe Kelly wasn't crazy when she thought people were following her, maybe something else was go-ing on in Chesapeake. I tried to let these imaginings just roll off my shoulders, but Alice didn't let it go.

She would listen to that voicemail from Kelly late into the night, she would stare at the picture that Kelly sent her. I would catch her staying up all night and blowing off patients in the morning. All the while my habits got worse and worse, I know she saw me looking at stuff one night, and just walked on by without saying anything. That might have hurt me more than the obsessive nature of her following Kelly's trail.

She kept showing me this photo on her phone, one that Kelly had sent her before she died, one of a tree with some kind of symbol on it. I just told her it was nonsense, that I didn't see any shape, or that there wasn't even a carving in the door. I know it was shitty, telling her that her eyes were lying to her, but I didn't know what else to do, how else to stop her from getting wrapped up in just one of her many clients.

KF: Alice was on a few different kinds of medication to help manage the symp-toms of (redacted) and (redacted) correct? Was she taking these medications?

SC: Religiously, that made it worse. I couldn't just blame her behavior on forgetting her meds or whatever. She was choosing, willingly, to just ignore me over a woman she didn't know until a couple months ago from her hometown.

Things came to head when I prepared a nice dinner, kind of a last-ditch attempt to save our relationship. I thought the night was successful for the first hour or two of our conversation. We remembered why we actually liked each other, what we found attractive about each other.

After the dishes were cleared and both of us were on our fourth glass of wine, Alice said she was thinking about going to Chesapeake, something about her aunt.

I tried to let it roll off of me, tried to be noncommittal. But she kept pushing, kept trying to get me to commit to going down with her.

And then she started talking about the body, saying crazy things about digging it back up, looking inside, finding out what "really happened." All legally of course, all going through the police, but there was something in her tone that made me realize she was never going to let go of what had happened to Kelly. When she started talking like that, well, I snapped.

Now I know that I said some things that were way out of bounds that night. Alice gave just as good as she got, tearing into my internet activities and other insecurities, but I don't know if it was the wine or just the anger over how we had been the past few months, but try as hard as I can, I don't remember what I said to her. Everything just came out of my mouth, every practiced insult and cut I could think to make against her. All that resentment just boiling out until I was out the house, slamming the door.

Whatever we did say, it made me angry enough that for months I didn't look her up, didn't try and find her. I figured we were done and that was that. Only when I started to see the list of the missing from the storm did I see her name and I felt some real remorse.

I was young, is what I tell myself, it was a short relationship, we just weren't meant for each other, all of it is what I tell myself at least. I guess I just hope that she's ok somehow, and not washed out to sea with all the rest after the storm hit.

30

Four Days Before Hurricane Ophelia

(The following was a sermon posted on the Calvary Baptist Church Website on September 1st by Reverend Philip Gordan. The sermon was titled "The Righteousness of God" and the associated scripture reading was Revelation 2:18-26. This sermon was not posted to the church's Youtube channel. The sermon was the final message from Reverend Gordan at Calvary Baptist available on their website.)

(Final chords of a worship song finish, and the minister steps up to the stage.)

Good morning good morning Calvary Baptist Church, do we feel the spirit of the Lord here today?

(Applause and cheers)

I said do we feel the spirit of the Lord in here today!

(Escalating cheers. The congregation seems nearly half again as big as the largest crowds from previous videos.)

That is more like it Calvary Baptist! I see a whole lot of new faces here today, and I just want to extend my sincerest thank you to everyone who has filled our church's pews these past few weeks. Thank you so much for helping us in the work God has called us to do to help this nation turn back to the love and the light of God. I think the mission that we have been engaged in here in Chesapeake has been deeply important, and I am happy to report that the sinful book entitled (redacted) will no longer reside in the Cedar Road branch of the Chesapeake library. Praise be to God.

(Applause)

It would not have been possible without you church. Thank you to all who worked together to win this victory for the Lord's kingdom. Before I get into my message today, I just wanted to recognize one person who without their commitment to what is right, and their fire for the Lord, we could not have won this great victory. Charlotte, would you please stand for us.

(Charlotte Harden, a middle-aged woman wearing a pearl necklace and a Save our Children T shirt stands and waves. On Charlotte's shirt is a pin of what looks like two black slashes blossoming upward with seven golden circles situated in the middle of the pin.)

Charlotte, you are such a great witness for the Lord. You who have dealt with unfathomable grief, but have turned it around to make our church, our city, and our state a more Godly place. This woman right here is one of my great inspiration's folks, let's give her one more round of applause amen.

(Applause, various cries of Amen.)

Alright folks, I want you to all remember this moment, remember this celebration, because this is but a taste of what is waiting for us when the Lord finally returns, and wow I cannot wait for that moment.

But it's not here yet. While we have won a victory, while we have helped prepare the ground for our Lord and Savior's return, we are not done yet. The race is not yet finished, and it would just be such a tragedy if the passion, and the energy, and the fire for God in this room dissipated. If the only thing Calvary Baptist could claim is that it removed a book from a library I would think it is a massive disappointment. I say that because I believe in you church, I believe that you have in your hearts and in your minds the ability to change the world, amen.

So, let's get into the word, shall we? I know recently we've been talking about the end times, and the final victory Jesus will win over the powers and authorities of this world. However, the Lord just really laid it on my heart to go back to those letters to the churches that John wrote at the beginning of that joyous book of Revelation. One in particular was laid onto my heart to share with you today. A letter to one of the first churches from Revelation 2, which we should have up on the screen behind me? Good it's there.

Alright, so this letter, starting in verse 18 is to the church in Thyatira. That's a fun one to say, let's all say it together.

(Church murmurs Thyratira in unison.)

Another funny name, but we know the Bible is timeless and true, so much so that I think that this verse really can apply to our church today. So, taking a look at the start the passage says, "I know your deeds, your love and faith, your service and perseverance, and that you are now doing more than you did at first." I read that passage, and I just thought that might describe us here at Calvary Baptist. When I look out at you folks on Sunday morning these are some of the ways I would describe the believers gathered here today. Love, faith, service, all of these words apply to each and every person in this room, and I thank God every day that I am able to serve as your pastor. Amen!

But that's not all, look at the second part of this verse here, where it says that the people in Thyratira have done more than they did at first. And I don't know church, but I can think of several big things we've been doing the past few weeks that have pushed us beyond our comfort zone. Our actions are like those of the church in Thyratira, where we are doing more than we did before. John, the apostle who wrote this letter, is telling us and that ancient church that there is a progression to doing the Lords work in your community, in your city, and in your nation, and like John I want to praise our church for doing that good work. Amen!
(Church roars Amen)

But…

(Pastor holds up a finger)

There's always a but isn't there when it comes to being holy in God's sight folks. But John does not let this church off easy and neither does he let us here at Calvary Baptist off either. Even though the church in Thyratira is doing more, it's still not enough. Let's take a look at what God's word says next.

"Nevertheless, I have this against you: you tolerate that woman Jezebel, who calls herself a prophet." Now folks when I first read that, do you know what the first thing that came to my mind was? Me and my wife have been married now for almost thirty years, and the first thing I saw is that if I ever referred to my wife Lindsey as "that woman," she would knock the teeth out of my head so fast that I wouldn't even know what happened. How many of ya'll fella's in the room feel the same way about your wives? Oh get those hands up there, I know that almost all of you wouldn't dream of ever referring to your ladies as "that woman." Chris, get your hand up, we know dang well that you wouldn't dream of referring to Pamela in that way.

(The camera zooms in on a seated man with white hair grinning as he reluctantly raises his hand while the crowd chuckles. On his chest is the same pin with black lines and seven golden circles.)

But look, if you let me get serious for a second, the reason we wouldn't dream of referring to our wives that way is not just because of our fear of lets just say, retribution, but also because we here at Calvary Baptist respect our women. We know our women are Godly and good witnesses for the word of God, we know our women have turned away from worldly desires and worldly sins and instead serve a heavenly father who is coming back soon to make all things new. Amen?

(Crowd chants Amen.)

My men in the audience could be a little louder on that one.

So this brought me to my next question, why would John the apostle while he is writing down the sacred word of God refer to anyone as "that woman?" It seems kind of disrespectful doesn't it? Well lets see what the scripture says this woman Jezebel was doing.

From the word, it says, "By her teaching she misleads my servants into sexual immorality and the eating of food sacrificed to idols. I have given her time to repent of her immorality, but she is unwilling."

So "that woman" in the scripture it turns out is not talking about one of the lovely, beautiful, and wonderful women of God in our audience, but instead about someone who is a false prophet. Who misleads people into sin, and I don't know about you, but I can certainly see some false prophets today in our culture. Amen.

"That woman" is the proper response to someone who is doing the work of the devil. And what makes it worse is that this woman, Jezebel, she knows what she is doing! She knows that her work is that of the enemy, that she is leading God's people away from his saving word. Literally, according to John, she is defiling the word of Jesus Christ and practicing explicitly sexual sin. It would be one thing if she was just unaware of the gospel of God, like Mary Magdalene who gave up her immorality, but she's that worst kind of person. Someone who knows better, but does evil anyways!

The Lord also put on my heart as I read this passage, one of the words used here in this chapter which is tolerance. Man, isn't it awful how one of the enemy's best tactics is to take a kernel of truth from the gospel, and twist it for evil. It's just a shame that the lying tongues of the powers of the air can take a word that was invented to describe something good and turn it to evil, and folks hasn't that happened with the word tolerance?

Tolerance used to mean that you and I could disagree about something that is earthly. Something like sports teams, or politics, or whether country or praise music is better, but at the end of the day we could still respect each other's views. Nowadays, that isn't the case. You've always gotta watch yourself to make sure that your words don't hurt anybody's feelings. This world, and this culture here in America have taken the good and godly meaning of tolerance and twisted it to mean that everybody has to agree on everything. In fact, the new meaning of tolerance requires us Christians to call evil good and wickedness righteousness. The enemy has twisted the word to mean the exact opposite of what it used to mean. So now if you are like me, or like Charlotte, or like Alex and when you see evil in the word you have to say something you get branded as being "intolerant." You get shunned, you get canceled, you get arrested, and I've only got one thing to say to the powers and authorities and nations that let this happen which is "have your fun now, because my God is real and he is coming back to make all things new." Amen?

(Congregation shouts amen.)

But thinking about this word tolerance, I don't know about you but instead of going with the world's definition of tolerance, maybe let's go with the biblical one. How does that sound? What's funny about this passage is that usually in our everyday life, tolerance is considered a good thing, but here in the word, it's the opposite.

John says to the believers in Thyateria that tolerating that woman Jezebel is what he holds against the church. Because you know folks, one thing God cannot tolerate among his people is sin. The bible in fact calls us to be intolerant to sin, to cast it out of our homes, our libraries, our cities until that blessed day where it is defeated forever. Jesus does not tolerate sin, so why should we? If you and I have a disagreement over a sports team we can work through that, most likely, because the sports team is a worldly matter. Sin is different, sin is something that separates us from our heavenly Father and cannot be allowed to continue in any true group of believers. Amen!

In fact let's read what is said about that woman Jezebel. The word of God says, "I will cast her on a bed of suffering, and I will make those who commit adultery with her suffer intensely. I will strike her children dead. Then all the churches will know that I am he who searches hearts and minds."

I don't know, but according to our modern culture that doesn't sound very "tolerant" to me. In fact, I bet if I said this up in Washington DC, or New York, or San Francisco they'd have me locked up in no time. But remember church, these aren't my words, they are God's. God tells us in no uncertain terms in his word that evil, that sin, that the work of the enemy should not be tolerated by his people. Amen!

So, I only have one question for you church, are you going to tolerate evil and wickedness? Are you going to tolerate sin, even when it comes from people inside or around the church? Or are you going to stand with God in rejecting the work of the enemy at every turn. Are you going to stand with God to make his kingdom a reality down here on earth? Stand with God until he returns to punish the wicked, exalt his people, and reign forever and ever! Are you with me Calvary Baptist Church?

(Congregation stands and cheers. The camera goes to a wider angle and seven circles in between two gently diverging lines are visible at the front of the church exuding a warm, yellow glow.)

31

Four Days Before Superstorm Ophelia

(The following is a (redacted) video made by Alex Ellington that was uploaded to the site on September 2nd at 4:02 PM. The video is shot from within Alex Ellington's sedan, and objects of note include discarded militia fatigues in the back seat, a "live free or die" hat on Alex's head. Alex wears an unbuttoned shirt and khaki slacks. A shirt with a red pill in the center and the text "you are not alone" underneath is visible underneath the unbuttoned shirt. The video was made private after my report on Calvary Baptist Church.)

I think that we, as men, need to remember the times we are living in are really flipping hard. I see videos of men like me, men whose women have been corrupted by this weak and failing American culture, and all the focus is on how to rebuild their confidence or what to do next. I think that, sometimes, we really have to just take a second and think about how dang hard it is to be a man in this country right now. I'm trying to live my life the right way, teach my children how to be Godly, and at just every opportunity, this culture, this cauldron of sin just takes my knees right out from under me. The works of the enemy have turned my own wife against me, and now my family, my rock, my foundation is just crumbling in front of my eyes. And I know I'm not alone, I know a lot of men either on the internet, or at work, or at church who have the same thought I did. Where they just came home one day, and bang, everything they'd worked for, everything they'd built just came crashing down on their head.

Now I know that I'm not a perfect person, I know that I've made mistakes, but I'm only human like the rest of us. I wake up every day and try my hardest to walk in God's light, and while I fail sometimes, at least I am trying. At least I haven't already succumbed to the workings of this world, and decided to dive deeper into sin instead of repenting and moving on. I mean doesn't it mean something that I want to work on myself, and be the man for my wife that she married twenty years ago? Shouldn't that matter? Shouldn't I matter?

But no, our whole life, our children's lives, are just getting thrown away because she doesn't want to do the hard work of reconciliation. That's what's wrong with people these days. No one is interested in hard work, everyone just wants to do what's easy, or what feels right, forget the consequences. It's what we've been taught, and it's absolutely what women have been taught. Did you all know that a lot of women are actually changing the vows for their wedding? Instead of "as long as we both shall live" some ministers are saying "as long as love shall last." As if one of our most sacred traditions needed to be disrespected even more in this country. All my wife is doing is just following the rest of the culture, doing what is easy, and maybe I could forgive her for that, it's understandable. But what she did today, I just need to tell people because I think it just shows how hard it is to be a man in America.

(Rustling sounds as Alex takes the camera and shows his clothes to the video. A large pistol is visible in the passenger seat.)

As you can see from my attire, I am dressed up. I think I cleaned up pretty nice, but today was not a nice occasion. I was dressed for family court, and had some paperwork that my wife wanted me to sign to make it clear that we were separating and she was taking the easy way out. We go through things, sign some documents, confirm that she wants a divorce, and I think that's that and we can go our separate ways until we have to fight over the kids. I had moved on when her lawyer, some other woman in a pantsuit with some dye or something else in her hair, entered another item into evidence in preparation for the fight over child custody. I think it's clear I should have more access to the kids given I'm not the one that started the divorce proceedings, but we all know how men fare in the legal system when it comes to custody battles in this country.

Curious, I ask what this new piece of evidence is, and my wife looks me dead in the eye and tells me that it's a recording from a private conversation me, her, and my pastor had a few weeks ago.

(Alex's face turns red and tears bead in the corner of his eyes.)

She took a private conversation that occurred in a holy place, and submitted it to a worldly court to take our children from me. I didn't know she could find another way to stab me in the back, but somehow, she betrayed both my trust and God's trust. She should know better, she should fricking know better than to do something like that.

I haven't seen my wife smile since I confessed my sin and tried to start the process of reconciliation. But when she told me that our conversation between our pastor and God was now going to be part of the custody battle? That woman's grin was ear to ear.

And I know I'm not alone. I know a lot of people out there feel the same way, where they don't even recognize the cruelty and evil of these women as they tear apart our families. There is a war on men in this country, and sometimes it's really hard to just keep going. Especially when things are so stacked against you. I know that my wife is going to come out better when it comes to custody of our kids, even though she's the one that's going through with this divorce not me.

I really only have one hope at this point, and that is more men will wake up to this system that is throwing us in the garbage. That more men will, and excuse me for being crude, find their balls enough to stand up and say no to this immorality that is twisting our women's brains. And when that happens, oh man, I think I'm going to be the one smiling. So to all you feminists, socialists, and other gender theory people, watch out, your game is almost up because soon the "men" are going to remember who we are.

If you resonate with anything I said today, please give me a like and a subscribe. Be safe out there men of God, we do not know the hour or the day he will return, but me and mine, we will serve the Lord.

32

Five Years After Hurricane Ophelia

Ernest Mobley Interview

Ernest Mobley - Fourth Recording 02/29/2032

Speakers are Ernest Mobley (referred to as "E" throughout the transcript) and Kellen Faulk (referred to as "KF" throughout the transcript)

KF: Were you a participant in the protests outside of the Chesapeake Public library?

E: I was a participant, a ringleader, whatever else you could say. I'm fairly certain that my photo appears if you google the Chesapeake Library protests. I also participated in demonstrations near the women's health clinic, the courthouse, any major religious event, I was there with Mr. Chris and Mr. E.

KF: Even after your strange experiences at All In night?

E: Home got worse in August. Dad wasn't home hardly at all, and neither was Mom. I felt forgotten, ignored, and could go days without speaking to either of them. So, I gravitated towards the two men who I believed still cared about me. When the library blew up in the news it was all that was on either the talk radio Mr. Chris listened to, and the subject of Mr. E's frequent rants. Often, he would tie his various shouting sessions back to his soon to be ex-wife.

Mr. Chris was quieter, but still paid attention to events. I'll never forget the day the president spoke on the issue. He had the volume high and we both sat in silence as the most powerful man in the country spoke forcefully in defense of our Christian faith. I think that was the only time I'd seen Mr. Chris with a wide smile on his face the entire time that he was listening to the radio. When we arrived at our destination for that day, the shooting range, he put the car in park and pulled out a small item from his glove box. It was a pin, a pin with two almost parallel lines that suggested a tree and seven dotted circles in the center. The symbol was plated in gold. He held it out to me.

"The time is almost here Ernest," he said, his smile fading. "You have heard the voice of God, more than once I'm sure. He has called you to be one of Gideon's three hundred. The question is if you are willing to take up the burden."

I reached out to grasp the pin, but Mr. Chris pulled it away from me.

"There needs to be no doubt in your heart if you want to serve the Lord. I feel as if you still have some concerns about God's word to you. Last time we spoke, you said that you were not sure the voice was from God."

KF: Did you still doubt God was speaking to you?

E: My concerns were less about God, but more about the people around me. Mr. E was scaring me, the cavalier way he brandished his weapon, the constant talk of his ex-wife in the car, I didn't like it all.

But Mr. E was not the one offering me the pin, it was Mr. Chris. The man who once again was telling me that I was special, chosen, selected by God. The opposite of being ignored and forgotten at home. So even though I was scared of Mr. E, even though there was a voice in the back of my head questioning why there had to be so much suffering at All In night, and why the voice made the noises it did, I told Mr. Chris I had no more doubts.

He placed the pin on my shirt and smiled. "I'm proud of you son, the path you have chosen is not easy." He then asked me to repeat a few words after him.

KF: What did he ask you to repeat?

E: If I could remember I would tell you, but it was the same as when he prayed over me in the truck before. Even now when I try to recall the words they only sound like the buzzing of insects in my mind. But I repeated every word, and I don't know today if all the words were even in a language I recognized, but at the end of the words Mr. Chris smiled at me and clapped me on the shoulder. He told me that I was ready for the fight, and never to let the pin out of my sight.

I took the metal and it burned in my hand. The gold became more vibrant in color, and in that place in my head where the voice spoke to me, I felt an opening, an awakening I guess you could say. Like when you dial a phone number and the person on the other side picks up the phone but doesn't speak. That same low buzzing sound with the anticipation that something could, if they wanted to, speak to you.

Before we pulled away, Mr. Chris spat out some of the tobacco chew in his mouth and said, "Son, I'm going to tell you something that I haven't told anyone but my wife and God."

I asked him what, feeling that gravitas you do as a teenager when a respected adult wishes to say something important.

"I always wanted a son. I prayed to God, I begged God, me and my wife for years. It never happened for us, we never could have a child. I thought I'd made my peace with it, until about ten years ago, I heard the voice, the voice of God, and it told me I would still have a son."

If I was certain of anything, I was certain at this moment at least, Mr. Chris was telling me the truth.

"I laughed, my wife laughed, we could not imagine how we would have a child at our advanced age. It shook my faith for a time, made things difficult between me and God, that was until I met you."

Mr. Chris offered his right arm and I nestled within it. He pulled me close and murmured, "I trusted God and he has provided, you can trust him too son, I know that the world is difficult and it is hard to be a teenager and hard to be in your situation, but I'm so grateful we met."

I can't remember the last time either my parents had embraced me, not since I was a child, and here was this man who I had the utmost respect for drawing me close and claiming me as his own. I could not have been happier, even if the crackling phone line in my head worried me about the voice from outside.

KF: It's reasonable, you took comfort and care that was offered, I don't think anyone would judge you for it.

E: I tell you this to try and help you understand what happened next. What I said that day as we drove to meet Mr. E at the shooting range in the early August heat. That I would say anything to keep the one adult who said "You matter" in my life.

I would ask you to remember that I was fourteen. What happened after my words at the range, it still is with me today, and I don't want to put my own guilt over the suffering I caused, but please remember, I was a child. I didn't know what I was doing, the effect it would have, I was just so stupid.

I deserve what's waiting for me after the end, I fucking deserve it, I don't even know why I am making excuses, but what happened was wrong to everyone, and to me too. I was wronged too damn it, and that should fucking matter.

33

Four Days before Hurricane Ophelia

(The following is the (redacted) search history of Alice Crenshaw's personal computer. These searches were all made between the dates of September 1st and 3rd 2027. The searches have been organized beginning with September 1st and ending with September 3rd for clarity purposes. All searches occurred after the end of Alice Crenshaw's relationship with Sean Clark. Searches have been consolidated to only include relevant (redacted) searches to this story.)

Wednesday, September 1st

2:05 AM Nightmares and Anxiety - (Redacted) Search

2:07 AM Anxiety Dreams: Causes, Meanings, and Tips - Healthline.com

2:09 AM Recurring Nightmares - (Redacted) Search

2:10 AM Here's What Your Recurring Nightmares Actually Mean - Time.com

2:15 AM Recurring Nightmares: Causes, Treatments, and How to Cope - Choosingtherapy.com

2:18 AM Stop Recurring Nightmares/ Dreams and Hypnosis Audio - hypnosisdownloads.com

2:25 AM Nightmares that Stop and Start - (Redacted) Search

2:26 AM Nightmare that stops then starts after you back to sleep -

(Redacted) Search

2:26 AM Why When You Wake Up After Having a Nightmare and Go Back to Sleep It's the Same Nightmare - quora.com

2:27 AM What Are My Nightmares Telling me? - (Redacted) Search

2:28 AM What Do My Nightmares Mean? - Vivapartnership.com

2:32 AM How to Interpret Dreams You Have About Practically Anyone - The Cut.Com

2:35 AM What does the Bible Say About Nightmares/Bad Dreams? - Gotquestions.org

2:37 AM Guilt Nightmares - (Redacted) Search

2:40 AM Roles of Guilt Cognition in Trauma Related Sleep Disturbance- ncbi.gov

2:41 AM Guilt Cognition Dreams - (Redacted) Search

2:43 AM Nightmare After Trauma as a Paradigm for all Dreams- pubmed.org

2:50 AM How Trauma can Effect Dreams: How to Cope - sleepfoundation.org

2:54 AM Counterfactual Cognitive Operations in Dreams - asdreams.org

2:57 AM How to Sleep After a Nightmare - peacefulsleep.com

3:02 AM Soothing Lofi Beats - google search

3:03 AM Lofi Beats to fall Asleep to- Youtube.com

(No more relevant google searches were recorded in the early morning of September 1st. Relevant searches begin again at 4:17 PM on the afternoon of September 1st.)

4:17 PM Bob the Necromancer does an Unboxing- youtube.com

4:18 PM When Do Police Exhume a Body - (redacted) search

4:19 PM § 32.1-286. Exhumations - law.lis.virginia.gov

4:23 PM What Happens When a Body Is Exhumed for a Criminal Investigation? - aetv.com

4:25 PM Exhumation Guide Rowland Brothers Exhumation Services - rbexhumations.com

4:27 PM Court grants permission for exhumation, after suspicions arise over death of deceased churchtimes.co.uk

4:33 PM Police to exhume body of woman featured in (Redacted) The (Redacted)- wbaltv.com

4:35 PM Police Exhume Body Chesapeake - (Redacted) search

4:38 PM How Much Proof Do You Need to Exhume a Body in Chesapeake - (Redacted) search

4:43 PM Can you Exhume a Body if you are not a Family Member - (Redacted) search

4:47 PM How to Get the Police to Believe You - (Redacted) search

4:55 PM The Process for Getting a Body Exhumed - (Redacted) search

5:07 PM Will I go to jail and for how long if I exhumed my father's body myself without a permit? - Legal Answers avvo.com

5:10 PM How to Dig a Grave - (Redacted) search

5:14 PM DIY Gravedigging - youtube.com

5:15 PM How to Dig a Grave By Hand - (Redacted) Search

5:18 PM How to Dig a Grave By Hand - carolinamemorialsanctuary.conm

5:27 PM Are Graves Really Six Feet Deep - (Redacted) Search

5:32 PM How Hard it It to Dig a Grave - (Redacted) search

5:33 PM What's it Like to Dig Graves by Hand? - nhmagazine.com

5:37 PM Amazon.com: Shovel

5:38 PM Amazon.com: (Redacted) Heavy Duty Digging Shovel

5:41 PM Amazon.com: (Redacted) Full Size Digging Shovel

5:42 PM Amazon.com: Trench Shovel for Digging

5:45 PM Laws around Exhuming Corpses in Virginia - (Redacted) search

5:49 PM Penalty for Disinterring Corpses in Virginia- (Redacted) search

(No more relevant searches were recorded in the afternoon or evening of September 1st.)

Thursday, September 2nd

12:42 AM Symbols in Nightmares- (Redacted) search

12:45 AM Symbol of Tree - (Redacted) search

12:47 AM Trees and the Occult - (Redacted) search

12:48 AM Willow Trees and the Occult - (Redacted) search

12:49 AM Willow Mythology and Folklore - TreesforLife.com

12:51 AM Willow Trees and Nightmares- (Redacted) search

12:52 AM Willow - Illusion - Tree Spirit Wisdom- treespiritwisdom.com

12:55 AM Why are Willow Trees Depicted as Evil? - Reddit.com

12:58 AM Willow Tree Lore- Druidy.com

12:59 AM Soothing Music for sleep - (Redacted) search

(The Final collection of relevant searches were conducted later that morning.)

4:12 AM Tree with Seven Eyes- (Redacted) search
4:13 AM Tree with Seven Yellow Eyes - (Redacted) search
4:15 AM Tree with Seven Eyes Symbol - (Redacted) search
4:17 AM Tree with Seven Eyes Symbol Occult - (Redacted) search
4:19 AM Tree with Seven Eyes Symbol Right Wing - (Redacted) search
4:23 AM Right Wing Militia Tree with Seven Eyes Symbol - (Redacted) search
4:34 AM Ancient Mythology Tree with Seven Eyes - (Redacted) search
4:52 AM The Importance of the Number Seven - (Redacted) search
5:01 AM Christ as the Stone with Seven Eyes - agodman.com
5:03 AM The Stone with Seven Eyes - ministrysamples.org
5:11 AM Seven Yellow Eyes the Bible - (Redacted) search
5:20 AM The Stone with Seven Eyes for God's Building - premieplus.org
5:32 AM Seven Eyed Tree Worship - (Redacted) search
5:43 AM Appearances of a Seven Eyed Tree in Old Stories - (Redacted) search
5:52 AM Has Anyone Heard or Seen Stories About a Seven Eyed Tree - (Redacted) search
6:01 AM Calvary Baptist Church Library protests - (Redacted) search
6:04 AM Striking Photos of the Religious Protests at Cedar Branch Library -wavy.com

34

Five Years After Hurricane Ophelia

Ernest Mobley - Fourth Recording 02/29/2032

Speakers are Ernest Mobley (referred to as "E" throughout the transcript) and Kellen Faulk (referred to as "K" throughout the transcript)

KF: What happened at the shooting range in early August?

E: Please know that I'm telling you what happened and easily could have left out my part in all of this. It's important people know what happened to Whitney Ellington, and important that I admit my part.

I walked with Mr. Chris that day to the firing range, and Mr. E was already there. He wore a (redacted) shirt and had the large handgun he purchased on a table next to the target. A collection of large bullets and various weapon modifications were spread out on the table in a haphazard manner. I remember the metallic smell of the ammunition and the muffled bang of the other patrons at the range. Mr. E smiled at us and motioned to his handgun, asking Mr. Chris some questions about its assembly.

Mr. Chris walked through the loading and firing process for the weapon and handed it over to Mr. E. The gun went off, and Mr. E cursed as the bullet missed the target. Over the course of the next hour, Mr. E practiced again and again trying to hit the target.

There were two kinds of silhouettes that you could practice on at the range. One was of a burly man, with short hair and broad shoulders. The other was of a long-haired woman making a suggestive pose. I think the original purpose was to practice on a smaller target, or perhaps old Cold War stereotypes of female Russian spies were in vogue when the firing range originally opened.

Mr. E used the woman's silhouette exclusively.

About halfway through our allotted hour, Mr. Chris suggested that Mr. E change targets. The male target was larger and easier to aim for.

Mr. E shook his head, and kept missing wide for the rest of our session.

Towards the end, Mr. E got frustrated and told the two of us that he wanted someone else to try firing the gun. I don't remember how many times he shot, but only one or two of the bullets even grazed the target.

Mr. Chris shrugged and loaded the weapon. I expected to see a shake in his arm as he lifted the comically large handgun and extended it out. Instead, his grip was solid and the barrel still. Even when the gun recoiled, Mr. Chris didn't flinch, holding the weapon like a much younger man who recently returned from war.

Mr. Chris fired ten shots. All of them were clustered around the heart and shoulder of the target just an inch or two apart.

Both men looked at me.

Mr. Chris held out the weapon in a silent offer. To be honest, I had no desire to hold the gun, let alone fire it. I didn't grow up around guns, and my thoughts teemed around worst-case scenarios where the gun misfired and hit either of them in the shin, in the stomach, or God forbid in the head.

Nowadays, when I think of that moment, I wish I had taken the gun and shot them both. Not that I expect it would have killed Mr. Chris, but it is good sometimes to imagine their looks of surprise and fear as I turn the gun towards them.

(Ernest smiles, eyes glazing as the narcotic inside the vaporizing device begins to work.)

But I didn't take the gun, and both looked at me in disappointment. They ignored me the last few minutes, until we finished putting up the weapons and started to walk towards the car.

On the way over, Mr. E started to talk to Mr. Chris about Whitney and the divorce.

He was almost foaming at the mouth, he was so angry. Screaming about pictures of Whitney he had seen on (redacted), talking about how she was going out to bars, getting drunk on alcohol, and speculating about her corrupting influence on 'his' children. Mr. Chris did nothing to calm Mr. E, starting new rounds of speculation, and agreeing with the worst charges that Mr. E laid at her feet. Charges of sleeping with multiple different men, taking hard drugs, and bringing their children to the bar.

I stood there silent and uncomfortable. My mind wasn't focused on the increasingly deranged speculation of Mr. E on his ex-wife's sins. No, instead I was worried about feeling invisible, frightened that neither of these two men who I thought the world of would ever speak or acknowledge me again. My mind racked for ways to think of how to reenter the conversation, how to make both of them acknowledge me again. I really wanted to hear about how I was special, I was chosen, I was important, that was what I wanted to hear again.

Right before we reached the car I looked at both men and said, "and that's not even the worst thing she did."

All four eyes of the men met mine, hardened with anger. They gave me the look an adult gives a kid who intruded on a conversation that was not intended to be in their presence. Like the look my parents gave me when I walked in on my Father's ultimatum to my Mother.

They asked me what I meant.

"I was at the women's health center for a protest two days ago," I told them, even though I called it a different name that I will not repeat. "When I was there, I saw Whitney walk through the doors with her eyes down rubbing her stomach."

KF: Was this true?

E: No, a complete lie, made to get back into Mr. Chris and Mr. E's good graces. A stupid, thoughtless lie of a child.

Have you ever been cliff diving?

KF: A time or two, maybe at a camp when I was younger.

E: It's something of a right of passage for children. All that stress waiting in line to get to the top, watching the kids that aren't able to jump, your own heart pounding in your chest as you get closer and closer to your turn. And when you finally get to the top, you get up to the ledge and some combination of fear and anxiety fills your mind. Fear of the drop, and anxiety that you will be one of the kids that cry their way back down to the bottom.

Often you edge up to the side of the cliff, not wanting to slip, getting as close as you can before you take that last step. There's that moment right when you step off, when you know that there's no going back. You can't get back on the cliff, you've made your choice, and now you're falling.

When I finished my lie, and saw Mr. E's face, I felt the same way I did when I jumped for my first cliff dive.

Mr. E took me home that day, and didn't say a word the whole drive back to my house.

35

2 Days until Hurricane Ophelia Makes Landfall

(The following is a voice memo recorded on Alice Crenshaw's phone. The voice memo is time stamped at 4:27 AM on September 3rd, 2027)

I became a therapist because my life improved dramatically after I got help. Talk therapy, medication, it all worked together to help me just feel better than I did before. Often, I read self-help or other experts speak of therapy as a dead end or cul-de-sac because you're never really "cured" of chronic mental conditions. This idea is nonsense because the conditions are chronic, lifelong, and require constant monitoring.

Or else you end up like me, up at nearly five in the morning, staring at a photo and fighting the dread coiled in my stomach.

I'm on my meds, I should be stable, what is happening at Calvary Baptist, what happened to Kelly, fills me with terror.

Me and my mom have both struggled with anxiety, constantly preparing for the worst-case scenario. Before I got help, I would sometimes sit up at night and worry about outlandish tragedies that could befall me or my parents. Whenever Dad would leave town for work I would imagine him on the side of the road, a victim of a car accident, or a murder, or even attacked by some sort of monster or alien. I thought everyone had those worries, and to a certain extent everyone does.

But not to the same degree, not enough to keep a little girl awake deep into the night. Not enough for me to be here, as a grown woman, who has figured out a few things about herself, just staring at a photo on the internet trying to reconcile what I've seen.

The thing about anxiety is that when you grow up with the condition, you build some systems for yourself to stop the destructive cycle of worry. I often explain to patients that anxiety is like looking down a dark hallway and seeing shapes at the end. You can't make them out, but your mind starts filling in the blanks, and when you have severe anxiety, those shapes are always terrifying. Your adrenaline kicks in, as your body gets ready to fight off whatever imminent threat is barreling down the hallway to rip your throat out.

But most of the time a dark hallway is just a dark hallway. Darkness is just the unknown, what we can't see, and in life you always don't know more than you know. When my Dad went on a work trip, I knew he was gone and I didn't know what would happen to him. My mind, and my condition, makes it so that I invented shapes in the dark that placed him in danger. Once that happens, once your body responds to the worry with adrenaline, that's when you can end up staying up all night waiting for a loved one to come home.

That level of fear and worry is not sustainable, not at all, so what I do and what I tell other people to do when they come to me with these problems, is build a set of tools to stop that bodily reaction to worry and anxiety. Sometimes it's music, sometimes it's counting, sometimes it's distraction, but the point is to help a person look into that dark hallway, into the unknown and accept that they don't know exactly what the darkness holds, but in almost every case, it's going to be alright.

But what happens if there is a real monster at the end of the hallway, something evil that does want to hurt you?

The panic response, the adrenaline, I've built so many defenses to stop it from surging through me, that I have to check and double check when I feel actual fear, like I do right now. Fear I feel for Whitney, and dread that whatever Kelly saw and felt in her last moments might have been more than the delusions of a paranoid woman.

This photo I'm staring at. It's of Calvary Baptist's protests outside the library and I see so many people I know. Kelly's Mom, Alex, pastor Gordan, and of course Mr. Chris, their faces twisted in anger. I should know these people, I grew up around them, but I don't recognize the anger and the rage in their faces as they hold signs that say just the most deranged things. I could be there, if a few things had gone differently, I could be in that protesting crowd.

Or I could have ended up like Kelly.

But that's just the dark hallway, the unknown. I don't know what's in the hearts of the people at Calvary Baptist when they spew hatred, and it's not good to try and fill in the blanks. I have defenses, I have coping strategies, I am a therapist for fuck's sake, I'm the one who helps people get over these cyclical thoughts that do nothing but cause incessant worry and fear. I should fucking know better.

Then I looked at Mr. Chris's jacket.

He's always been a veteran of some foreign war. He seems too young to have fought in Vietnam, but too old to fight in Iraq or Afghanistan. But the jacket has various right-wing slogans, as well as the Semper Fi motto of the Marines. On his left shoulder is a patch, a patch that had two parallel black lines blossoming up in the shape of a tree, and seven circles on its trunk.

I googled that shape over and over again. I looked at far right militia groups like the (redacted) and the (redacted.) I couldn't find anything. I've only ever seen that symbol, that shape in one place, carved on Kelly's door before her accident.

Kelly said that Mr. Chris was following her. I didn't believe her, I couldn't believe her, but too much just isn't adding up. Why was Mr. Chris the one who reported the accident? Why was he wearing the only other example of that seven eyed tree symbol she sent to me that was carved on her door? I didn't believe her, I couldn't believe her, and now she's gone.

I'm worried about Whitney. Scorning the church, scorning Alex, I don't know. There are dangerous people, deeply dangerous people there, and if something happened to her, I could never live with myself.

But I'm a therapist, I'm not a detective, I'm not a police officer, and I have no idea what to do. The dread that I've felt, that I've put off these past weeks, since me and Kelly started talking, it's taken a shape. Something awful is at the end of that dark hallway, I know it.

(The following is a phone call made to the anonymous tip line set up in relation to the fatal hit and run of Kelly Harden. The officer who answered the hotline was John Harrison. The call was placed at 8:15 AM on September 4th, 2027.)

John Harrison: Chesapeake Police, how can I help you?

(Redacted): Hi, I'm here to call with a tip on the fatal hit and run from earlier this month? That girl on Battlefield?

John Harrison: That is what this line is for. What new information do you want to report?

(Redacted): Well I was talking to Kelly before the accident and she claimed that she was being followed, by a Mr. Chris Durose in the weeks leading up to the accident.

John Harrison: Were you a friend of Kelly's?

(Redacted): Sort of, we had a professional relationship.

John Harrison: Ok, so Kelly said that she was being followed. Is there any other information you want to share with me?

(Redacted): Before Kelly died there was vandalism done to her home, she sent me a picture, a symbol was carved into the door.

John Harrison: Vandalism? I'll check to see if anything was reported to us about her door.

(Redacted): No, I don't think she would have reported it, she was apprehensive about the police.

John Harrison: Believe me, I know.

(Redacted): Well, the same symbol, the same vandalism, I saw a picture of Chris Durose having the same symbol on his jacket.

John Harrison: Ok.

(Redacted): I just wonder if the two are connected.

John Harrison: Do you have any information on the vehicle that struck Kelly?

(Redacted): No, but I thought it was notable that a man she claimed was following her was wearing the same symbol that was carved into her door.

John Harrison: I have to check on the symbol, but I have here a list of reports that indicate Kelly "struggled with delusions" as well as repeated attempts to fill an antipsychotic medication. I'm sorry to tell you ma'am, but Kelly may have been in the grip of one of those delusions when she spoke to you.

(Redacted): But the door damage, the patch.

John Harrison: Thank you for your tip, unless you have any information about the vehicle, I think we are done here.

(Redacted): No wait there's–

(Call Ends)

(The following is a voice memo recorded by Alice Crenshaw. The memo is time stamped at 10:21 AM on September 4th, 2027.)

It's time to go and I'm shaking.

I've called Whitney, I've put in my PTO, I've sent my medication refill down to Chesapeake. I hope that the dread coiled in me is just my overthinking. There's nothing I'd want more right now than just to be proven paranoid and wrong. I hope that Kelly just was delusional, that my old church is nothing more than another dime a dozen cesspool of hatred and bigotry, and that Whitney is safe.

But I don't know anymore. I don't know where I grew up anymore, I don't know what the people who I would have sworn by when I was younger are capable of. I feel familiar with the form of the church, Sunday sermons, Wednesday night meetings, worship, the service, the car washes, the vacation bible school, the fall festivals all of it. But what is being preached, being spoken off at these meetings is totally unrecognizable.

Whitney should not be alone right now. I didn't drive down to help Kelly. I called my refusal a boundary, when I really was just afraid. Afraid of what I would find if I uncovered what my home, and my past hold now.

I am still afraid, I'm more afraid than I was when Kelly emailed me that last night we spoke, but I won't make the same mistake.

It's time to go home, God help me, it's time to go home.

(Car Engine starts)

PART THREE

36

5 Years after Hurricane Ophelia

(Gary Vinnic retired from a distinguished career with the (redacted) aid organization. As a leader in this charity, he has visited multiple disaster sites and war zones touching the lives of hundreds that have been affected by superstorms, earthquakes, wildfires, and the continuing war in Eastern Europe. After six months of intense chemotherapy, Gary rang the bell signifying his cancer was in remission.

Gary was the leader of the aid team that found Calvary Baptist Church some three weeks after Hurricane Ophelia decimated the Hampton Roads Area. After multiple requests for an interview, Gary finally responded, asking what news organization I was writing for. At this time, I had been let go by (redacted) and was working independently. Only once I revealed this information was Gary willing to meet.

Gary stays in a small house in Bridgewater by himself. He never married due to his constant world traveling and explained to me how any woman he had in his life couldn't handle "not knowing if he was dead or alive." Gary offers me a drink and reclines in a chair before he tells me his story.)

Gary Vinnic first interview. 09/13/2032

Speakers are Gary Vinnic (referred to as "G" throughout the transcript) and Kellen Faulk (referred to as "KF" throughout the transcript)

G: Yes, I led the team that found Calvary Baptist. One of the reasons why I wanted to work with (redacted) aid was because we didn't have to wait for the government to get into an area and help people. Was it dangerous? Of course, but that was part of its appeal. If we waited until the situation was "safe" every time we hauled freshwater and medical supplies to poor folks trapped by the elements, or in a war zone, well let's just say a lot more folks would have died.

So we were ahead of the cleanup effort after Ophelia. Around Calvary Baptist there were still major floods, and the damage was catastrophic. It reminded me of some of my first missions in Indonesia after the tsunami. Nothing was left but debris and destruction. Splintered wood, downed trees, the whole nine yards man. Mt. Pleasant was supposedly one of the fastest growing areas inside of Chesapeake but you couldn't tell it from what we saw. The place was a ghost town, with people either having gotten out or being carried away by the storm.

We saw a lot of dead folks on the way out to Calvary Baptist. Corpses that wouldn't be recovered until the waters finally receded two weeks later. They are still updating the death count to this day, every time a new body floats up from the Chesapeake Bay or in the Great Dismal Swamp.

We were nervous, we still weren't hearing anybody. Maybe some lucky SOB was able to hole up in their house until the rushing water withdrew, or was on some of the precious little elevation in the area. Calvary Baptist was a storm shelter and we thought we'd find whoever had made it there. The only noise I remember was the drone of the mosquitos and other parasites that thought Christmas had come early with all the stagnant water lying around.

Then we saw the church, and from the moment I saw the site, things just stopped making sense.

Everywhere you walked was covered in birdshit. Thick, white and clinging. The scent was terrible and I remember stuffing cotton up my nose to keep out the smell. No bodies of birds though, couldn't find a single one, just their shit everywhere. Like a whole flock of them holed up, soiled the place, and then left like nothing happened.

And that's before we saw the lack of water damage.

Look, Hampton Roads is a super flat area, it's one of the reasons the hurricane was so devastating. The whole area lacked natural barriers to prevent the water from the historic storm surge washing in, and on top of that the hovering nature of the storm dumped feet of water on top of the already inundated coast.

But around the church, the ground just dried up. Almost like it was built on a hill or something that kept it safe. Except that didn't make any sense because the church was on the same flat ground as the surrounding area. Not only did it look like the floodwaters hadn't reached the church, but it didn't even look like the place had gotten wet. Now it had been a few days since the storm had passed on for good, so it made sense the sun might dry some places out, but there wasn't even a sign of mild water damage around the place. Whereas half a mile away it looked like the Day After Tomorrow.

Butts station, Princess Anne, Abermarle, Hickory, everywhere even close to the church was still dealing with floodwater. Storm surge got as high as forty feet in some of those locations, wiping out everything. But Calvary Baptist didn't even look like it had been hit by a stiff rain.

Not to say the church was in one piece which brought us to the second thing that didn't make sense. The debris field.

The church collapsed in on itself everywhere but the main sanctuary. The cinder block buildings behind the house of worship were scattered all across the ground in random directions, like they were hit by incredibly high winds. Fine, I thought, I don't totally understand storms, let's just say that this particular spot was hit by high winds, but avoided the waves. I'm sure there's some meteorological explanation for something like that.

The weather couldn't explain the sanctuary though.

The roof was ripped clean off, shingles and ceiling beams scattered all across the ground. Stained glass crunched under our feet the closer we got to the site. Me and the team thought at that point there was no chance anyone would have survived. A feeling confirmed by the eerie silence around the church. No human voices calling for help, just the drone of mites and mosquitoes.

KF: Could the roof have been destroyed by the winds?

G: Yes, easily, with the speed of the wind during Ophelia it would have been more notable if the winds hadn't caused major damage.

The problem was. The front of the sanctuary, where I guess the pulpit or stage used to be, was just gone. A crater where that fourth wall should have stood.

Look, I did some of the aid operations up in DC where that government building was destroyed by that nutjub a year or two ago. The blast in the side of the church looked intentional, like someone detonated a bomb inside with the intent to blow out the side of the church.

KF: Could it not have just been wind damage?

G: Not unless wind damage makes a clean crater, not unless wind damage leaves a blackened blast zone almost a hundred feet from the building it destroys. Wind damage doesn't look systematic, it's not neat it's chaotic. No way a high wind would just leave the other three walls of the sanctuary up, while obliterating the front of the worship center.

We also started finding pieces of people. An ear here, a hand there, a few feet, and one desiccated head. At first we thought there might have been a graveyard uncovered by the wind and human remains brought to the surface by flood waters, but Calvary Baptist didn't have a graveyard attached to it, and the remains were in a neat semicircle around the blast radius. A storm wouldn't do that, we would have been finding human leftovers all around.

The injuries were wrong too. Wind injuries are often blunt force. Yes the wind can blow hard enough to tear people up, but often the most gruesome things you see are a result of blunt force impact. You know, when a piece of debris, or something slams into the human body. Often the wind doesn't kill people, flying objects accelerated to ungodly speeds kills people. The trauma you see to the human body resembles a car crash, gruesome, but chaotic.

Wind doesn't blow hands and ears off of people in a neat separation. No, in order to get that kind of evidence, you need some sort of explosion.

KF: Did you think that when you got there or is that more of a belief you've developed in hindsight?

G: To tell you the truth, I was mostly just confused, and tired. We had been working non-stop for weeks, and now I was looking at a situation that defied my instincts. The church looked like a warzone, not a natural disaster. But having a job to do is a great cure for confusion. Maybe there was a gas accident, or maybe the church stocked illegal explosives, being a detective trying to figure out what happened wasn't my job that day. I had one of my team call in for a cleanup team, and told them we were gonna spend just a couple more minutes to see if anyone was left. There were other places on our route, and time was of the essence if we wanted to save as many people as possible.

Me and one of my team, Edgerin, started scrambling over the debris to get into the sanctuary. He was ahead of me, Edgerin always had a much better eye for hazards than I did, he was just better at sweeping an area, especially one like this where we really should have waited for a cleanup team. But we had to know if someone was in there, if someone needed our help.

We got over the rubble scramble, and Edgerin stood at the top of the collapsed debris, face mask filtering the unholy amount of dust that was floating inside the church. He didn't move, just stared down into where the sanctuary was. Have you ever seen those videos of antelope getting caught by lions, or crocodiles in the wild? How they go rigid right before the end? Edgerin was standing up above me in that same stance of panicked stasis.

I'll never forget the look in his eyes. Pupils wide in shock, but fixed ahead of him to the sanctuary beyond. Edgerin had been with me a long time, he had been there for the DC bombings, for a few runs in eastern Europe, a couple in Sudan. My point is he'd seen some shit, just like me. Torture victims, people trapped in houses that flooded, at a certain point seeing dead bodies becomes just another part of your life. But we what we saw in that church…

KF: No one was alive?

G: No, and we expected that. I think back on that moment, and I think what stopped us both was confusion. I've heard that people who see the dead, who work in my old line of work use their memories of previous horrors as a way to categorize whenever they see something awful. You're able to turn off the part of your brain that imagines what the dead person you are looking at went through, you stop writing their story and instead fit the pattern into something you've seen before. It makes you clinical, efficient, and helps you repress seeing people in their last moments.

But inside that church, there was no pattern to fit the dead, it was so bizarre that we couldn't help but try to understand what happened.

For one thing, the bodies weren't decomposed. We were weeks after the hurricane, if these people died then most of the soft tissue on the bodies should have been gone, and evidence of teeth and nails falling away should have been there. These people looked much fresher. A few still had their eyes, blood was still leaking from a few of the closer bodies from blisters across the skin. Every one of the bodies was rigid, upright, like they had died days not weeks after the hurricane. The smell got in your nose, your mouth, and your eyes. My stomach clenched up when a breeze blew their stink towards us.

They all were sitting in the pews, except for two or three who seemed closer to the front of the church and were lying straight on their back. All of them staring up at the clear sky. Their faces with most of their features, nose, eyes you know, and rigormortis locked in their final expressions.

They were grinning, smiling in elation as they stared up at the sky, while their bodies fell apart around them.

KF: What killed them?

G: A nasty surprise I didn't learn about until about a year ago.

(Gary rubs his bald head.)

Have you ever seen someone with late stage radiation sickness? Someone who's been exposed to a lethal dose? Scientists will tell you radiation attacks the integrity of the cells, which sounds painful but you don't understand unless you see it. The people in that church, men, women, children sitting in the pews, blood dripped out of their mouths, ears, and noses covering the floor of the church, and their skin. God almighty their skin.

If you had gone up to one of those poor folks and placed your hand on their skin, you could have pushed through it as easily as if it was wax.

As soon as me and Edgerin saw the radiation burns, we scrambled out of there. A few minutes later the cleanup team got there, the same organization we worked with, all going through the convention.

The man who landed with the helicopter, told us not to worry about what happened and that a full investigation inside the church was upcoming. I remember being in a daze trying not to sound insane as I described what I saw. He patted me on the shoulder and said it would all be alright and they would find out what happened.

I wanted to believe them, so I did.

A month later an internal report came out about how the victims at Calvary Baptist were killed in an "electrical fire" and me and Edgerin are sitting in a cold room with a bunch of goddamn lawyers. Both of us signed documents out the ass agreeing with the official story, honestly, I think we both were trying to forget what we saw in that church.

KF: Are those documents still binding?

G: You bet your ass.

KF: Then why are you telling me this? Can't they come after you?

G: Me and Edgerin worked together for almost fifteen years, he was a bit older than I was and early on helped me out with a lot of things, I won't get specific. He retired a few years ago, and I was so happy that he was able to live the rest of his life with his wife and kids. If anyone in the world deserved a happy ending it was him.

He hadn't been retired for six months when his symptoms started. At eight months he was in intensive care, and within a year he was gone. Leukemia, they said, took him out of this world as soon as he was done saving people. It wasn't fair.

I almost went to someone then, but people get cancer, it's tragic but it happens. Then last year I got my diagnosis.

It can't be a coincidence that me and Edgerin were the only ones to go into that church. Something happened there, something awful enough to leave a taint that followed me and Edgerin for the rest of our lives. We saw something we weren't supposed to in there, and it killed Edgerin. I needed to tell someone before it killed me too.

37

38 Hours Before Hurricane Ophelia Makes Landfall

(The Final voice memos from Alice Crenshaw's phone were recovered from an SD card held within the Convention's 'vault.' Recent reports from (redacted) have revealed that the convention kept archives of 'sensitive information' in order to stay ahead of major problems or scandals the denomination faced. Buried within the data on sex pests, abusive ministers, and various scams were the final recordings of Alice.

The following is a voice memo recorded on Alice Crenshaw's phone timestamped at 2:30 PM September 4th, 2027.)

I made good time,

Driving down 95 always is a crapshoot. I think my strange departure time helped me out, beating the traffic. I never really thought about how fortunate I was to work virtually my whole time at full cup. Commuting is not my favorite, I've always said if I could have a single power it would be teleportation. Just get me to the place I need to be.

Aunt Whitney called me back about halfway through the drive. She was worried for me, worried about me I guess. I know my text to her probably wasn't coherent, probably sounded a bit like Kelly's emails to me, but I made contact and she's safe. I had her share her phone location with me, and the location has stayed stagnant for the past two hours. I also asked her about people tailing her, but she didn't say anyone was following her around. Her handoff of the kids with Alex a day ago hadn't been pleasant by any means, but she didn't expect it to be fun.

For a moment I felt silly, inventing in my head a bunch of horrifying scenarios. That's one of the hardest parts of being anxious, the shame that surrounds you whenever you realize those wild daydreams you had about incoming doom just don't come true. My imaginings just felt so real, I could see the men of the church, led by Alex and Mr. Chris, both with the seven eyed tree sigil pinned to their chest looming over Whitney and Kelly's bodies. The experience is like a nightmare, but you know you are awake, and whenever you try to explain it to someone they look at you like you are explaining a particularly vivid dream, not a worry that feels as real to you as breathing.

I haven't told Aunt Whitney about the pins, or Kelly, or really anything but being worried about Alex. I figure that is better, more grounded, Alex doesn't need to be part of some strange religious group with odd iconography to be dangerous. Best not to worry her about both my mental state, and any more than absolutely necessary.

Besides, the shame cooled after I went to Kelly's memorial by the side of the road.

I was less than five minutes away from Whitney's house. Her "find my friends" still had her inside the house, and I saw the cross by the side of the road where Kelly was killed in a hit and run. I don't know why, but it just felt right for me to stop for a moment. Whitney wouldn't be hurt or killed by the church in the five minutes it would take me to stop at the memorial. I slammed on the breaks and pulled over on the shoulder coming to a stop a few feet before the roadside cross.

Cars honked behind me as they swerved to avoid my braking vehicle. I flipped on my hazards and opened the passenger side door. The spot was in front of a small, squat tree and at the traffic light that led to a small shopping center. It was easy to imagine a driver running the red light without seeing Kelly walking across the intersection. If it were me, I'd like to think that I'd check on the person I just hit with my car, but a small voice in my head wonders if I would just run.

I can't stop seeing Mr. Chris's face in the driver's seat of the white truck.

I opened the driver's side door and walked to the squat tree. My knees got dirty on the ground as I leaned closer to the marker of the accident. The cross was a small wooden thing, barely a foot tall and less than a foot wide. A few wilted flowers lay at its base, and a small picture of Kelly when she was a girl had fallen flat on the ground and was covered in dirt.

People go to graves for a lot of reasons, to talk to their loved ones who are gone, to place respectful items on the grave, to remember how that person impacted their life, both positively and negatively. Honestly, the purpose of a graveyard is not that far removed from therapy. Someone who is six feet under the ground can't speak, they can only listen. That's my job too, to listen, to let a person talk about their issues on their own. To help guide, not to save.

But I felt like such a stranger at Kelly's marker. I wasn't family, I wasn't even a friend, not really. Staring at that little cross my failure seemed to close in around me. What if the reason I'd raced down from Falls Church to Chesapeake, the reason I convinced myself Kelly's death was more than just a hit and run was just my own rationalization of my failure? You see, it wasn't that I didn't do enough to help Kelly, instead it was the work of my old church for reasons that I did not understand. Looking for someone to blame is a common stage of grief, and sitting there in the dirt, car hazards flashing behind me, staring at the small wooden cross the shame of "overreacting" or "making shit up" hit me like a wave.

In the bright light of day, on a busy street, the fevered imaginings of the night before seemed so far away.

I gripped the ground and took a deep breath. I still have some of the dirt under my nails. While I brushed off my pant legs, my eyes went to the shrub behind the cross and that same panic from before froze my limbs.

I blinked once and took a step closer to try and understand what I was looking at. There was something carved onto the trunk of the shrub, something carved above the small wooden cross. My eyes darted around, but I couldn't see anyone looking at me, so I reached up my hand and touched the marks made in the tree, tracing their lines. My hands shook as I traced the seven circles carved into the trunk of the shrub.

They were deep cuts, made with a knife, and dug deep into the bark. If I returned a week later, I was sure the interior of the tree would already have been hollowed by parasites. Already, insects seem to swarm around the slashes. Each of the circles had a small pupil carved into the center, pointed to the cross. I took a step back and saw that all seven eyes were carved to stare directly down at the memorial for Kelly.

I took a picture and ran back to my car. I almost hit a bus merging back onto the road, I had to get to Whitney. I decided that I was going to tell her, no matter if it made me sound insane, I would show her the picture and she would take me seriously, be certain that she was in danger, that something wrong was happening around here. I pulled into her driveway, and saw her dog scratching at her door and barking at me. I pulled out my phone and looked for the photo.

It was gone.

I must have gone through my pictures a hundred times looking for the one of the crucifix with that damned sign carved above it. The eyes in the tree watching my every move. It's not in my phone, it's as if someone deleted the evidence, or the picture just was never taken at all. I checked over and over again while Aunt Whitney waved at me and made her way to my car door.

No matter how hard I looked, it was just gone. Even if I know what I saw, I can't tell Whitney about it now, not unless I take her back to the site. And if the image still doesn't appear, like it didn't for Sean, will it mean I really am just losing it?

38

33 Hours Before Hurricane Ophelia Makes landfall

(The following is a voice memo recorded by Alice Crenshaw. The voice memo is time stamped at September 4th at 4:56 PM.)

I'm scared and I don't know what to do. I feel like I should talk to someone, tell the police, but I don't even know what to say. I don't know how to not sound like Kelly.

I just need to talk it through, be clinical, and then I'll listen back and see if what I'm saying makes any sense at all.

When I drove down here, I had to make a few calls to make certain that my medication, both my (redacted) and (redacted) would get refilled. Chesapeake is a big city, even if I was worried about something being wrong with Calvary Baptist Church, that shouldn't have a reach to the nearest Kroger. Over a million people live in Hampton Roads, and a couple hundred thousand live in Chesapeake. I got Whitney to drive me to the pharmacy, keeping my eye on her the whole time. I just wanted to pick up my prescription.

I have been on this medicine for years, it helps me regulate my feelings, helps me stay in the present instead of constantly imagining horrible fates for the people I love. And now, damn it, now I don't have what I need and what's worse is I can't go back to get my medication.

I'm getting ahead of myself, I need to wrap up this story in a bow, figure out a version that doesn't make me come across as paranoid. Doesn't make me come across like Kelly. God, she was trying to tell me and I just pushed her away, I didn't listen.

At the counter, the bored college student who was interning took my information and my driver's license. She went into the back where they keep the medication.

She wasn't the only one working there, I saw the flash and swish of another white coat moving around behind the counter. They moved with a bit of a limp and I saw a shock of white hair on the top of their head. I stood there at the counter for ten minutes while there was some conversation behind the aisles.

When the cashier came back, she took my credit card. While the card was docked in the machine, I saw the other figure walk around the corner.

Standing in a white coat was Ron Harden, Kelly's father. He quickly averted his eyes from mine and shuffled back towards the rear of the store, but I recognized him. He was a deacon at Calvary Baptist when I was younger, one I didn't care for, and had been in all the news stories about the hit and run after Kelly died.

What I don't know, what I can't trust, is the glint of light I saw from his lapel. I keep thinking about that moment, when he turned, and sunlight shone in from the window to the glint of his chest, and wondered what the shape of the pin on his collar was.

All I know for certain was that there was a pin there, on his chest, with seven points of lights reflected off of the shape. I'm not sure they were eyes, they couldn't be eyes, there's no way Kelly's own father would wear a pin that matched the symbol carved above her grave. Right? I have to believe that.

As soon as the transaction was processed I sprinted out of the pharmacy to Aunt Whitneys' car. I must have been pale, because she asked me what was wrong. For a moment I thought about telling her everything, every intrusive thought and fear that's haunted me since I heard about Kelly's accident. But I didn't, I can't, not until I can give more answers, not until I can get my story straight, and then it won't be Whitney who I tell, but the police.

We drove home, and I went up to the room I am staying in to take my medicine. I ran out last night, must have lost track, usually I'm better about being on top of how many pills I have left, but with the last few weeks I've been distracted.

I opened the first bottle and saw a different shape of pill.

Now the casings for my medication change colors all the time, that's not the problem, the problem was that it was in a completely different shape and structure than my medication. I lifted the bottle over my head and looked at the label.

My name was on the bottle, but in the wrong place. I prescribed this medication to Kelly.

I shrieked and threw the pills across the room.

If I had taken her medicine, God knows what would have happened. And I guess pharmacy mistakes happen often, millions of them a year. If the cashier just wasn't paying attention she may have just grabbed the first medication with my name attached.

But Ron Harden was there, he was in the pharmacy, and the two of them talked for a long time before she came out with my medicine.

Ron, more than just about anyone, should know his daughter's name. How could he just make a "mistake" to give the medicine to the wrong person? What if it's a message, a sign? Telling me to get out of town, to not keep looking around about Kelly's "accident?"

It doesn't make sense, why would Kelly's own Dad be a part of the 'conspiracy' or whatever else I am calling it? Every one of my supports telling me I'm overreacting is screaming for me to tap the breaks on my mind. So far, I've managed to keep myself out of trouble, out of major trouble at least, but my mind keeps wandering to a place where I might be able to find proof about what happened to Kelly. Closure, understanding, and if I'm right, justice.

Her body.

I know where she's buried, the cemetery is one mile away from Calvary Baptist. I was there once or twice for a funeral for an old person in our church. If I could just look at her body, look at the injuries from the hit and run, see that part of the news story was right, I might believe the rest.

But if not, I'd have physical evidence, something besides just my fears that points to Kelly being right about the end of her life.

I don't even know what I'm more scared of, that I do something rash like try to dig her up and end up in prison for nothing, or if I'm right.

If I'm right, if Kelly was right, then her blood is on my fucking hands too.

(The following is a voice memo recorded on Alice Crenshaw's phone. The memo is time stamped at 7:42 PM on September 4th.)

I need to sleep.

I've called and hung up the tip line for Kelly's case five times. There's no version of my story that doesn't sound insane, especially now that I'm running on no sleep from the night before. I know it's bad when I'm entertaining graverobbing just to set my mind at ease. I am going to go downstairs, be around my aunt and her very lovely dog, and think about something else. I've been spiraling for weeks about Kelly, and Chesapeake, and Calvary Baptist. I need to stop, I need to be with a person I love for a few minutes and then I need a real night's sleep.

Things are going to be ok, I'll switch my pharmacy, I'll be fine. I just need to breathe.

Everyone can get a little paranoid coming back home.

39

Ernest Mobley - Fourth Recording 03/01/2032

Speakers are Ernest Mobley (referred to as "E" throughout the transcript) and Kellen Faulk (referred to as "KF" throughout the transcript)

E: It did not take long for my lie about Whitney Ellington to bear fruit, even if it was not the kind that I desired.

It was the night before the storm. September 4th, or the morning of September 5th, these things blend together in the early hours of the morning. I dreamed of the yellow eyed tree again that night, its eyes rolled back in ecstasy, except instead of screaming I heard gunshots. Loud ones, like I was back at the range. I started awake at the sound, sitting upright like something out of a movie.

When I woke, the taste of blood was in my mouth and my room was no longer pitch-black dark. Instead a dull yellow glow came from my bedside table. The mustard color was emerging from the pin of the seven eyed tree that I took off before I slept. I turned over to grab it and it was hot to the touch. The light of headlights shone from outside of my house door, and I felt dread and nausea in my stomach.

KF: What time was this?

E: Past midnight, I'm not sure, I know I had my phone but I can't remember the time.

KF: *And there were no adults in your house? No one who would be disturbed by a loitering car outside the driveway that early in the morning?*

E: No. And I wish there were, to stop me, tell me that whatever a person who was at our door that late in the evening wanted to do could not be good.

But no one was there, and I was certain as if I had ever been of anything that it was Mr. Chris outside my door. My suspicion was proven correct when I saw the white Toyota in my driveway. Over the bed of the truck, was a cover of some kind, one of those hardshell plastic roofs that fit snugly over top of the bed. I didn't give it much mind and opened the passenger side door. My hand went for the handle when Mr. Chris rolled down the window and hissed at me to get in the back instead.

I opened the rear door of the truck and scooted into the cramped quarters of the vehicle and blinked my eyes to try and shake off the sleep in my eyes. Something clinked on the floor of the truck when I sat. The wooden stave and metal head of a shovel glinted up at me in the past midnight light.

"Where were you," hissed Mr. Chris, not turning around to look at me. "I've been calling for twenty minutes."

I mumbled sorry and went to check my phone to see if I had missed a call from Mr. Chris. He grabbed the phone and held the sides turning it off in one smooth motion.

"Not on this son," he said. "You have to leave this here tonight, you can't bring it with you."

I started to protest when Mr. Chris cut me off with a wave of his hand.

"Now is the time son, either you stand with God and you do what I say, or else I leave you here. But I'll need your pin and I won't be back to pick you up again. This is the big leagues son, where you decide if you are in or if you are out. You have to decide right now."

KF: *You didn't find his request odd?*

E: Of course I found it odd. But honestly that was part of its appeal. If it wasn't scary, it couldn't be from God.

I left my phone at the house, and we started driving in the truck. I didn't know where we were going, and quickly lost track of the turns. I was young so I didn't pay much attention to the roads and other important markers of exactly where we were. Mr. Chris was nervous though, I could smell his sweat through his vest and he chewed through an absurd amount of tobacco on our way down.

To get from the Greenbriar area out to Mt. Pleasant and eventually to the beach, you needed to travel on a dark two-lane path called Elbow Road. Mr. Chris kept checking his rearview mirror as we got further and further down the road. In the distance, ahead of the truck, I saw Mr. E's car in the dark, the beat-up Sedan parked off the side of the road.

Mr. Chris swore to himself and pulled the truck off to the side of the road.

"Ernest," he said, his voice full of steel. "Do not, under any circumstances, get out of this car, do you understand me?"

I asked him why.

Over all my time with Mr. Chris, he had never snapped at me. I had endured some sullen silence every once in a while, but never did he raise his voice. Until that moment where he said, "You don't need to know why, but stay in the Goddamn car, do you understand me?"

His volume, the tone of his voice, scared me enough to remain silent in the back seat.

Through the windshield I saw Mr. Chris and Mr. E yelling at each other. I could hear muffled voices but couldn't make out any of the words they were saying. As they argued, I heard that frequency, that open land line in my head to "God" started making noise. The same groan of release over and over again, like it was locked in a cycle of intense ecstasy. The noise overwhelmed me until I covered my ears and closed my eyes.

The next thing I knew, the two men were behind the truck, and I felt the vehicle shift as they removed the plastic hatch. There was a muffled thump, and both men came to the front seat.

I saw a yellow glow in the side mirror of the truck, like some source of light was coming from the bed cover.

"You will listen to me, you will do what I say, or your life will end tonight," Mr. Chris said to Mr. E, grabbing him by the shirt. "You have no idea what you have risked, what you have put in jeopardy tonight with your idiotic short sightedness."

"You can't talk to me like that," Mr. E said, reaching down towards his belt where I assumed his weapon was holstered. Before he could grab the gun, a flash of yellow shined in Mr. Chris's eyes and he slammed Mr. E against the window by the throat.

"I'll just bury you in the same place, would that make you happy?" said Mr. Chris, applying enough pressure to make the window groan. Mr. E feebly clawed at the wrist constricting his throat but could not push the older man away. His breath came in ragged bursts, until Mr. E nodded his head and gasped out his consent to Mr. Chris.

"You will get back in your car, you will follow me without question, if you get pulled over you will say that the two of us are working late and will be pleasant and polite to the officers. When we arrive at our destination, I will give you further instructions."

"Why not just do it here? Or at the church?"

Mr. Chris pointed out the driver's side window. "Because there's houses and a major shopping center less than three miles away. We need to get out into the real country, not this boutique version."

"But the church—"

"Has the same problem, it's less than half a mile from the suburbs. You've ruined the chance for this to matter, for it to serve a higher purpose, may God have mercy on your soul."

Mr. E turned on his own car and both vehicles moved to drive down the road.

Static buzzed in my head, enough to give me a splitting headache. I could still hear the voice from outside, that thing that was groaning and smiling without a mouth, but it was muted, like a cell phone was in the same room on speaker phone but not making noise directly into the receiver. I welcomed the static for the rest of our drive.

Mr. Chris didn't turn the radio on once.

When we arrived at our destination, Mr. Chris left the engine on and told me to wait. We were in some open country out near Smithfield. Large houses and suburbs grew up around there about a decade ago, but given the long commute to where most work was in Norfolk or Portsmouth, the houses outstripped the demand leading to wide abandoned lots that no one had set foot in for years. Mr. Chris directed Mr. E to drive deeper into the lot towards a thicker copse of trees. The branches tangled up at the top creating a gnarled roof above our heads, and I kept my eyes away from their trunks because I was afraid to see yellow orbs staring back at me, rolled back and pupiless.

After a few minutes in the truck, I started to see the smoke drifting past the rear window. Mr. Chris opened the door and pointed at the shovel.

"We need your help son."

The smell of burning rubber rushed down my nose and made me clench my stomach. Mr. Chris placed a few empty cans in the trunk bed and closed the hardshell plastic cover with a dull thump. He murmured a phrase under his breath, and a yellow sign appeared on the cover as he resealed it. The static in my head spiked until I looked away from the truck bed.

Mosquitos swarmed above Mr. E, a few landing on his neck and poking their needle mouths into his flesh. I swatted at my arm to knock one of the bugs away. I remember that as soon as the insect bit me, the static decreased and the ringing in my head gave way to a clarity I had not felt since waking up that evening.

I took the shovel and strode to the spot that Mr. E was standing with his own shovel, and we dug. I don't know how long I was out there with Mr. E and Mr. Chris digging, but I still can recall the sting of the mosquitos, the taste of burnt rubber in the air, and the repetitive clink of the metal shovel into the ground. We dug and dug in that stagnant August air. The heat was intense enough that Mr. Chris took off his vest baring his arms while we worked. Chorded muscle and upraised veins flexed in the dim light of the moon. The longer we worked the more defined his arms became as two sigils of some kind started to glow a sick, mustard yellow on either of his shoulders. The static or buzzing in my ears intensified every time I stared at those glowing symbols.

My neck itched and my arms burned when Mr. Chris finally said, "That's enough." He looked at me, eyes glowing and said "Ernest, get in the truck."

I didn't want to go back, not when I had finally gotten some relief from the buzzing in my mind with the physical labor of digging the hole. I didn't want to ask why we were digging, why I was needed, because I knew I didn't want to know the answer. I walked back to the truck being careful not to look at the bed as I got into the back of the vehicle.

The buzzing stopped. My mind was finally clear, and the collection of inches, scratches, and aches from the in all likelihood several hours of hard labor I had engaged in made themselves known in a sort of glorious uncomfortability that banished the open land line in my mine.

Something tapped in the bed of the truck.

It wasn't a loud sound, quiet enough that I didn't know what the noise was when it began. Just a light thud, repetitive and muffled. I looked up at the sky to see whether or not rain or other detritus from the trees could be responsible for the noise. The sky was clear, and quiet except this muffled thumping behind me.

The sound came from the other side of the plastic cover on the truck bed. It picked up in intensity, turning from a tap into a dull thud, like a fist or palm was repeatedly slammed against the plastic.

The voice, the voice from outside, the groaning sound of something in the throes of deep pleasure, of coming near its end returned loud enough to fill my mind. It drowned out the tapping, drowned out the sound of Mr. E and Mr. Chris coming back to the car. I covered my ears, maybe I screamed, I can't remember.

The profane thing howled in a final release and the world went silent.

Mr. Chris came back into the car behind the driver seat and Mr. E entered the passenger seat. A glow of a fire in the distance colored the edges of Mr. E's blond curls. We drove in silence, until we came near to my house.

I think that could have been it, could have been my last encounter with either or them, with Calvary Baptist if when we stopped outside my house both of these men who had supported me, who I believed loved me, didn't turn and place a hand on my knee.

Mr. Chris smiled and said, "I'm proud of you son, you didn't let us down."

Any thoughts of what we had just done, what I know I helped out on that quiet night before the storm evaporated from my head in the warm glow of pride.

Mr. Chris and Mr. E said the voice, the buzzing, everything that made me feel like something about this place and these people were wrong, was actually a gift, actually was good.

And God knows, it was fucking easy to believe.

40

19 Hours Before Hurricane Ophelia Makes Landfall

(The following was a voice memo taken by Alice Crenshaw at 2:02 AM on September 5th.)

I got some sleep at least, before the dreams.

Whitney is still in the house, just a few rooms over. It's alright, I need to just keep telling myself I'm alright, she's alright, nothing is coming for us here in our own house. I've tried breathing deep, tensing my muscles, going to my happy place, nothing is working, so I'm recording myself.

I've had dreams before, more recently, but none this vivid.

It's a dream that's waiting for me whenever I close my eyes. Like a show that I've put on pause, but reruns whenever I get close to sleep. Maybe describing it will let my mind do what it needs to.

I know that dreams are generally our brain's way of sorting information, a key process to prepare our minds for the next day. I also know that people I have helped think their dreams have a deeper meaning, or are trying to tell them something. Dreams can be revealing, but it's just the brain sorting information, doing what it needs to do to be ready to be active and awake the next day. Sometimes it seizes on anxieties, symbols, whatever that a patient, or me in this case, attaches meaning to.

I had a friend who swore they dreamed of (redacted) before it was invaded, and when they flipped over and checked their phone they saw that the tanks had moved in. Some people would say that's a sign of a kind of collective consciousness, that some acts are so evil they scar into the subconscious of all of humanity. I think it's more likely my friend really cared about (redacted) and coincidentally dreamed of the invasion before it happened.

But I don't want to go back to mine yet, I want to move on.

I was at Kelly's grave. A congregation of people were gathered around the open hole. The dirt was piled up in a mound nearly next to the grave, the coffin somewhere deep below. I couldn't see her, but since it was a dream, I knew it was her down there.

None in the congregation were facing towards the grave. They were all turned outwards, their heads staring at the sky. Their faces were nothing but a blur on top of their black clothes and dresses. Directly in front of me was a willow tree, not a small shrub like I saw at Kelly's memorial, but a great branching thing, tall enough to block the sun.

On the willow's trunk were seven yellow eyes, each the size of a dinner plate. Insects crowded around the eyes, and some sort of liquid dripped and pooled near the roots of the tree.

I wanted to turn, I wanted to run, but my muscles were rigid, frozen in place. Only after I stopped struggling did I recognize that the eyes were not focused on me, but instead stared down into the grave.

Thumping, I heard thumping from below, a tapping on the coffin from Kelly. I couldn't see her, but I could hear the dull thud of flesh against the wood of the coffin. On top of the casket I saw a glowing yellow symbol, it looked like a letter but not one from any alphabet I recognized.

I opened my mouth to scream, to cry out to the congregation for help but I couldn't speak, I couldn't move, couldn't do anything until the tapping stopped. Until everything went silent.

Do you ever get towards the end of a dream and hope that it's about to end? Like the ending of a story, you feel like the scene is over and it's time to move on, but you don't, feeling the dread pool in your stomach?

The dread grew with every passing moment after the tapping stopped, and every time I close my eyes, I'm back there with the congregation facing away, Kelly's movements below ended, and the seven eyed tree looming above all of us. I am frozen, just waiting for what comes next.

(Silence)

Those yellow eyes, dripping and wide. I'm terrified when I go back to sleep they will be fixed only on me. That whatever is in that tree, that I will have its attention.

I don't want to see the end of that dream. Please, may I not see the end of that dream when I close my eyes.

Please…

Please…

(After another 3 minutes, even breathing begins, the phone dies ten minutes later ending the recording.)

41

6 Hours Before Hurricane Ophelia Makes Landfall

(The following voice memo was recorded on Alice Crenshaw's phone at 2:30 PM on September 5th. Behind the content of the memo there is a steady drone of rain.)

I am creating a record of the past few hours. I want to remember what happened, and if I'm wrong about Calvary Baptist Church and the death of Kelly Harden, I want to have a clear record of my story. I hope that whoever is listening, even if it ends up being a court of law looking to put me away, can understand why I am about to, well why I need to see for myself what happened to Kelly.

I have only been off of my medication less than two days so major side effects of withdrawal have not kicked in yet. Even so, hallucinations or delusions are not side effects of either medication. I also want to state for the record that I have no history of paranoia or delusion, and I would fucking know because I am a therapist.

Please just try and understand, why I have to see for myself, why I have to dig until I find the fucking root of what is happening here.

This morning, my, shit–

(Rapid tapping on the steering wheel. Rain continues to drone.)

You can do this, stay clinical, it's just a report, you can do this.

(Shuddering breath)

I should start further back, I'm from Chesapeake originally. Currently I live up in Falls Church, but I grew up around here. I came back home because I was worried about the safety of my Aunt Whitney. Recently she pursued a divorce to her long-time husband Alex, and I had reason to believe that her church, Calvary Baptist, may have some dangerous people in its employ including her soon to be ex-husband. I wanted to be there because I thought that she shouldn't be alone during this transition. My Aunt Whitney's life was the church, and I was worried that they would hurt her in some way.

I was more concerned due to the strange circumstances surrounding the supposed hit and run of Kelly Harden. Kelly also had connections to Calvary Baptist, and reported to me before she died that she thought she was being followed by members of the church. Those same members of the church were involved in the majority of the reporting that surrounded the hit and run. I was not sure if Kelly was hurt or killed by some of these people, but I wanted to keep my aunt safe.

As soon as I arrived in town yesterday, I had my Aunt share her location with me and asked her to be careful given the circumstances I have just described. She agreed, and I stayed at her house overnight.

This morning–

(Shuddering breath.)

This morning, I was woken up by my Aunt's dog Vince barking and howling. I went to check my phone and found that it had died in the night. Last night I had, strong dreams, and apparently forgot to plug my phone back into my charger. I found my charger and plugged it in while calling out for my aunt. While my phone was charging I washed and ran downstairs to find Vince still in his cage. A puddle of acrid liquid sloshed around the bottom of his crate.

Whitney went out with that dog every morning. I ran back upstairs and knocked on her door over and over. There was no response, but I couldn't get into the room because the door was locked. My phone charged enough to turn back on, and I heard it trill a few times with the noise of a text message. Whitney texted me sometime last night saying that she was going out, that she would be careful, and not to worry.

After inputting my passcode incorrectly four times, I finally got back into my phone and checked find my friends. Her phone was in the house, in her room.

Vince kept howling.

I don't know if a bad hangover would be enough to keep Whitney asleep through my pounding on her door, but it at least was an explanation. One that I desperately hoped was true. I went back downstairs and the clock read sometime after two PM. Without an alarm, without my medication, without my supports, I could easily have slept later if not for Vince. I put the dog on a leash and went out to the backyard to let him do his business. I called Whitney's phone twice while Vince barked and howled outside, with no answer.

When I brought the dog inside, he ran directly upstairs to Whitney's room and started scratching at the door. I again tried to call out for my Aunt with no response, I called her again and when it went to voicemail, I decided to get into the room one way or another. I brought a hammer.

It took me longer than I expected to get the door open, Vince barked the whole time. When I got inside the room, I saw Whitney's phone, placed neatly by her bedside. Vince started sniffing and rolling in her sheets, crying in escalating decibels, but she wasn't there.

I just stood there, frozen. I couldn't get the same phrase out of mind, couldn't stop thinking "it's happening again." I don't know why but I went into the bathroom to check if she was in the shower even though I didn't hear any running water. I think I even checked under the bed, calling Whitney's name over and over again.

The dog brought me out of the panic. He started snarling and whimpering. The poor thing was my Aunt's since he was a puppy and his attempts to be fierce and intimidating were constantly undercut by those high-pitched dog sobs. When I sat up from under the bed, his teeth were bared at the opposite wall. He gave two more barks, then leapt over me. His nails clicked on the wooden floor as he sprinted down the stairs.

I closed my eyes. Dread deadened my muscles, made me stay there for I don't know how long before I turned my head to the far wall above Whitney's wardrobe.

Black and yellow paint decorated the wall, in a shape that I wish to God I had never seen.

Two black lines blossomed upwards, and between them were seven yellow eyes with black pupils. The most detailed depiction of the symbol that Kelly sent me after it was carved into her door, the symbol on Ron Harden's lapel, and the shape on Mr. Chris's jacket.

The eyes were the key to the piece. Someone had taken the time to give them texture, to make them look viscous and wet, as if they were the orifices of some unknown thing that watched the room now. The painting towered over me, some of the branches of a tree being painted on the ceiling as if its limbs grasped towards me. I felt watched, and my revulsion at the painting for a moment overwhelmed my dread at what it meant for my aunt.

I called the police and held out my phone to take a picture. A hold signal answered me, and I just stood there, frozen, waiting. The eyes, they weren't looking at me, they were looking at my Aunt's bed. Try as I might, I could not find an angle where they looked anywhere else but directly down at where she slept.

While I waited, I took a picture of the wall. Evidence or something, I had to have a real reason to talk to the police when they got to the house. Absolute evidence that something awful was happening. I flipped back to the picture Kelly sent me to examine them side by side, make sure the symbols matched.

When I went back to the photo of my Aunt's wall, there was no painting.

I looked up and saw yellow paint dripping down the wall to the top of the wardrobe.

In a panic I took another picture, and then another, and another. I must have taken a hundred photos of that God damned wall and in every one, the symbol, the key connection between Kelly and the lead ball of worry in my heart was gone.

I stared at the picture and the wall, my heart pounding. Sean couldn't see the symbol on Mr. Chris's vest, Kelly had never reported the vandalism on her door to the police, and the picture I took at her grave site self-deleted. Now my symbol wasn't appearing on a phone's camera. It didn't make sense, and I couldn't know if someone else came to the house, if they would see the abomination that decorated Whitney's wall.

Finally, a voice came through the phone, "9-11 what is your emergency."

I was silent, trying to gather my thoughts, trying to figure out what to say. To me it must have felt like just a minute, but it could have been any amount of time. I was unsure, I am still unsure of what was happening. Before I could speak the operator said "I don't have time for this," and hung up.

I sat there for another two hours trying to get the line back without success, those awful, yellow eyes still staring down at my aunt's bed. To tell them, to make someone besides me see that something awful had happened and was close to happening again. For someone to tell me that I wasn't just projecting, or having a breakdown, or that I wasn't fucking crazy.

Fuck, I sound like Kelly.

(Thuds of a palm slamming against the driving wheel are audible. The drone of the rain intensifies.)

Calm down, get through it, calm down.

(Muffled counting backwards from ten.)

Kelly, Kelly is the key, she has to be. There's one thing I can do to reveal if this is just a creation of my mind, just me not being able to hack getting too close to a patient and it not working out, or if it's something else. One piece of physical evidence that can reveal the truth about Kelly. I have to know, I just have to know what happened. I have to know if the people that I grew up around, people that I looked up to, if they did something unspeakable.

I have to know if it's all in my head or not, and there's only one place that will tell me.

Because Kelly could have been me. That's what I didn't understand, but if the people who loved me made just a few different decisions, if the path deviated just a little bit, I could be the person in the coffin down there. I could have been tormented just like Kelly, and died, God I don't even know how many times. Died when she was bundled off to Wilderness Camp, died when she got home and didn't feel any different, died when she cut off her family, died when people started to follow her, until she was actually dead and underground.

She reached out to me for help and I failed. I know that, but I have to know what happened. I want to find her body at peace, bearing some of the scars of the accident. God knows I want that; I want to go back to my aunt's house and find that the painting isn't there, that it never was there, that I made it up in my mind. I want to be wrong, more than anything I want to be wrong.

I'm crouched at the end of a long hallway, praying that it's just a hanging jacket or coat at the other end instead of a monster lurking in the dark.

I am in my car at the Harold Gossem cemetery, one mile away from Calvary Baptist Church. I hope this recording along with my other oral diaries can explain what I'm about to do. Under the cover of the rain, I am going to find out what happened to Kelly Harden.

(A car door opens. The wind and rain roar. Voice memo ends)

42

Five Years After Superstorm Ophelia

(Hillary Young contacted me with the cryptic message "I might have something you want" after I started looking around for stories about Calvary Baptist. She claims to have worked at the cemetery next door, a small spot named after an old church member called Harold Gossem. I met with her after dark on the third floor of her short pump apartment.

Hillary is a tall woman in her early thirties with a full head of dark hair and a stylized pair of glasses. Her palms are sweaty when she greets me, and she apologizes for the heat inside of her apartment. She assures me that it is not always this warm, but she's "trying to save some money on the electric bill." Hillary opens a drawer in her kitchen and pulls out a small thumb drive and places it on the coffee table in her living room. She sits on the floor with her back against the far wall and offers me the large recliner in front of the television.)

Hillary Young interview. 10/3/2032

Speakers are Hillary Young (referred to as "H" throughout the transcript) and Kellen Faulk (referred to as "KF" throughout the transcript)

H: Do you know what happens to a graveyard after a flood? Let me give you a hint, one of the most powerful forces on this planet is rainwater, when deposited in high enough quantities and given enough time, rainwater could reduce the world's largest mountain to a neat little hill. Have you ever been down to the Grand Canyon? It's an incredible sight, looking down at a seemingly endless gorge, no wonder the first guy who saw it must have thought it was carved by the Gods, or the sight of some great natural catastrophe, but nope, just a river, plus rain, plus time. Point is, high volumes of floodwater and storm surge are responsible for the majority of the world's landmarks, and Hurricane Ophelia brought both of those things to a degree Hampton Roads hadn't seen in centuries.

So, if you bury a casket, let's say 52 inches underground, but it gets hit by a high storm surge or is pummeled with rain water for days, that earth holding the casket erodes and runs off fast. It's really just one of nature's arms races between the integrity of the soil and how fast and strong the flooding is. Generally, it requires an exceptional catastrophe to disturb the dead that far underground, but that might be one of the best ways to describe Hurricane Ophelia, an exceptional catastrophe.

But let's say the people running your cemetery are cheap. Let's say they didn't give your loved one the burial they deserved and maybe only dug down forty or thirty-six inches and called it a day. What's worse is they didn't build a concrete vault to hold the grave, but instead just placed the coffin underground and decided not to worry about the ground shifting. The only one who will know is the dead right, and it's not like they can complain. Hypothetically, if that were to happen at a small, cut-rate cemetery like say Harold Gossom, it wouldn't take much at all for the soil to erode out and your loved one's final journey to be very wet.

Once that happens it really depends on how much money you spent on the casket. If the deceased is buried in a wooden casket, guess what, it's going to pop to the surface like some deranged old pirate ship floating on a final voyage. Depending on the height of the flooding, like say a storm surge higher than thirty feet, you could have these ghost ships stuck in tree limbs when the flooding finally recedes.

However, if you splurged on one of those nice caskets, one of those boxes that sends your loved one into the next life like some kind of Egyptian Pharaoh, well those are generally sealed up airtight to preserve all the aromas of the dead and stop them from leaking. So, you tell me, what's lighter, air or water?

KF: I assume air.

H: Bingo, so those nicer boxes, the perfect way to send grandpops to the afterlife in style. That thousand-dollar box the funeral home upsold you on because it's what "they would have wanted" is going to pop up and float like a cork until that seal breaks.

KF: Then it sinks?

H: Not only does it sink, it fills with water. Whatever the weight of that coffin was in the past, well it's now probably three to four times as heavy as every cubic inch of air in that puppy is replaced with heavy liquid. Totally impossible to move, seen coffin handles pop right off if you try.

KF: So, what do you do then?

H: Drill a small hole in the side to drain the water, and then pray to God that your nose plugs are working. All those fun aromas that have been marinating in there for who knows how long finally escaping to the big wide world can give you a condition of permanent nausea.

So, if you're like me, and you worked for a cut-rate cemetery, after you get back from your evacuation, the cemetery might as well be destroyed. Problem is, after a family attends a funeral and puts their loved one to rest, they expect to be able to come back to the same spot to pay their respects. Makes sense right? Well, easy enough, just go find the coffins, gravestones, and whatever else and just put them back after the rainwater recedes and you're fine.

Well, unless you have a doddering old idiot for a boss who kept the records of all the dead in a three-ring binder and didn't back up the files on a computer. A three-ring binder they "forgot" during the evacuation that has now been inundated with enough water that to call the pages which held the precious records "paper" is no longer scientifically accurate. So now not only do you have to repair your cemetery and put the dead to rest, you actually don't have any idea who's even buried on your little plot of land.

Luckily, you have a twenty-one-year-old kid doing a series of odd jobs around town and your cemetery is one of them. Also luckily, you are a paranoid old fart who has security cameras placed around the entire premises and those kept transmitting data at least for part of the storm. Put two and two together, and you end up with me, twenty-one-year-old me, watching some hundreds of hours of security camera footage and trying to reconstruct every grave that went missing based on blurry footage matched with the government's worst run database to find and return the large number of missing coffins from after hurricane Ophelia.

I won't lie, it was deeply miserable work. Tedious as hell. The first steps were easy, pausing the cameras before the storm struck and inputting the names and dates on the gravestones into an excel file. Only took me a few days to figure it out from the blurred and scratched names on those stones, a few times I wouldn't know what a gravestone actually said and would have to dig through the footage to find the funeral. Let me tell you, that was not a good realization, as it exponentially expanded the amount of footage I had to sort through.

See, my boss didn't understand how to sort the video data. Everything had a timestamp, sure, but before that timestamp was just this long line of computer speak words that were identical in the folder that the cameras were transmitting to. After staring at Ex3041ZtP enough times every file starts looking the same. But I managed to fill in the gaps and we finally had a list of names of people who were buried in the cemetery. Then I started to try and watch some footage from the storm and things got weird.

KF: Weird how?

H: Well, I could see the different coffins that got dislodged and started taking down the names of the people who were buried and matching them to the gravestones and one was missing. I must have combed through that footage a thousand times looking for my mistake, but I could not find evidence of the coffin matching one gravestone in the corner of the cemetery. A new one, the last one we dug before the storm.

K: Kelly Harden?

H: Yeah, that's the name, sometimes I still see that gravestone in my dreams. Evidence that my strategy, my method to get the task of matching gravestones with coffins was flawed. I second guessed myself over and over about what I saw, it was like when you are missing a single piece of a puzzle. No matter how much people tell you that it doesn't matter, or the puzzle still looks good, your eye is drawn to the gap every time you look at it. Not being able to finish the puzzle, or in this case my tedious task can be enough to drive you nuts.

Finally, one day, I just marched over to my boss's room and demanded to know what the date for Kelly's funeral was. I told him that it was driving me bonkers because I had matched up every other gravesite. He seemed evasive, giving me a few different dates. This was odd because early on he had been so confident that he remembered every funeral, not accurate, just confident so I stopped asking him because I didn't appreciate being sent on wild goose chases through thousands of hours of footage. When I asked about Kelly though, he got distant and gave me an imprecise range, and I don't know, it seemed like he was making a performance out of being vague, like he didn't want me to look.

I took his range, and I took every day before the hurricane for the month of September, and looked through each piece of footage. Took me another week, but I couldn't find Kelly's service. It didn't matter how much I looked, the footage just wasn't there. It got weirder when I found a gap, a place where it seemed like the video files were just deleted. Early August, I think like the 8th or 9th, there weren't any files. Now tell me how my boss, who had this folder as an amalgamation from data collection hell, had the wherewithal to find and delete footage from a specific day. It didn't add up.

(Hillary picks up and holds the jump drive in her hand.)

I wasn't even looking in this time frame, it was a mistake, a misclick that I ended up in this specific file. Timestamped late afternoon, early evening the day of the hurricane and I saw a person walking onto the graveyard grounds in the rain. It was a woman, young, maybe in her thirties, and she was dripping wet from the rain. She wore tennis shoes and had a hooded sweatshirt, but nothing that was waterproof, and she walked directly over to Kelly's grave.

Look, graverobbing is a thing. I wasn't kidding about some people loading up their dearly departed's caskets like Egyptian pharaohs. All those pearls, precious earrings, memories, whatever sitting underground attracts the worst kind of people. You know, I can even understand the thought process. I know when I die, I'm probably not caring about the ten-thousand-dollar engagement ring on my corpse.

But this woman, she was different. There was no nervousness you expect from a thief, just straightforward determination. She went over to the headstone and started to dig.

When I showed my boss, he had us call the police, and I turned over what I saw, every moment of it but it still didn't feel right. My boss was really nervous the whole time the police were there, and insisted on deleting the record off our computer as soon as they were gone. Before they did though, I made a copy, mostly to cover my own ass if the police ever did follow up on the footage.

But they never did, and when I quit working for the cemetery in early October, my boss was almost transcendently happy. He had gotten some new money from some denomination bigwigs out in Texas, and was planning expansions to the cemetery. I didn't want to be a part of that, no matter how many times he offered me.

(Hillary takes a deep drink of her beer.)

I did finally find out why I couldn't find a coffin to match Kelly Harden's gravestone though. She didn't have one. About an hour, hour and a half after that woman finished her, well what she came to do, the floodwaters swept in. Before any of the other dead were disturbed, I saw a body bag floating to the surface, a hand and a foot hanging out of the side, both looking much fresher than anyone who had been in the ground almost a month should.

I'm not an idiot, I know that with all the trouble you went through to get this footage you're going to watch. Just be prepared, it's not easy, I wish I'd never seen it. I wish I'd never worked so close to the dead at all.

43

3 Hours Before Hurricane Ophelia Makes Landfall

(The following is a written description of video footage from security camera #5 at the Harold Gossmer cemetery. The camera did not capture any audio, but instead only captured video of the incident. The video itself is included in this compilation, and the description was written by me after multiple viewings. Discretion is advised as the video may be disturbing to some viewers.)

Relevant footage begins at 5:21 PM and continues until 9:32 PM. Objects of note within the frame include the headstone for Kelly Harden, approximately fifty other headstones, a small wire fence that surrounds the cemetery, and a large tree about thirty feet due north from Kelly's headstone. Rain falls in moderation and intensifies throughout the footage. Wind and other storm conditions also intensify throughout, culminating in major flooding towards the end of relevant footage. A red sedan with the headlights on is the only vehicle in the parking lot for the entirety of the video captured during this time.

At 5:27 PM, the driver's side door of the red sedan and a woman (assumed to be Alice Crenshaw) exits wearing a yellow hoodie, washed denim jeans, and a pair of blue tennis shoes. Alice carries a large garden shovel in her right hand and a pair of wire cutters in her left hand. She cuts a hole in the fencing, and enters the graveyard.

By 5:30 PM, Alice examines each of the gravestones. She puts up her hood during this time, and often squats down to the ground to read the tombstones. Alice shakes her head and moves between three separate gravestones.

At 5:42 PM, Alice looks at Kelly Harden's gravestone. She places the wire cutters into her back pocket and takes out a flashlight. She turns the flashlight on, and places it on the ground. Alice then puts her shovel into the earth down point first. Alice pauses for several minutes, her body weight swaying on top of the shovel making small indentations on the ground. After a few halfhearted strikes on the ground with the shovel, Alice drops the shovel onto the ground and walks back towards the Sedan. She stops in front of the gnarled willow tree to the north of Kelly's gravestone. Her fists clench and she freezes while the rain runs off her. Her head bobs and she says something, but her words are unintelligible because she faces away from the security camera. Alice strides back to Kelly's grave, and picks up the shovel.

At 5:46 PM, Alice begins to dig into the earth.

At 6:02 PM, Alice digs six inches into the ground. She covers her nose and drops the shovel. The rain intensifies, and she sits on the ground near the hole she has dug. Alice rocks back and forth several times, never turning her back on the willow tree to the north.

At 6:09 PM, Alice stands up and continues to dig.

At 6:32 PM, the wind and rain intensify. The willow tree starts to sway and bend. The wind pushes the tree in the direction of Kelly's grave. Alice continues to dig.

At 6:42 PM, a small branch about three feet long and two to three inches thick breaks off of the willow tree and impacts Alice's shoulder. Alice falls to the ground from the impact and holds her shoulder. A large rip is visible on Alice's yellow hoodie. Alice holds up a middle finger in a rude gesture to the tree and continues to dig. The pile of dirt beside Alice now comes up to her knees.

At 7:14 PM, Alice doubles over and hangs her head. She falls on her hands and knees and vomits beside the grave, wrinkling her nose, and positioning her shovel near her shoulder. The rain intensifies and the wind knocks Alice down at her first attempt to stand up. Her hands grip the ground, and she pushes up to stand in the wind and the rain. She continues to dig.

At 7:22 PM, Alice stops digging. She pulls the shovel up and stares down. Her face scrunches in disgust and she covers her nose. The shovel drops to her side and she steps into the grave. The hole is shallow, no more than two to three feet deep. Alice pulls out the wire cutters from her pocket and leans down to where no part of her is visible but her yellow hoodie. The hood shudders and flaps in the wind.

At 7:26 PM, Alice becomes visible again and her mouth is stretched wide, her eyes bulge, and a vein stretches taught in her forehead. After ten seconds she inhales again and seems to scream some phrase or word (assumed to be "no" or "fuck.") Her hood falls to the side, and rain runs down her cheeks. She grips her hair and pulls a fistfull off of her head. Her spine curves and she screams the same word (assumed "no" or "fuck") at thirty second intervals. Her face and hair are completely waterlogged by the driving rain. The flashlight goes out in the rain.

At 7:30 PM, Alice hugs her arms around her chest and starts murmuring repeatedly. In the low light and the lack of audio make it impossible to determine what she says. At 7:31 PM, Alice stands up in the grave and screams again, her hands balled into fists. Alice screams at the willow tree bending in the wind some feet away. Visual analysis thinks the most likely phrase is, "look at me!"

At 7:33 PM, Alice bends down into the grave with her wire cutters in her right hand. After a few seconds she stands up with a cut pair of (assumed) zip ties. Alice turns around and bends down into the grave about a foot in the opposite direction of the tree and emerges a few seconds later with another pair of (assumed) zip ties turning her back on the tree. The wind accelerates, and a large tree branch breaks off the willow tree. The projectile slams into Alice's back, and she arches in pain at its impact.

At 7:34 PM, another piece of debris flies towards the security camera impacting its view of the western side of the cemetery. Alice Crenshaw is no longer in view.

At 9:07 PM, a severe gust of wind rips the Willow tree from the ground and hurls it out of frame.

At 9:32 PM, floodwaters inundate the cemetery grounds.

44

(The following is an email draft saved on Alice Crenshaw's cloud from her professional account used for full cup solutions. The draft was still in her google drive when it was recovered for this story.)

[DRAFT]
7/14/2027

Dear Kelly,

I am sorry to tell you this, but I really do not think that I will be able to continue being your therapist for the foreseeable future. I think that I accepted your case out of selfishness, that I had unresolved issues surrounding Calvary Baptist and religion. I've found that I've not had your interest at heart in all of our discussions, but instead have been distracted by my own baggage and past. I know that may be difficult to hear, but in the best interest of my safety and yours, I think we need to end the professional relationship between us. I am sorry that things have turned out this way, and wish that I had known both myself and your situation better before we started talking, but I have a host of other therapists I may refer you to after our conversations end. I don't want you to feel like I am leaving you out in the cold, but when a therapist is too invested in their patient it can end up hurting the healing process instead of helping.

However, just because I think that our professional relationship should come to an end does not mean that we should no longer speak to each other. I want to extend an invitation to you, one I should have had a long time ago, an invitation to come up here to Falls Church. I have some money, a few connections, and can help you get on your feet if you want a fresh start. When I started trying to take apart my upbringing and unlearn some of the unhelpful ways of thinking around church, I had to get out. College wasn't enough, I had to go somewhere new, somewhere I didn't know to get some space and some distance. Without that opportunity I never would have healed, and I don't really know where I would be right now.

Kelly, you have impressed me so much, because you managed to do some of that healing on your own and under much more challenging circumstances than I had. My family was understanding, yours wasn't, I had the ability to find a different job, you didn't, I could leave, you are still there at home. I want to pass on the support and help that I had unlearning what got put into my head to you. Because you deserve it, and because I should have done it earlier.

I understand if you didn't read this email past the first paragraph, I also understand if you feel uncomfortable accepting my offer. Just know that even though I don't think I can help you professionally, that doesn't mean I don't want to help. Please just think about it, anytime you want, I'll be ready for you to drive up and leave everything that happened to you behind.

Sometimes, rooting around in our past just makes us bleed more. Sometimes what is best is just to bind the wound and move on. I can't heal your hurt for you Kelly, but I can buy the gauze and remind you to replace the bandages.

If you let me.

Think about it, call me before you drive up, or don't. The offer is open.

-Alice

45

Five years after Hurricane Ophelia

Ernest Mobley - Fifth Recording 03/05/2032

Speakers are Ernest Mobley (referred to as "E" throughout the transcript) and Kellen Faulk (referred to as "KF" throughout the transcript)

KF: After that night in the vacant lot, what did you do next?

E: Stayed awake and watched television until the sun rose. The stereo connection to whatever spoke to me through the pin on my shirt was buzzing away, muffled noises of ecstasy or screams of pain rocking around in my head like someone who is watching a movie on full volume downstairs while you try to sleep. I was terrified to close my eyes. Worried about what I might see, might come in contact with in my dreams.

The seven eyed tree had always had its gaze directed elsewhere in my dreams. I still worry, still fear that one day it's eyes will be fixed on me. That I will gain its attention.

Even though I was exhausted, burnt out, and covered in mosquito bites, that fear kept me awake in the early hours before the storm. Early enough to start catching that the weathermen were freaking out.

KF: When did you decide to leave the house?

E: As soon as Calvary Baptist declared itself a storm shelter. That moment I texted Mr. Chris, and he said he would be there to pick me up soon. I mentioned my Mother since she was in the house, but she had been out drinking late and we hadn't spoken all day.

I still thought she was going to come with me, even when we hadn't had longer than a three-word conversation in months. I took it for granted, that of course she would be willing to come with me to the church.

KF: She didn't?

E: I asked her twice, I don't know if she was awake either time I stood in the doorway. The first time I asked quietly, the second I screamed out for her. Neither time did she respond. I think in a way she welcomed the storm, or maybe she got out right before the winds and rains hit. I don't know, what I do know is that I stormed out of the house and Mr. Chris's white truck was waiting for me.

One of the things I always appreciated about him, even in spite of everything else, was that he knew when to keep his mouth shut. Obviously, I was distressed, and when my mom didn't appear behind me coming out the door, he said nothing about it. Instead he just acknowledged my presence, turned on some local Christian weatherman and neither of us said a word all the way to the church.

What I remember most was the birds. While the storm was still ominously creeping across the Atlantic, birds started roosting on the church in large numbers. Seagulls, Herons, even deep waterfowl like Albatrosses or Cormorants. I still don't know why they thought the church would be safe, but they covered every inch of the property they could. The great willow trees in the backyard of the church groaned and creaked with their weight, as some hundreds of gulls sat on top of the branches like a collection of writhing gargoyles.

When I arrived at the church, there was still enough space for more birds. A few hours later, even the roof of the church was dotted with stoic creatures, who bit and screamed at each other for any inch of space. Their blood and shit covered the church while all of them screamed at the storm. A few of the larger birds that weren't used to people stayed away from the arriving cars, and tried to keep their distance the best they could. The seagulls, or beach birds that were used to people though, they dove and cawed at the food brought for the shelter, none got aggressive with people, but I remember thinking as some of the last cars pulled into the church, that if those birds wanted too, it was hard to imagine anyone stopping them.

People came in batches, the first groups looking sure that the church would protect them, but the closer we got to the storm, we saw some people who were just scared. One family managed to make it to the church after the bridge collapsed. I didn't like the way Mr. Chris looked at them as they arrived, like he was sizing them up, for what purpose I didn't know. There was only one or two of those groups, before the storm started getting bad.

Before no one could get to safety.

Pastor Phil greeted people with handshakes, I remember Ms. Harden took pictures of the surrounding clouds and the clear sun shining down on the church building. I thought it was strange the church windows were not boarded, not even the massive stained-glass portal on the front of the sanctuary. I asked Mr. Chris about the storm, and he just said that, "Remember Gideon son, God keeps his people safe. We will see it before this storm is over."

Mr. E was there, his two children in tow and his gun still poorly concealed. I didn't speak to the kids, but I remember feeling guilt whenever I saw them throughout the day. I begged off helping work with children to stay with Mr. Chris laying sandbags outside the sanctuary to avoid looking into their eyes. If one of them had asked, questioned about their Mother, the careful illusion of not looking into the eyes of what I had done would have crumbled in my mind.

Maybe that would have been better. Maybe I would have grabbed them and run into the storm if I knew what was coming, or if I decided to understand what I had done.

The hours before that evening, all I can remember is snapshots. Like one of those old-time projectors that clicks before each still image.

A pelican with a broken wing limping through the parking lot, trying in vain to fight off a hoard of seagulls.

The floodwaters down the street rising to cover one of the nearby houses, but stopping at the edge of the church property.

I remember the smell of rain and smoke in the air from electrical fires sparked by the storm.

And the dark clouds that swirled right outside of the property as the sun set.

The storm surrounded the church, but not a single drop of rain fell on our roof. We didn't even lose power. The sun set illuminating the sky in its normal reds and oranges, but I remember a miasmic yellow light remaining, like the afterbirth of the sun still faintly glowing from outside while the mosquitos and birds screamed and buzzed outside the church window. Even by nine o'clock, that yellow glow backlit the church property.

The connection in my head, the stereo line to the voice from outside, didn't stay quiet for long, even with the loud cawing of the gulls. The presence seemed agitated, angry even at the situation. At the time I did not understand the tone and tenor of its sighs and grunts, but now I feel certain that the thing was acting like a partner who had not been intimate in weeks. Like my father who would try and kiss the back of my mother's neck and would be rebuffed or pushed away. The creature was sitting in an attic, or garage, or wherever else it could pout in silence.

There was a barrier between it and the suffering surrounding Calvary Baptist Church. Some veil that prevented the pain, terror, and anguish of the storm from reaching its ears. From covering its senses, from giving it the release it desired more than anything.

Slowly, as the day wore on, I felt the voice from outside's attention shift. No longer were those yellow ones focused on all of Hampton Roads as the hurricane ravaged and destroyed hosts of lives. Instead I felt this unknowable creature turn its face towards me and towards the church.

I was in the social hall, sitting at one of the metal chairs, listening to the thud of worship and praise in the background from the sanctuary. The guls were cawing and screaming outside and I tried to use the noise to drown out the ominous feeling in my head. The worry that the thing's sullen pouting was morphing into anger. That any second, it would emerge in a rage, angry that its needs had been put off for too long.

The dread built until I found myself fingering the small pin on my lapel. The static peaked in my head and I pulled the pin off of my lapel and placed it on the white plastic table. For a blessed moment, the noise stopped, and I was alone in my own head.

Out the window, the largest and oldest of the willow trees was visible. Each of its branches were crowned with gulls and pelicans fighting for space, their bodies backlit by the mustard glow that seemed to surround the church. As if they were all possessed by the same thought, the birds took to wing, flying away from the tree and screaming at the birds on the roof of the church. I can still hear the scratching of their feet on the roof of the building as they all fled the tree.

In the trunk of the great willow, the bark moved like water. Shifting and running until a cavity opened up in the center of the trunk facing directly towards the church, towards the window, towards me.

Trails of red and black insects ran from the cavity in the tree, showing it's form as a great eyelid wider than my outstretched reach from one hand to another. I prayed that the eye would stay closed, that the yellow orb from my dream would stay rolled back in pleasure or closed completely.

The door between the social hall and the rest of the building opened, and I heard a clatter as a metal object was dropped on the ground. I could not turn my head to see who was there.

All I could do was meet the yellow gaze of the eye in the tree, staring through me with impossible malice.

46

1 Hour Before Hurricane Ophelia makes Landfall

(The following is a voice memo saved on Alice Crenshaw's phone. The recording is timestamped at 8 PM, September 5th, 2027. Rain and wind are not audible in the background, only a low buzzing of some kind of insect and the cawing of a great number of birds.)

Kelly, I believe you, I should have believed you from the moment you reached out. I believe that you were followed by people from Calvary Baptist Church everywhere you went, I believe they tormented you at work, at home, in your own fucking mind. And when that wasn't enough, they killed you. I'm so sorry that I didn't listen, I know it doesn't matter now, but I'm sorry, I should have listened to you. I could have told someone, I could have done something. If I actually wanted to help you, I could have gotten you out of this place before things got really bad, before they killed you.

I wish I had dug you up from the ground before now. That I was able to show someone else, anyone else, what happened to you. Maybe then, maybe your death could have been useful, helped someone else avoid your same fate, but no, they took my aunt too. They could have her right now, Mr. Chris, your parents, Alex, all of them. I hope they don't cut into Whitney the same way they cut into you. Are her hands going to swell to the size of baseball mitts when they've been bound with wire?

Are mine?

Why would they do that to you? Why would they do that to her? How could they, people I sat in the pews next to, people who sang praises to God, how could they do what they did to you? I'm so sorry that I didn't see, they killed you but I let them put you in the ground. How could I?

Even the hurricane spares this church. There's no rain here, the clouds surround this place but I'm right outside the edge of the parking lot, and everywhere here at the church is dry, not ravaged by the wind or the rain. Instead it's clear, and I can hear singing from the sanctuary. Are the knives that cut into you still in the church kitchen? Is my aunt still alive or has she already been cut up to pieces? Is something worse in store for her?

The church is the same, a steeple over a modest sanctuary that juts out past a mid-70's brick building two stories high in a large L shape. The smell of the wetlands nearby is a perfect mix of sewage and mold, and the ferns and trees that grow behind the church makes it feel tropical. And while the storm rages around me, and I remember what you smelt like when I pulled you out of the ground, please tell me why this place still feels like fucking home.

(Dragging of a shovel on the ground echoes in the recording. Labored breathing and steps are audible. Quick intake of breath and fast movement as the phone is jostled for the next minute all that is audible is Alice Crenshaw's heavy breathing and loud squawking of seagulls. After 72 seconds of these sounds Alice's voice returns in a whisper.)

Alex, my old anger issues youth pastor Alex, he's here, he stepped outside and looked at the parking lot. He had a gun, I don't think he saw me, but he had a gun and his finger was on the trigger. That same look was on his face, the look he had when he knocked my coffee from my hand. I wonder if that was the same look he had when he took my Aunt. What happened to him? Was he always like this, just in need of one good push to send him down the road to insanity, to have him start wearing old symbols and hurting people? Did I just not see it all along?

She might be in there. God, I'm so fucking scared. I'm scared to look at the Willow trees in the backyard of the church, scared they will look back at me. I'm scared to go inside, what happened to Kelly's hands, fuck, why would they do that to her hands? It makes me cold, even thinking about going back inside that church, back to a sanctuary, a social hall, that I've been to a million times. A place that feels like a dream, where it takes a moment but I can remember every room in that building.

It feels like another life, another person walking inside those halls. Were the symbols of this fucked up tree and the hurt the people I sang Amazing Grace next to dealt out there the whole time? Did I just not see?

Did I just not want to see?

I can't leave, I can't look away again. I don't know what I'm going to do, but I have this shovel, and these wire cutters, and I remember how to get around that church. I have to try and save someone from what's happening inside this time. I can't leave again. Kelly, you were right, and I'm sorry I didn't see. I'm sorry I didn't see how they were hurting you every day, I'm so fucking sorry.

I'm terrified to go inside, but I can't leave, I can't look away again. If there was any good in me projecting, and lying, and everything else I did to you Kelly, I have to stop the people inside from hurting someone I love.

(Squawking of seagulls fills the recording. A limping gait and scrape of a shovel over concrete is heard for a moment then the recording ends.)

47

Five years after Hurricane Ophelia

Ernest Mobley - Fifth Recording 03/05/2032

Speakers are Ernest Mobley (referred to as "E" throughout the transcript) and Kellen Faulk (referred to as "KF" throughout the transcript)

E: I kept expecting the eye to disappear. To vanish like the specters and demons I saw in the movies. The beat was played out, the music peaked, and now it was time for the thing that should not exist in that tree to disappear. Instead, its lidless eye kept boring into me, through me, becoming more tangible with each passing second. A roar of anger built in my mind, leaving me frozen to that metal chair unable to move.

Mr. Chris, because of course it was Mr. Chris at the door, strode over to the window where the eye gazed into Calvary Baptist Church and closed the blinds. A dull mustard glow still creeped along the edges, as if reaching fingers from yellow eyes still crept through the barrier. True fear was in Mr. Chris's eyes that night, not annoyance, or anger over the sloppy way that Alex had done, whatever he had done, the night before, but actual panic and fear at the presence outside. I didn't even need to ask him if he saw the seven-eyed tree, his eyes told me enough.

The rough hands of Mr. Chris took both of my shoulders, and

helped me calm my shaking. He tilted his head down and made his voice gravely and solemn. His eyes pointed to the pin that I swear was vibrating on top of the white tabletop of the social hall.

"Keep in on son, no matter what happens tonight, keep it on."

I told him that I was worried something was wrong, that I was scared.

"Come with me," he said, pointing back towards the sanctuary. A few classrooms were nearer to the front door, beside the awning that Pastor Phil was standing under only an hour before greeting the collection of people taking shelter from the storm.

I followed him mute, but looked back over my shoulder every so often to make sure that the yellow eyes were not following me down the hall.

Mr. Chris closed the heavy wooden door to the church classroom, past the "secret" passage that led upstairs to the youth room and the supply closet. He sat down beside me and looked out the window to the frothing sky around the church. Clear where we sat, but not a hundred feet from the property, I could see the line of rain and wind ripped apart the neighborhood. Floodwaters seemed piled up like at the glass edges of a fishbowl.

"Are you losing faith?" Mr. Chris said. "Even now when God's providence is keeping us safe in the storm?"

I couldn't meet his eyes and stayed quiet.

"Now is not the time to lose faith but to gain it, only in times of great hardship do the true believers in God's plan reveal themselves."

I finally asked him, probably too sharply, the question that had weighed on my mind since those first car rides after All In Night. Since my strange nightmares, and the crackling malice in my head.

How did Mr. Chris know that thing outside was God?

For a moment, the question seemed to catch him off guard. Throw him enough that instead of the easy explanation he always seemed to have, he had to actually think about my question.

Often, I think about another world, one where he yelled and screamed like a revival pastor or turned away in icy silence. If then, I would have finally pulled myself out of the spiral of madness that enveloped me at Calvary Baptist.

But instead, he took my hand and said, "it is alright to be frightened, are you afraid son?"

I shook my head yes, blinking back tears.

"To be frightened is normal, the things of heaven are not the things of earth. Why else do you think angels' first words are always 'be not afraid?' Because God is powerful and mighty and we are weak and sinful."

I asked him why God was angry then, why he was staring at us with such hate.

"It's not hate son, it's disappointment. God has provided us protection from the storm, you can see out there how the rest of this place is under his wrath and we have been protected. God does not do this for free, he calls for a sacrifice on our part to show our devotion."

Mr. Chris's eyes started to shine with tears. I didn't like the way he looked at me, like a man dropping of their child to study in a foreign country, or like my fifth-grade teacher who I loved sending me off to middle school. His face was more lined than I had ever seen it before, and for just a moment he looked like the old man I knew him to be instead of someone who walked and moved with timeless speed.

"Before God blessed Abraham, before he said Abraham's descendants would outnumber the stars in the sky, God asked for a sacrifice. A sacrifice of what was dearest to Abraham in the whole world. Only when Abraham was ready to plunge his knife into his son was God satisfied with Abraham's display of faithfulness."

Mr. Chris pulled me into an embrace. The tobacco scent of him clouded my nose.

I let him hug me. Let him pull me close as I murmured the word ok over and over. I still was afraid, and I still felt that whatever lurked outside was something wrong, and I worried over the story he was telling, but to be held, to be embraced was better than to face whatever was outside alone.

I believed Mr. Chris, because I wanted to. Because it was so much easier to come to terms with my part in that wretched summer if we were working at the direction of God instead of the evil presence that lurked outside of the church windows.

Mr. Chris did not let me go. Even when I started to push him away, his weight kept crushing me, until I could barely breathe.

I remember him muttering under his breath, "please, not him, please."

The voice crackled in my head in anticipation. I remember distorted voices murmuring 'so close.' It sounded not like a single voice, but a cacophony of partners right on the edge of pleasure.

Sometimes I'm back in the crush in my nightmares, with that voice in my head.

Suddenly the pressure was gone. I gasped for breath and rubbed my arms to get feeling back in my extremities. Mr. Chris's face broke into a wide grin, tears still shining on his cheeks.

When I asked him why, he pointed out the window. Down the street, making her way towards the church was a rain-soaked woman with a shovel in her hand. She walked with a limp, and sparks flew from the shovel's blade as she dragged it behind her. She stared at the church, shuffling her way almost like a zombie in an old Romero movie.

"And so, God provided a ram for Abraham to sacrifice instead of his only son," murmured Mr. Chris.

For the first time that night, the voice growled in anticipation instead of anger.

48

30 Minutes Before Hurricane Ophelia Makes Landfall

(The following was the final voice memo recorded by Alice Crenshaw. The voice memo is time stamped as 8:22 PM on September 5th 2027.)

I'm going to die tonight. After the storm is over, after the wreckage is removed, if someone finds this recording please know that it was not an accident or a tragic mistake that killed me. It wasn't even the storm, there's still no rain here. Even the weather reserves its justice for the people in this building. I am going to die at the hands of Kelly Harden's and Whitney Ellington's murderers. I don't know how long I have until they find me, but I will say all I can before they…

Before I…

Before it's over.

I made it inside the church without being seen. My right leg is still hurting badly after the tree branch slammed into me at the graveyard, but I thought it was strange that no one was watching the door after Alex popped out to survey the yard. He looked over the yard twice then went back inside letting the door slam behind him. He stood near the front of the building where the awning covered the entrance to the church. I made my way towards the back.

I picked my way through the cars to the church door, staying as quiet as I could, and thankfully there were no eyes from inside the church on me. No faces looking out the window to pick out me hobbling towards the door, no Alex holding a shaky hand to his oversized pistol. Outside the church, birds crowded the roof of the church fighting and pecking at each other. None roosted on the three willows, and I did not dare look at the trunks of the trees.

I made my way to a side door of the church that I remembered was sometimes left unlocked. It led to the kitchen and the social hall, and once inside I knew I could navigate the church easily. The sanctuary boomed with music so there was a chance I could sneak in without being spotted.

That's what I thought as I opened the door and stepped inside. A smell brushed my nose as I entered, one of rotten leaves. On the back of the door, something glowed, a yellow mark I didn't recognize. The hair on the back of my neck stood up, and one of the seven yellow eyes on the nearest willow trees stared through me.

I slammed the door. Stupid, idiot thing to do, but I felt like something had seen me, something impossible, something that did not make sense. I waited there, hunched, until my back grew stiff listening to the birds scream outside and trying to make out the sound of footsteps on the cold linoleum tile. I don't know how long I stayed there in that kitchen, but I couldn't go back past that tree. The only option was farther in.

I walked forward, opening the social hall doors. If they were holding my Aunt in this building it would be upstairs. Several rooms that were adjacent to the youth room upstairs didn't have windows, and were insulated from the rest of the church. The opposite end of the church also held a few old restrooms or classrooms that could be converted to hold Whitney, or maybe even others. I remembered there was a side staircase, a "secret passage," when I was attending the church to the left of the fellowship hall, just past the social hall, a way upstairs that could avoid walking any closer to the sanctuary where I knew there would be people who could spot me.

That was when I thought I could actually get my aunt out, that I was some hero, some detective, that would rescue her from the terror I uncovered. That "secret passage" also had a door to the exterior of the building, and if Whitney was being held nearby we could run out the side door and take our chances with the hurricane.

We'd have had a better chance of living, I know it.

A sweet smell filled the hall, one of bags of leaves mixed with bad mushrooms. A dark yellow glow drifted down the hall and the stink intensified. I stood there, frozen, my hand on the doorknob to the staircase, terrified. Something moved in the shadows at the end of the hall, a shape that looked like a man except for two yellow pinpricks for eyes.

Adrenaline kicked in, and I opened the heavy wooden door and pressed the small lock in the center of the doorknob. I dropped the shovel on the other side of the door, and scrambled upstairs on all fours, hearing something shake the handle downstairs. I ran faster, faster upstairs, hoping to put some distance between me and the yellow thing downstairs. At the second floor, I shut the door behind me and listened for footsteps.

I hobbled to the corner in the L shaped hall, youth room behind me, the rest of the church in front of me. I didn't want to find my aunt in the youth room just to run into the yellow thing before we made it to the side stairs. I peered down into the long dark hall past the stairs that linked the first and second floor, heart pounding, waiting, my hands grasping the cable cutters I had in my back pocket. I held my breath to try and hear the fall of footsteps on the bottom floor. None came.

But that musk, that smell of dead mushrooms and bags of fall leaves filled the hallway. Down at the other side, where I could not see the doors due to the darkness of the hall, a single yellow eye opened and blinked twice. I met the gaze.

The eye blinked one more time and, fuck me, I saw a man walk out of the door. Not through it, he stepped out inch by inch, like a snake shedding its skin.

I ran, pulled the doors to the youth room open, and dived underneath on one of the awful checkered couches which was still there from my time as a kid. Holding my mouth to stop from coughing dust and revealing myself, the doors to the room opened. Someone walked in the room, The smell of rotting leaves became overpowering, sticking the dust in my throat.

The floor creaked, and I saw a brown dress shoe through the flap at the bottom of the couch. The foot was sockless in the shoe, and the tendon between the foot and the calf stretched taut like the string of a fleshy harp. I inched my hand to my back pocket to pull out the cable cutters, holding my breath as the same mustard light flooded the room. The floor creaked with the yellow eyed thing above me shifting his weight.

I got the cutters into my right hand. If I could've just inched them out, gotten the outstretched blade on either side of the tendon, I could have cut, could have hurt this thing. But before I could fit the foot of the man who walked out of a wall in the cable cutter, he turned and strode away, leaving me frozen under the couch.

I hear them now, with my ear to the cold linoleum floor. I can hear the people moving below me, looking, searching. It's only a matter of time before they pull me out from under here, I don't think it's going to be easy or quick. I keep telling myself I need to move, I need to run, need to search the other rooms, but I'm scared that they will see me the moment I leave this couch. Maybe it's better if I stay here, maybe when they start to move the couch I can cut them with my weapon before…

Before they…

I wonder if they will sing a hymn while they kill me? Will it be one of the old tunes or a contemporary song? Will I know the words?

Please know, I hope someone knows, that I died scared, just like Kelly died scared, just like I'm sure Whitney died or is scared right now. I don't understand, I don't understand why they are doing this, I should know them, I did know them, but now they're going to kill me and for what? For that smell of rot? For that glare of yellow? For the yellow eyes that followed me around this building? It doesn't make sense.

But whatever these people worship now, whatever they killed Kelly for, and will kill me for, was there the whole time. I just didn't see it. I didn't see it because I wasn't the one on the altar, I was in the congregation, and until I was the one who was hurt, who was directly hurt, did I see this place for what it is. For who it hurt, and killed, and devoured, and for fucking what? Why?

I don't know, and I don't want to understand. I thought Kelly could help me, help me deal with the shit I went through. Dig to root and fix some of the things inside me that were still broken, but sometimes you dig down to the heart of what happened to you, and there's nothing there but blood.

(Rustling comes closer, a door opens and two men's voices are audible.)

(Recording Ends)

49

Hurricane Ophelia Has Made Landfall

(The following was retrieved from archival footage held by the denomination of the final live streamed sermon from Calvary Baptist Church. At the front of the congregation is Pastor Philip Gordan with dark circles under his eyes and a damp three-piece suit. The livestream has been running for seven hours, and Pastor Phillip has been preaching intermittently during that time. Relevant footage begins at 9:02 PM and the livestream ends at 9:22 PM.

At the front of the sanctuary, the podium and the altar have been removed. Two sets of stairs covered in red velvet carpet lead up to the stage where the pastor stands at the center of some sort of sigil, or marking. The edges of this sigil are six feet apart and stretch nearly ten feet long in nearly parallel lines. Seven circles are visible in between the two long marks on the ground. Behind the minister is an eight-foot stained glass window, where light streams through giving the room a mustard yellow color. Two heavy wooden doors flank the stage, with the one on the right slightly open. One person, a young man with a head of sandy blond hair, exits the open door, closes it, and nods towards pastor Phil. He smiles and faces the congregation as the piano plays the soft tune of (redacted,) a popular Christian song. Pastor Phil begins speaking with his hands open wide.)

Pastor Phil: Dear God, thank you for your provenance in this dark time. We know that nothing we could do would wash away the taint of sin and death from our souls. We need you Lord Jesus, need you to heal our hearts and our souls, we need you to help us fix our eyes upon what is of heaven, not upon what is on earth. We recognize now dear God, the miracle you have blessed us with, how you are preserving your people through the storm just like you did for Noah all those years ago. Please fill this place with your presence, we know there's nothing we can do to deserve your grace so we thank you God, we thank you with all our heart, and we praise you and will until our last breath. And All God's people said.

Congregation: Amen.

Pastor Phil: Well Calvary Baptist Church, how does it feel to witness a miracle?

(Cheering and whooping breaks out in the crowd.)

Pastor Phil: Praise God, I hope the whole world will see soon how his power has protected us from the storm. I pray that when we walk out of here after this hurricane is over, we will become a story people will pass around to prove once and for all that God is real, God protects his people, and God's presence resides here on earth, Amen?

Congregation: Amen!

Pastor Phil: But church, let us not become complacent. I bring you a passage today from Genesis 19, a difficult story, and a warning to us here not to take our eyes off of the heavens to focus on things of earth. Remember that when Simon Peter believed in the power of God, he walked safely upon the waves, only when he began to doubt did the waves start to wash over him. Let us as a church not be like Simon Peter, who was chided after he fell into the water, as "of little faith" because I know that the faith of the people of Calvary Baptist Church is strong Amen!

Congregation: Amen!

Pastor Phil: The teaching that the Lord has placed upon my heart is a story you all may know, one of those old testament stories that our culture, our modern sensibilities recoils at. A story that seems mean, and hateful, and not the image of love that people have of Jesus. This is a story about a wrathful God, and how our focus should never be on flesh and blood but instead upon heavenly things above. The Lord has placed the story of Sodom and Gomorrah on my heart.

Sodom and Gomorrah were cities of such incredible sin that even when God sent his servants, the angels, down to the city to find just seven righteous men, they could find none. Instead they found a city so utterly controlled by sin, and hatred, and unnatural attraction, and lust, that God in his infinite wisdom decided the only way to fix the sin in these cities was to wipe them from the face of the earth with a great natural disaster. Today, we see degeneracy and unnatural lust consume our own country, and God has seen fit to send another punishment, a great storm to purge the sin that surrounds us, and you know what church, I know that it's only by the grace of God that we have been spared. Only by his grace and our obedience are we saved amen!

Congregation: Amen!

Pastor Phil: It is good we serve a good and kind God who saves those who are faithful to him. At Sodom and Gammorah, he outstretched his hand to Lot and his family, telling Lot, his daughters, and his wife that they could escape the coming doom. Because they knew of God, and protected his servants, they had a chance to escape the judgment. Like you today, who have come to this church to let God work and witnessed an incredible miracle that I believe the whole world will see. But God did not just deliver Lot from destruction, Lot had to keep faith, keep his eyes focused on God. The angels said to him in the scripture, "Don't look back, and don't stop anywhere on the plains! Flee to the mountains or you will be swept away!" Lot didn't ask for an extension, didn't ask for more time, didn't ask for a donkey to carry his stuff, no he obeyed God and ran.

Because his eyes were fixed on heavenly things instead of things of this earth.

Towards the end of the story, there's a warning, for us, for those who are God's people, those who wish to serve him. God's word says,

"Then the Lord rained down burning sulfur on Sodom and Gomorrah from the Lord out of the heavens. Thus he overthrew those cities and the entire plain destroying all those living in the cities and also the vegetation in the land. But Lot's wife looked back, and she became a pillar of salt."

Seems harsh right? If everything you ever knew, everyone you had grown to love was being destroyed in a holy fire, it would be hard not to look. Hard not to look back for your house, or your friends, or whatever else was left behind. But the story of Lot's wife is one of warning to believers like us today. God's grace and providence is protecting us from the storm, but that grace is contingent on us keeping our eyes fixed on him, fixed on things above, as opposed to things of this world. Lot's wife was turned into a pillar of salt because she could not keep the discipline to obey God, she was unable to keep her eyes fixed on God but instead worried and wanted for her past life. Because of this, God let her share in the demise of worldly things that she valued so highly.

We must keep our eyes on God, church! That's the only thing that will let us be a witness and example of his power and his grace. We must keep our eyes above the waves, we must look up to God or this miracle can be snatched away in a heartbeat can I get an amen!

Congregation: Amen!

(The door on the left side of the stage opens revealing two men, one identified as Alex Elington on the left and the other identified as Chris Durose on the right. In between them is a badly beaten woman identified as Alice Crenshaw. She is not moving as Chris Durose and Alex Elington drag her past pastor Phil and place her face down in the center of the symbol in the center of the stage. Alex Elington takes an object from Alice Crenshaw's back pocket and slams it into her cheek. Blood runs onto the stage. Alex drops the object several feet from Alice Crenshaw. The congregation is silent.)

Pastor Phil: People of God, I call on you to remember the story of Lot's wife now. I have sympathy for Lot's wife, everything she knew was being burnt and destroyed by fire from God. It must have been terrifying, it must have been strange. Remember whenever an angel speaks to someone in scripture their first words are always "be not afraid." We fear the things of God because we know they are above us, we know that heaven is eternal and is in control of all things here on earth.

So tonight, this is my call to you, what you need to do to keep the miracle of God's providence, to be like Lot instead of Lot's wife. I need you to keep your eyes fixed on the heavens, not on earth.

(Chris Durose steps in front of Alice Crenshaw's immobile body. He takes off his shirt revealing a host of tattoos of various religious and political causes. Of note is the double lightning of the Waffen SS, as well as the anagram 6MWE on each of his shoulders, next to a political slogan on his back that says (Redacted.) On his chest are the tattoos of seven yellow eyes in between his pectorals down to the bottom of his abs. He spreads his arms and starts to speak in a low tone, the words he says are unidentifiable.

Alex Elington has a gun holstered in the front of his pants and his eyes trained up at the ceiling of the sanctuary. The music continues, a more forceful piano ballad ringing out in the sanctuary. This is an old song, a hymn with booming bass notes, and belting melody.

Alice Crenshaw twitches. She crawls forward closer to the discarded object on the ground.)

Pastor Phil: Turn your eyes upward. The Lord says "set your mind on the things above, not the things on earth." Keep your eyes focused on God church, keep your eyes on him, our wretched souls do not deserve his forgiveness but he gives his grace freely. Keep your eyes focused on that truth church–

(The melody and the words of the pastor become inaudible. Screams and caws of seagulls from outside of the church drown out any audio.)

Pastor Phil: Open the eyes of my heart Lord, I want to see you.

(Alice Crenshaw holds an object in her hand. Blood smears the ground where she had been laying. Her nose is disfigured, and her left hand is missing two fingers. She reaches her arm out towards the foot of Chris Durose. He is sweating and chanting, his hands trembling. She crawls on her belly towards him.

The object in Alice Crenshaw's hand disappears from view beneath

Chris Durose.

Chris Durose screams in pain and collapses to the ground, a flash of yellow escapes from his chest. More blood runs across the stage and Alice Crenshaw looks to grip and rip chunks of his flesh off with the object in her hands. Chris Durose rolls on his back, and Alice starts working on his tattoo of the seven eyed tree.

Screams echo throughout the sanctuary. Alex Elington pulls out a large pistol from his pants and starts shooting. Alice Crenshaw and Chris Durose recoil and blood bursts from their back. The object in Alice's hand is revealed to be a pair of cable cutters, blade thick with blood and gore. The blade is clamped around Chris Durose's lips.

The stained-glass window above the stage shatters. The wooden ceiling of the sanctuary groans and one of the light fixtures falls to the ground.

The lights cut off. Screams clip out the audio.)

(Recording ends)

50

Five years after Superstorm Ophelia

Ernest Mobley - Fifth Recording 03/05/2032

Speakers are Ernest Mobley (referred to as "E" throughout the transcript) and Kellen Faulk (referred to as "KF" throughout the transcript)

(Livestream archival footage from Calvary Baptist Church ends. Ernest puts down the vaporizing device and leans forward in his chair.)

KF: Is this how you remember the events during Hurricane Ophelia?

E: That's not the question you want to ask me is it?

KF: Ideally no, I'd like to know what happened next, after the footage ended. How did you survive while the rest of the church was found dead inside the demolished building?

E: You think I might have had something to do with the end of Calvary Baptist?

KF: I think you have functionally admitted to being an accessory to murder and are the only survivor of a natural catastrophe that killed everyone else in that building. Either you were involved or something else, something more extraordinary happened.

E: Yes, to both of your questions.

KF: Explain.

E: I was one of the reasons the extraordinary events as you describe occurred and I was involved in the death of every member of Calvary Baptist Church in that building.

KF: How did you do it? How did you kill them all? Did you have help? Someone still at large?

E: (laughs) Oh yes, I do think that 'they' are very much at large. I hope that when I finally pass from this life they aren't waiting for me.

KF: This is nonsense, I'm–

E: You are the one who has pushed me for the truth. You are the one who has wanted to have the answer every time I have warned you about its nature. You are the one who wanted to hear about my dreams, who wanted to hear about the voice in my head, and who wanted to hear about the fate of the church. Even now, you have to know what happened, you have to know so bad that it is burning you up inside. If you want to leave, publish my words in the paper, maybe put me in prison for the last few months of my life, you can certainly do that.

But I don't think you want to. You don't think I'm crazy, I think you believe me, and know that right now is your final opportunity to learn what happened that night. This is the last chance to pull up the bloody root of Calvary Baptist. Could you live with yourself if you didn't learn the truth?

After all you've done, after all I'm sure you've given up, can you afford to turn back now?

(Long pause in the recording)

KF: Tell me please.

E: I'll spare you the details of how they found that woman. How they dragged her down to a room beside the sanctuary, of the noises I heard from that room reached a crescendo even as the screams were drowned out by the thumping bassline and reverberating lead guitars. Safe to say, the thing from outside, the seven eyed tree, was deliriously happy with what was happening in that small room adjoining the sanctuary.

When the worship finally calmed, and the cries and screams from the antechamber stopped, Pastor Phil motioned for me to check the room. His face was ashen, sweat beaded on his forehead, and I got the sense he wanted me to check what had happened in there because he could not face it himself.

When I opened the door, the room stank of sweat and blood, and red spread across the linoleum tiles like spilled ink. Mr. E had in his hand a pair of cable cutters, the stainless steel rimmed with red. The woman wasn't moving.

I pointed to the sanctuary floor, and they dragged her out.

She lay in the center of the sigil. Mr. E swung the pair of clippers at her head impacting her temple. Her body writhed like a dead deer absorbing a bullet. The blood on his hand made the clippers slip onto the ground and he turned towards the congregation instead of picking them up. Before I could point out how close they were to the woman, Mr. Chris held out his hands in prayer and motioned for the congregation to do the same.

The call of the gulls on the ceiling of the church was the only noise left in the room.

Mr. Chris removed his shirt, revealing sets of hateful tattoos and three glowing sigils of the seven eyed tree.

I wish I could tell you there were gasps at the provocative nature of his tattoos, or the glowing yellow from his torso, but the whole congregation just stared. Charlotte Harden looked at him with hungry longing as his mouth opened and he prayed aloud.

The words, they were not in a language I knew, but I could hear the syllables. Low and guttural and seemingly from another time and another world. Even though I did not know their meaning, I could understand their purpose, could understand that he was calling something, begging something to be in our world that should not be. On the stage, behind Mr. Chris, I saw an outline of a willow tree, its branches reaching up to the roof of the sanctuary, seven yellow eyes rolled in ecstasy.

The same willow from my dreams, now becoming more tangible by the moment.

I wanted him to stop, but I could not move. A foul smell came from my pants and my limbs started shaking the more solid the seven eyed tree became in the room. A constant scream ripped through my mind, and I knew more than I knew anything else in my life that whatever was in that room was not any God I knew, it was something else. Mr. Chris's eyes were closed tight in concentration, sweat pouring down his naked back as he spoke every syllable that froze my heart.

The woman moved.

With every word Mr. Chris said the gulls and birds outside shrieked and cried. I could see their shadows through the stained glass flying up, fleeing from whatever was being summoned, whatever was being called at this church. The roof groaned in relief as the sheer weight of the sea birds rushed upwards

The woman inched her hand forward. Bloody stumps were where her middle and ring finger used to be. She graspedthe bladed instrument lying on the ground. No one saw her, Mr. E, Pastor Phil, the congregation, all eyes were fixed on the spectral tree looming over all, moss creeping out along the walls.

Her eyes bloodshot, her teeth clenched in effort, the woman took the weapon carelessly left on the ground and crawled along her belly towards Mr. Chris. I could've said something, could've called out a warning, but I wanted the voice from outside to stop, I wanted everything to stop. For the flickering image of the seven eyed tree to disappear.

She bit her bottom lip in concentration and fitted the blade of the clippers around the back of Mr. Chris's heel. He did not notice her, all his concentration bent towards whatever presence he labored to bring into this world. I reached and grabbed the pin on my lapel. My chest burned and pulled, but I ripped it off and cast it onto the ground.

The wire clippers made a soft click and Mr. Chris screamed in pain. He collapsed onto the ground, blood flowing from his heel, the woman crawled on top of him cutting with the blades over and over again. She grasped his ear, his nose, and was working on his lip when gunshots ripped through her back.

She and Mr. Chris stopped moving and the church went silent.

I looked behind me and saw that the tree was gone, and for just a moment I wondered if it was going to be ok, if whatever we had called out had returned to the dark.

The birds weren't cawing anymore.

Like heavy hail, they slammed into the ceiling. All the thousands of seabirds that sought refuge in the pocket of safety from the hurricane fell out of the sky. The sloped roof of the sanctuary guided their corpses to the ground, and the mass of their bodies filled the view from the stained-glass windows on the side of the church.

The voice from outside bellowed, "FINALLY," in my ear as if it stood behind me, and the rest of the congregation seemed to hear. People started to scream as the roof splintered and was ripped off flooding the whole place in yellow light.

All of them looked up, turned their eyes to heaven. Mr. E, Charlotte Harden, Pastor Phil, Whitney's kids, all of them stared up into that yellow light. The screaming stopped, and those who had stood to flee instead sat down as if in wordless worship.

I ran from the light, ran as fast as I could to the floodwater around the property, and towards Hurricane Ophelia. The sanctuary collapsed behind me without a scream. The yellow light ending where the storm clouds began.

I ran, and then I floated, until I was found. First by rescue teams, then by the denomination. I told my story once, and ended up institutionalized, waiting to finally find someone who might believe me.

Waiting for someone like you.

KF: If I believe you, why would the thing you describe let you live? Why would it let you go?

E: I like to think because I turned away at the last moment, because I let the woman end whatever rite that Mr. Chris was performing, or because I threw away the pin. The happy ending for me is that I ran from it at the right time, that I am redeemed.

KF: And the unhappy ending?

E: We don't know if it did let me go, or if it will be waiting for me when I die, greeting me as an old friend.

You have another question I feel, something else that's digging into your skin.

KF: Did you see it? Did you look up when you ran?

E: Does it matter?

KF: What did you see?

E: Have you ever been down to the small church down the street here in Bedford?

KF: That's not my question—

E: It's a little sanctuary and steeple. Charming and quaint, probably a congregation of fifty or so. I drove down this Christmas Eve, when I still could drive. I missed it, missed the ceremony, missed the peace I used to find when I prayed, actually prayed without that outside voice speaking to me. Besides, I felt like I could use all the help I could get when I passed to the next world.

The music boomed out from the sanctuary, a familiar hymn, a Christmas Carol I bet even the most ardent atheist would recognize. I hummed it to myself, and turned off my car. Taking communion, singing with other believers, listening to a sermon, the whole ceremony appealed to me. I told myself this time would be different, that not every church was Calvary Baptist, and I was starving for human contact.

I reached to open the car door when I saw the light. The dull yellow glow that spilled out from every window illuminating the cross on top of the sanctuary into an eldritch lighthouse. The whole structure backlit like some profane beast.

Acknowledgements

Without a few key people, there is zero chance this book ever sees the light of day. Thank you first and foremost to my wife Haley who gave me the confidence to publish Profane Beasts by looking up halfway through reading through the manuscript and saying, "this is like a book." Thank you to my dear friends Alison and Jared for both creating the wonderful cover and giving me the confidence to put myself out there artistically. Thank you to Mom and Dad for reading and reacting in a thoughtful way to the content inside. Thank you for understanding that we all remember our time in the Evangelical church differently and giving me space to process what happened. Thank you to Ket, Nik, and Lisey, who took time out of your busy lives to not just read, but also provide feedback on Profane Beasts. Thank you for your thoughtfulness and encouragement that what I wrote here was good enough to publish. Thank you to Knocked Loose for making a horrorcore album that captured the essence of what it was like to grow up in the Chesapeake swamp. Finally dear reader, thank you for taking a chance on reading this book. I hope it brought you some peace, catharsis, or understanding of yourself and the world we live in.